QUEEN of RUIN

QUEEN of RUIN

TRACY BANGHART

HODDER CHILDREN'S BOOKS

First published in the US by Little, Brown Books for Young Readers in 2019

First published in Great Britain in 2019 by Hodder & Stoughton

1 3 5 7 9 10 8 6 4 2

alloy**entertainment**

Produced by Alloy Entertainment
1325 Avenue of the Americas
New York, NY 10019
www.alloyentertainment.com

A CIP catalogue record for this book
is available from the British Library.

ISBN: 978 1 444 95532 3 (hardback)
ISBN: 978 1 444 94301 6 (paperback)

Printed and bound in Great Britain by Clays Ltd, Elcograf S.p.A.

The paper and board used in this book
are made from wood from responsible sources.

FSC
www.fsc.org

MIX
Paper from
responsible sources
FSC® C104740

Hodder Children's Books
An imprint of
Hachette Children's Group
Part of Hodder & Stoughton
Carmelite House
50 Victoria Embankment
London, EC4Y 0DZ

An Hachette UK Company
www.hachette.co.uk

www.hachettechildrens.co.uk

To the women of my family,
who have shown me so many
different ways to be strong

ONE

SERINA

With every breath, Serina Tessaro's broken rib flamed. The half-healed slash on her arm burned, the bullet wound in her shoulder ached, and her bruises from Commander Ricci's punishing fists screamed. In truth, finding a place where her hurts *didn't* lick at her, hungry and hot, was a difficult job.

But it was the memory of Jacana's small lifeless body, Oracle's sightless eyes, the rows upon rows of brave dead women that caused her the most agony.

She should have known that here on Mount Ruin, survival would mean pain.

Since the first moment she'd stepped on this island, condemned for reading—her sister's crime, not her own— she'd been surrounded by it. The pain of the shackles, of her fellow prisoners' sobs. The pain of being stripped down and inspected by Commander Ricci. And then there was the agony of the fights themselves, watching women kill each other for rations. Watching her own friend Petrel die. When it had been Serina's time to fight, she'd found she couldn't do it. She'd submitted rather than kill Anika, a girl from Hotel Misery. And she'd paid for that decision with pain as well. Banishment, attacks, and then, last night, Commander Ricci's revenge. He'd captured her and put her onstage, and told her to choose which woman she would fight.

When Serina had stood up to him and refused to fight another woman, when she'd invited *him* as her adversary instead, she'd assumed she would die.

She hadn't expected a rebellion.

But Slash and the Hotel Misery crew had attacked the guards; Oracle and Ember had attacked Commander Ricci; and Serina, unlike so many others, had somehow lived to see the morning.

Every painful breath was a gift, one given by Oracle and Slash and all the women who'd chosen to fight the guards instead of one another. Serina swore to herself, as she helped scrub away their blood from the floor of the amphitheater, that she would not let those women's deaths be in vain. She wouldn't let down the ones who lived either.

Dawn danced across the island like a Grace in a golden dress, lining each leaf and harsh volcanic rock with lacy filigrees of light, even as Serina and the others worked to erase the carnage of the night before. All the bodies were gone—the slain women committed to the volcano's red glow and the guards to the sea's cold depths. Soon, every trace of blood was gone too.

Biting back a groan, Serina carefully pulled herself to her feet. Sunlight warmed her face. Beside her, Cliff hauled up a bucket of bloody water. Her broad, sun-weathered forehead furrowed in concentration, or maybe exhaustion. The older woman had been in charge of the Cave crew's freshies and was one of the first women Serina had encountered on the island, along with Oracle.

Serina's breath hitched. She still remembered that night so clearly—how terrified she'd been, even before the fight had started, even before she knew women were about to start killing one another. How alone she'd felt, and how much she'd missed her sister.

That hadn't changed. Serina's separation from Nomi hurt more keenly—and more deeply—than her broken ribs and bullet wound.

Cliff carried the bucket to the edge of the cracked stone amphitheater, where Mount Ruin's hardy yellow grass waved in the breeze. Another woman, bent and weary from the night's work, gathered the dirty scraps of cloth they'd used to scrub the stone. Serina wiped sweat from her forehead with the back of her hand.

Nomi.

Serina needed to come up with a plan. Nomi was trapped in Bellaqua, one of three Graces for the Superior's Heir. Not that long ago, Serina had wanted exactly what Nomi had—a life of luxury and beauty on the arm of the most powerful man in Viridia—but to her sister, that life was a prison as real as Mount Ruin. And Serina was determined to liberate her.

Anika and Val appeared at the top of the amphitheater with a rusty cart laden with large burlap bags—the rations Commander Ricci had hoarded. As they pushed the bounty down the aisle toward Serina, a line of women gathered behind them, spreading out along the swaths of volcanic rock that had poured over one section of stone benches. More filed in from the base of the theater, where a handful of women had been resting against the wall of the observation tower. All told, Serina guessed there were a hundred and fifty women still here, still alive, give or take a dozen. Most of them stared hungrily at the cart of burlap bags.

Val and Anika stopped when they reached the dais at the bottom of the amphitheater.

Val's unruly brown hair curled in every direction around his tan face. His jaw was bruised, his neck streaked with dirt. Serina smiled at him a little giddily. He'd had the chance to escape, to leave her behind. But he hadn't. He'd stayed and helped them. He noticed her expression, and his own face relaxed into a grin.

"How do you want us to distribute the extra rations?" Anika asked. Long streaks of morning sun gilded her rich brown skin. One of her eyes had swollen shut and tufts of hair had pulled free of her tight braids, but she stood with the same confidence—the same defiance—she'd shown from the moment she'd arrived on the island.

Serina had heard a rumor that the women of Hotel Misery had tried to name her Shade, but she'd refused to answer to anything but Anika, saying her name was the only thing her mother had given her that no one could take way.

It was Anika whom Serina had submitted to, rather than killed, when it'd been their time to fight. That moment had started all of this, had put a target on Serina's back. If Commander Ricci hadn't tried to make her fight again, maybe there never would have been an uprising.

"The food will be easier to share fairly if we all stay together in one camp," Serina said. "Do you think Hotel

4

Misery is big enough for all of us?" They'd already set up an infirmary of sorts in one of the old ballrooms on the first floor.

Serina would be happy if she never had to sleep another night in the lava tube her crew had called home. Oracle hadn't seemed to care about the sulfuric winds off the caldera or how close it was to the living part of the volcano, but the rock had always felt like it was pressing down on Serina and she'd never been able to forget that rushing lava had carved out the space ... and could pour down upon them at any moment.

Anika glanced at the other women of her crew. In the hours after the fight, when their leader, Slash, had been killed, Anika had stepped in, shouting orders as she helped Val haul the seven surviving guards to the compound.

She turned back to Serina and nodded. "We have room."

"How can we trust Hotel Misery?" someone asked. "They'll kill us all in our beds."

Serina found the source of the voice in the crowd—a woman in her twenties with a sweep of white-blond hair and a pinched, angry pink face.

"What's your name?" Serina tensed her leg muscles to keep herself from swaying. She was so tired.

"Fox," the woman spat. "I'm in charge of Jungle crew now that Venom is dead." She turned her glare on Anika. "Thanks to *her*."

"Venom killed plenty of *us*," another sharp voice replied. A rumble of voices built, insistent and angry as a wasps' nest.

"Hey!" Serina called, raising her hands for silence. "That violence was demanded by the Commander, remember? Anika didn't kill Venom by choice. *None* of us killed by choice. We are not enemies. We need each other. We'll only survive if we work together, like we did last night."

"You think we're going to *survive*?" Claw, a gnomish woman from Cave crew, cackled. "We've little food and no way of getting more. We're all going to die here."

Serina crossed her arms over her chest, ignoring the sharp pain that radiated through her torso. "No, we're not. The next boat of prisoners is due in a week, maybe two. There will be rations on it. We can overpower the guards, take the food for ourselves. We can use the ship to escape . . ."

Her voice faded. Except where would they go? And what about Nomi?

Anika tilted her head. "Didn't the guards have their own boats? Why can't we use those? We can leave now, get off this rock, and go back to our families."

"*My* family sent me here!" someone shouted.

"There are no boats." Val raised his voice over the building din. "This island was punishment for the guards too. Even Commander Ricci. We all disappointed the Superior in some way—too ruthless, not ruthless enough. He sent all his failed soldiers here. We weren't allowed boats, not even for an emergency evacuation. The ships that arrive with prisoners are our only contact with the outside world."

He glanced at Serina, a question in his eyes.

She knew what he was asking. Val had a boat, a secret

6

he'd hidden for years. They'd planned to use it to escape, to go back to Bellaqua and try to rescue Nomi. With one discreet shake of her head, he would hold his tongue. The boat would remain a secret, and Serina's best chance at reuniting with her sister.

Yesterday, she'd been prepared to leave, but she'd found she couldn't abandon Jacana, who'd been helping her look for a way off the island. Now Jacana was dead. Serina hadn't been able to save her. There was nothing to keep her here, nothing to stop her from taking Val's boat and going to save her sister.

Nothing except for the women of Mount Ruin. Those dead, like Jacana and Oracle, whom she'd promised to avenge. And those living, whom she'd promised herself she'd try to save.

Serina couldn't sneak away in a secret boat and leave these women. Not even for Nomi. She would get her sister out of the Heir's clutches, out from under the cold, watchful eye of the Superior. But not like this.

"There *is* one boat on the island," she said, still meeting Val's gaze. He nodded a little, but his brows drew together, sharing her sadness. "But it's small, only big enough for two or three people. Still, it may be of use."

"And how do you know about this boat?" Anika asked, her eyes narrowing.

"It's mine," Val said. "Hidden so well no guard or prisoner has found it. I snuck it onto the island to rescue my mother, who was being held here, but"—his voice caught—"she was gone by the time I arrived."

Anika's suspicion eased slightly. She rocked back on her heels.

"But ... but I don't understand," another voice, a smaller voice, said. Theodora, who went by Doll now, so named for her tall, loose-limbed body and perfectly oval golden-brown face. She'd been assigned to the Cave the same time Serina had. "What are we going to do when the prison boat comes? You said we'd escape. Where will we go?"

Serina opened her mouth, but nothing came out. She didn't have an answer.

Val stepped up onto the dais next to Serina and turned to face the crowd of women filling the amphitheater. He cleared his throat. "There's a country called Azura, to the east of Viridia across the Gallatian Sea," Val said. "My father was a merchant and once did business there. He told me that in Azura women work, own property, even handle their own money. They can read. Our borders are closed to Azura save an occasional delegation invited by the Superior, but it's not so very far away. And *their* borders are not closed to us."

Val had told Serina about his father going to Azura. It's what had inspired him to teach his wife to read and, in turn, the girls who came to their house to be taught in secret. It's what had gotten him killed and Val's mother sent to Mount Ruin. It explained a lot about Val too.

"You want us to go there?" Fox asked, brushing her white-blond hair off her furrowed brow. "Why would they take us in?"

Val shrugged. "I can't say for certain that they would. But it will be safer than staying here or going back to Viridia."

That's when I'll go, Serina thought. *When we take the ship, when these women are safely on their way to Azura, when they don't need me anymore, then I'll take Val's boat and save Nomi.*

And if Nomi didn't want saving? Serina pursed her lips. There was a chance that her sister had taken to life in the palazzo, that she'd found her role as a Grace less abhorrent than she expected. But Serina didn't think so. When *she'd* wanted to be a Grace, when *she'd* told Nomi that she was willing, Nomi had said it didn't count when you weren't allowed to say no.

And she was right.

It didn't matter how luxurious Nomi's life was now. Serina was going to give her a *choice.* That's all Nomi had ever wanted. The chance to decide her own fate.

If it killed her, Serina was going to give that to her sister.

"So we take the prison boat," Serina said now, raising her voice over the skeptical murmuring of the crowd. "We go to Azura. We make new lives."

Anika's shoulders slumped. Serina noted her reaction, wondering at the girl's disappointment. Her gaze climbed to the women filling the amphitheater, some seated on the stone benches, some standing on the frozen wave of black volcanic rock that covered half the curved seating area.

There were so many gaunt faces, so many bruises, so many sunken eyes. Serina saw hunger staring back at her, and fear. Some of these women had been here for *years*, had watched countless fights, seen countless women die.

"You all have been fighting for so long," Serina said, the words catching in her throat. "It's hard to believe it's really over. It's hard to imagine things getting better. But they will. For the next ten days, this is our island. Just like our names, just like our lives, we've *earned* this. We've earned our freedom. No matter what happens when we get to Azura, this will always be true. We're not prisoners anymore."

The energy of the crowd lightened. She saw hints of hope scattered throughout the exhaustion, in the glint of a smile here and there. Even the leaders of the other crews perked up a little. Twig's steel-bar arms were relaxed at her sides. Among the Southern Cliffs contingent, a small smile flitted across their leader Blaze's scarred face. But Anika wasn't the only one who still looked troubled.

"We're not prisoners anymore," Serina said again, as much to remind herself as the rest of them. Even for her, who'd been on the island for weeks, not years, this truth still felt like a dream.

She turned to Anika. "Can you organize the sleeping arrangements and help distribute this food? Val and I'll check on the guards."

Anika straightened her shoulders and nodded. She pushed the squeaking cart up the aisle, calling out suggestions to the other crews: *Take your injured to the old ballroom. If you've got rations or belongings in your camps, bring them with you. We've only got so many rooms. You'll have to pair up.*

When Serina moved to follow, her legs wobbled. She paused to steady herself. She couldn't afford to collapse now.

"I can check on the guards by myself," Val offered, taking Serina's arm. "Why don't you rest?"

Serina shook her head and limped up the steep aisle of the amphitheater, using his grip on her arm to help steady her balance. "Soon."

He didn't argue, which was good, because she might not have had the energy to stand her ground. The truth was, Serina was afraid to slow down. She didn't want to rest. Didn't want to stop. If—when—she did, Jacana's small, broken body would fill her mind.

If Serina gave herself time to think, she'd drown in regret.

And Jacana wouldn't be the only one haunting her. Every time Serina paused, every moment she wasn't concentrating on the next task, she saw Oracle's head snapping back when the bullet hit her forehead. She felt the weight of the woman's body on her shoulder as they hiked to the summit of the volcano. She remembered Slash's bloody corpse draped across the men she'd killed.

"Serina?" Val asked.

"I'm okay." She realized she was leaning into him and forced her body to straighten.

They hiked slowly along the path to Hotel Misery, so slowly that when they reached the cracked marble, Anika was already shouting orders and handing out food. They continued on toward the prison compound. The building was deceptive; when she'd first arrived, Serina had assumed that's where she would be held, in a small cell like a princess in a grim tower. But the population of women sent to Mount Ruin had outgrown the building's capacity long before her time; now the cells were used for the storage of weapons and rations, and as the guards' own sleeping quarters.

The few guards who had survived the uprising had been locked in their "bedrooms," the rooms reverted to their previous use. The irony hadn't escaped her. The weight of the keys to their cells pressed against her thigh. She slipped her hand into her pocket and around the cold metal.

"You told them about the boat," Val said once they were away from the others. "What about Nomi?"

"I'm going to go after her, but not yet. Not until everyone else is safely on their way to Azura." She rubbed at the back of her neck, finding a sore spot. "Anika has family she's anxious to return to, I think. Maybe others do too. If I'm going back it wouldn't be right to go alone, to keep the boat a secret."

Val scuffed his boot against the rough rock of the path. "It's small, Serina. Anika could come with us, but no more."

"Us?" Her foot caught on a ragged edge of rock, and she stumbled.

Val pulled her closer. "I go with you. Whenever. Wherever."

Serina's heart turned over. "Won't they need you to navigate? To negotiate once they arrive in Azura?"

She wanted him with her when she went to find Nomi. But she wanted every woman on this island to find safety too. She'd assumed Val would have to go to Azura with them. Maybe she and Nomi would follow, if they could.

"Commander Ricci has maps. Some of these women come from boat families. Even if they can't read a map, I can show them. They'll know how to operate the ship." He rubbed his hand down her back. "And as for negotiating, they won't need a man for that. They'll want to speak for themselves."

Serina's throat closed as emotions swirled through her. "Yes, of course," she said, her voice thick. "They will want to speak for themselves."

For some time, they walked in silence.

Eventually, the prison complex rose before them, gray and imposing. Serina could still sense echoes of the terror she'd felt when she'd hiked up the uneven trail from the pier for the first time, this iron-barred monstrosity looming over her.

Her gaze shifted to the water, blue and sparkling, stretching out to the horizon. From here, she could just see the corner of the pier, and out beyond it—

"Val." She gasped, skidding to a stop. Her injured ankle screamed. Her stomach dropped.

She couldn't breathe.

She pointed, her hand trembling. "Val, a boat."

TWO

NOMI

Nomi stood on the boat's heaving deck, her heavy golden gown streaked with blood, and cried as the dark shadow of Mount Ruin rose before her. This wasn't the triumphant mission to save her sister that she'd envisioned. Nomi was heading for her own small cell, her own imprisonment. Asa had promised Nomi he'd reunite her with Serina, but she'd never imagined it would be like this. Not until she'd watched Asa slice his blade across his father's throat.

Maris, Nomi's fellow Grace, had seen it too, unfortunately. So Asa had sent them both away as prisoners, all so he could maintain the illusion that his older brother, the Heir, was the real murderer. A few feet in front of Nomi, Maris sagged against the gunwale, her straight black hair a snarl, her red dress soaked with sea spray. She slumped over the edge and stared into the water rushing by. Maybe she would have jumped overboard if her wrists hadn't been shackled to the boat. She hadn't said anything for a long time.

Nomi opened her mouth to offer something—a reassurance, another apology—but the wind stole her breath. Maybe it knew all she had were empty words.

They were close to Mount Ruin now, close enough to see the chipped concrete pier. Nomi swallowed a gulp of sea-soaked air.

The sailors moved to the bow of the boat, where Malachi lay. The Heir was a crumpled shadow on the deck, his burgundy velvet coat stained with his own blood and the blood of his father, the Superior. Asa had killed the Superior and tried to kill Malachi too.

All because Nomi had trusted Asa, had believed he would make a better Heir, a better Superior. She'd been wrong.

The sailors bent over Malachi's still form.

"Don't touch him!" Nomi screamed hoarsely, as she'd screamed a dozen times during the crossing, praying with every shout that they'd listen, that they'd notice his chest rising and falling. Asa had ordered them to throw Malachi overboard when he stopped breathing.

But he hadn't stopped.

"They said to throw him over when he died," one of the sailors was saying, the deep rumble of his voice barely audible over the constant thrust of the steam engine. "But he ain't dead yet and we're almost there."

"The prison don't know about our orders." The other sailor scratched his stubbled chin. "Less questions if we get rid of him now."

Nomi shouted again, but they ignored her.

"It's too late," Maris said, her dead-white cheeks whipped by her hair and her dead-dark eyes burning. At some point, they'd both lost their masks from the masquerade ball. Nomi couldn't remember the last time she'd felt the pinch of the stiff fabric across her nose. She couldn't believe the Heir's ball had been only hours ago.

Only hours since she'd told her brother, Renzo, to run instead of help her frame Malachi. She'd known by then that Asa wasn't to be trusted, but she'd had no sense of what he was capable of. She did now. She hoped Renzo had listened. She was certain Asa would kill him if he found him.

The sailors heaved the Heir to their shoulders. Malachi coughed weakly—"Can't you see he's still alive!" Nomi yelled—and his eyelids fluttered and opened, and he was awake and sputtering, and then he disappeared overboard.

A sob ripped from Nomi's chest.

Her chains clanked as she yanked herself toward the sailors, straining against the shackles. The skin at her wrists tore and bled. "You killed him!" she screamed, over and over. The sailors ignored her, and maybe they should have. She didn't know if she was speaking to them or herself.

You killed him.

This was her fault. She'd trusted the wrong brother. Asa had promised freedom, for Nomi *and* her sister. He'd promised an end to the Graces, a change to the laws of Viridia. He'd said he would let women have rights, let them read . . . he'd told her exactly what she wanted to hear. And she'd fallen under his spell. It had been easy, too easy to believe Malachi was as cruel and volatile as his father . . . because Asa had convinced her. But it had all been a lie. Asa was the cruel one.

The murderous one.

Malachi's words haunted her. *I've no desire for an unwilling Grace. I will force you no longer.* It was one of

16

the last things he had said to Nomi, releasing her from her obligation. He wouldn't force her to be a Grace.

And now he was dead.

The boat hit the pier with a shudder. Nomi's legs buckled, but the stiff brocade of her gown held her up. The sailors removed Maris's shackles, and then Nomi's. She spit in the closest one's face. He pushed her toward the gangplank, making her stumble. Maris kept her back mercilessly straight, but her cheeks were streaked with tears. Nomi couldn't bear it. Maris should never have been a part of this. She shouldn't be here with Nomi. She'd done nothing to deserve this suffering but witness someone else's crime.

But Maris was right. It was too late.

The sailors yanked Nomi and Maris onto the dock. A prison guard waited at the edge of the pier, his hat drawn low over his eyes.

"This is a smaller ship than usual," he said gruffly. "A smaller load too. Only two prisoners?"

The sailor gripping Nomi's arm shrugged. "Yeah. So?"

"And the rations?" he asked when the sailors deposited Nomi and Maris before him.

The other sailor scratched the back of his neck. "Rations? We were told to bring these girls here. No one said anything about rations."

"You've got their intake papers?" The guard put his hand out, impatience creeping into his voice.

Nomi wondered what would happen if she screamed out the truth—that Asa had killed the Superior and sent them here to keep them quiet. The guard probably wouldn't care.

"Got no papers," the sailor next to her said, shrugging. "This lot came from the palazzo. Don't know how it's usually done, but we were told very specific to bring 'em here. Which we've done." He wiped at his nose with the back of his hand. "Now they're your problem."

The prison guard stared narrowly at the blood on Nomi's dress and then at Maris's white cheeks. Was he worried it was some kind of trap? As if they were a threat.

Finally, with a curt nod and another long glance at the boat, he dismissed the sailors. Nomi's lungs constricted, bound by her corset and the horror coursing through her. She put her hands on her waist, wishing she could rip herself out of this dress, these mistakes, this life. Her fingers found a hole in the fabric; it took her a moment to remember that Asa had stabbed her too. He would have killed her, just like he killed Malachi—a sob lodged in her throat—but for the corset that was slowly killing her now.

In her mind, the Superior's icy eyes stared at her, his throat running with blood.

"Come on," the prison guard said roughly. When he grabbed Maris's arm, she whimpered.

Nomi glanced back once at the boat and the choppy waters off the edge of the pier. The sailors were watching her, even as they readied for their trip back. There was no sign of Malachi. Nomi turned and followed Maris and the guard, her feet dragging. The only thing keeping her from throwing herself off the pier and into the churning ocean was the hope that she would see Serina soon.

Please.

The guard moved quickly, pulling Maris up the steep path. He glanced back at Nomi often, his other hand on his firearm. His expression warned her not to fall behind.

Daylight warmed the blackened cliffs that framed the path, and soon Nomi was sweating, her dress heavy as iron. The footing didn't help; the strange, swirling rock caught at her impractical shoes. Twice she twisted her ankle.

Before her, the prison rose out of the rock like a cancerous growth, its steel-grated windows and concrete walls unnatural above the graceful whorls of volcanic rock.

Someone stood in front of the building's barbed-wire fence. At first, Nomi thought it was another guard. But there was something—she couldn't quite see around Maris—there was something familiar—

"We're out of sight of the boat," the guard said. He released Maris's arm. "You're safe."

"Safe?" Maris asked incredulously, shifting to put distance between them. The way opened before Nomi, fully revealing the figure waiting for them.

The woman flung her tail of hair over her shoulder, a move so familiar Nomi herself often subconsciously mimicked it.

Shock exploded through Nomi's body, electrifying every nerve ending. She forgot about the guard, the sailors, Renzo, Maris, Malachi.

All she saw was her sister.

"Serina!" she screamed.

She lifted her skirts, dodged Maris, and ran.

"*Nomi?*" Serina gasped, her eyes wide with disbelief, just as Nomi's arms crashed around her.

The force of Nomi's embrace knocked Serina back a step. But Nomi couldn't seem to calm down. She couldn't let go.

"Serina. Serina!" Her sister's name was sweet as an answered prayer in her mouth.

"How are you here?" Serina asked, her arms curving around Nomi. "You're hurt. Are you hurt? There's blood on your dress—"

"I'm fine. It's not mine. I'm—"

"You're here. You're *here*."

Apparently neither of them could form a coherent thought. Nomi sank into her sister's embrace and breathed fully for what felt like the first time in months. Nothing else mattered. The whole world became a blurry, forgotten dream. Nothing was real except Serina holding her close.

And suddenly, Nomi was weeping.

"I'm so sorry about the book," she said into Serina's shoulder. "I had no idea. I—"

"Hush, hush. I'm sorry too. I should have listened to you. I didn't see things the same way, but I do now. I . . ." Serina's grip tightened. "So much of what's happened is because of you."

Something inside of Nomi broke. Her sister said it, inexplicably, like this was a good thing, like whatever had happened because of Nomi was good. But Nomi had watched the Superior die. She'd felt the Heir's blood on her hands. She'd sent Renzo into hiding with a death sentence likely waiting for him. There was no good in this. In her.

"Oh, Serina. If you knew—" Nomi opened her mouth to tell Serina all that had happened, every shameful thing she'd done.

"Shh," Serina quieted her. "It doesn't matter. You're here now. You're safe. We both are."

At that, reality started to break through the haze. Nomi loosened her hold on Serina. Her sister's braid was untidy, her face bruised and swollen. It was such a departure from the perfectly polished, serene version of Serina—the only version she'd ever seen—that Nomi wondered how she'd even recognized her sister.

"How are we safe, Serina?" Nomi asked, staring at her sister's wounds. *Wounds.* Serina's clothes were torn and stained with blood. Where was her cell? And the guards? The guard who had met the boat . . .

She started to turn in his direction, but the look on Serina's face stopped her, with its mixture of weariness and pride.

"We *are* safe," Serina said. "For now, anyway. The women of Mount Ruin rebelled. We're not prisoners anymore. We're free."

Nomi's thoughts stuttered to a halt. She stared again at the purple bruises on Serina's face. "You're free? You look as if you've been beaten."

"I was. But I fought back," Serina said. "I am a rebel now, just like you."

With those radical words ringing in her ears, Nomi noted the new, commanding way Serina held herself, and she remembered the strength of Serina's embrace. "Not—not *just* like me," she said shakily.

Serina grinned.

Nomi smiled back, but the expression faded quickly. Serina didn't know why she was here. She didn't know what Nomi had done. She didn't know about Malachi and why Nomi's dress was covered in his blood.

"Serina, I—"

"This is Val," Serina said, gesturing to the guard. He wore an oddly joyful smile that Nomi couldn't account for. "He helped us . . . He's . . . well, not much of a guard, it turns out." Serina shared a knowing smirk with the young man.

Nomi gave him a little, awkward wave. She'd been terrified of him only moments ago. Every instinct within her still saw him as a threat.

"It's a shame we had no warning about the boat," Val said, his hand dropping from his firearm. "It was only two sailors."

"Only two?" Serina repeated, her eyes wide. "But we could have taken it, gotten out of here *now*. Why didn't—"

"I kill them?" Val asked, a sudden tension running through his frame. "They were innocent, Serina. They weren't the usual guards—they had no idea what the normal protocol was."

Nomi wanted to tell him that the guards *weren't* innocent—that they'd just killed the Heir—but she didn't understand what they were talking about or the stubborn set of her sister's chin.

"But we could have been off this island today," Serina said, sounding both wistful and annoyed at the same time.

"We're not ready." Val glanced at Nomi and Maris. "Had the boat not returned to the palazzo, we would have had mere hours before the Superior sent someone to investigate."

Val took a step toward Serina, and something in his expression made Nomi wonder at his relationship with her sister. Why did he look so pained at Serina's disappointment? "I'm sorry. I had to make a decision quickly."

Serina's expression eased. "You bought us time. That's good. We can stick with our plan."

Nomi was about to ask *What plan?* when Serina turned to Maris.

"Maris? That's your name, right?" she asked. "I remember you. You're one of the Heir's Graces too."

"Not anymore," Maris said flatly. "The Heir is dead. So is his father. Asa is the Superior now."

Serina's eyes filled with questions.

"I'll explain everything," Nomi said. She had to tell Serina about Renzo too. A sob lodged in the back of her throat. "It's . . . it's a lot."

"Grace! Grace!" A girl jogged down the path to them, her freckled cheeks stained pink with exertion. "We need you."

Serina tore her gaze from Nomi's. "What's happened, Mirror?"

Grace? Mirror?

The girl called Mirror paused, eyeing Nomi and Maris. "Who are you?"

"There was an unscheduled boat . . ." Serina hesitated. "It's complicated."

"So is this." Mirror beckoned toward the path.

Serina and Val followed her.

Nomi hustled after them, and even though she understood nothing, her heart still pounded at their urgency. Maris kept a hand on Nomi's arm, as if she were scared to let go.

"You found your sister," Maris mumbled. "That's something."

"This is madness," Nomi replied.

The black volcanic rock ebbed and flowed along the ground, forever frozen in its onslaught. Trees grappled toward the sky in small breaks, and a hardy yellow grass sprang up wherever it could find purchase. They passed the terrifying building Nomi had assumed was the prison. A few minutes later, another large building came into view, this one half-crumbled and yet somehow elegant, with a chipped marble fountain in front of it. Not a prison.

Serina and Mirror slowed.

"This way," Mirror said, and everyone followed her into the shade of a large marble-floored room that looked like it had once been the lobby of a hotel. In its center, a group of women huddled around something on the ground.

"What is it?" Serina asked. The women made room for her. Nomi and Maris paused outside the circle of women. But they were close enough to hear Serina's gasp, followed by, "I know him. That's the Heir."

Nomi's mind went blank. Then she was pushing through the others, ignoring their hisses and answering elbows, until she could see what the others saw. The body on the ground.

She fell to her knees at his side. Water puddled beneath him, wetting her heavy skirts. Whispers echoed behind her: *Malachi. The Heir. Is he dead?*

Nomi's hands flitted across Malachi's chest, over the deathly pallor of his cheeks, over his closed eyelids, purpled with cold. He was dead. Was he dead?

"What happened? Where did you find him?" Serina asked.

Another girl's voice answered, "He was on the beach south of the pier. Pretty bad wound in his side."

"He was on the boat with us," Nomi whispered. "They—they threw him overboard."

And there it was, so faint Nomi would have missed it if she hadn't been staring, hoping: the tiniest rise of his chest. "He's still alive." She could barely form the words.

"Maris said he was dead. And the Superior too. What happened?" Serina crouched by Nomi and put a hand on her shoulder.

"I was trying to save you," Nomi said in a rush. "I thought I could—I thought I was going to change Viridia. But Malachi's brother betrayed me. He—he killed his own father. And Malachi . . . What Maris said is true. Asa is the new Superior." The words sliced her throat like knives. "And it is my fault."

"Asa tried to kill his own brother?" Serina asked, staring down at Malachi, her eyes wide.

"If we don't do something fast, he's going to succeed," Nomi replied. Malachi had lost too much blood, had suffered for too long. He was strong, but he wouldn't survive in this state forever.

"Good," came a hard voice from the crowd of women. "Let them *all* die."

"His father killed my cousin," another call joined the first.

"His father took my sister as a Grace. She died two years later in childbirth. We should let his son die too."

Nomi brushed Malachi's cold cheek with her fingers. *No. No, he can't die.*

"Let him die!" The call was picked up. Magnified. The words echoed around her.

"No!" she shouted at last, above them all. Silence fell. She didn't stand up. She didn't look at the women crowded close. She kept her eyes on the faint swell of Malachi's chest, on the weak flutter at his throat.

"You do not want this man to die," she said, her voice ringing.

She knew what they did not. She had seen Asa's face after he killed his own father. She'd seen the emptiness, the lack of remorse. She'd seen how good he was at using people.

"You think the Superior was bad?" she continued, her voice pulsing with conviction. "You think he was capricious and cruel? You have no idea. His son Asa killed him, his own father, in cold blood. Asa fooled me for weeks, let me think he wanted what we all want—freedom and choice for women in this country. He convinced me entirely, so much so that I helped him plot to replace his own brother as Heir. He convinced me that Malachi was as volatile and awful as their father. But Malachi is *not*. He is *not his father*." The words filled her up, the fury spilled out. Nomi stood up and faced Serina. "You can't let him die. He's the only one who can stop Asa. And trust me, Serina, Asa *must* be stopped."

Nomi's heart beat so loudly she could hear it pulsing in her ears.

Serina glanced around at the women who encircled them. "Nomi . . ." she said, and Nomi could see as clearly as Serina the bloodlust in their eyes. These women had suffered. They wanted the Heir to suffer too.

Nomi reached for her sister's hands. She didn't understand what was going on here, why these women seemed to listen to her sister. But they were, to a one, waiting to hear what Serina said. "Malachi does not deserve to die," Nomi said, more softly. "He's in this position because of me. His blood is on my hands. I can't let him die."

Serina glanced down at Malachi's still form for a long moment. When she spoke, her voice was strong and the expression in her eyes was one Nomi had never seen before: hard and glittering, without a hint of serenity. "This is my sister, Nomi. She's been living in the palazzo. If she says the Heir needs to live, then he lives."

"What if she's wrong? What if he's as bad as the rest?" a girl with a swollen cheek asked, crossing her arms over her chest.

Nomi opened her mouth to say he wasn't, to tell them what he'd said to her at the ball. That he'd be willing to let her cease being a Grace if she chose.

But Serina spoke first. "She's my *sister*, Anika. I trust her, and we will try to save his life. He may die anyway. If he doesn't, if he recovers, we will watch him closely. Because Mount Ruin is no longer his to claim. If he threatens us in any way . . . if he's not the man my sister says he is, we will kill him ourselves. This is our island, won by our bodies and our blood. We will not give it up to him."

Nomi stared at Serina as she would a stranger. Her sister had lost all hint of softness, of submission. She looked *nothing* like a Grace. Instead of dance steps and face creams, she spoke of bodies and blood. Of murder.

The truth Nomi had been facing since the first moment of their reunion crystallized in her mind. Serina had become a warrior.

"Are you . . . are you their leader?" Nomi asked, in awe.

"She's the reason we're free," Anika said. "The guards forced us to fight each other. *Kill* each other."

Nomi's breath could barely find its way to her lungs. Nomi's secret had sentenced Serina to *this*? Serina had been sent here for stealing a book, for knowing how to read. But it had been *Nomi's* crime. This should have been Nomi's punishment.

"Your sister refused to kill me," Anika continued. "Grace was supposed to finish me off. Her crew would have gotten the rations, but she submitted instead. She refused to fight. No one had ever done that before." She glanced at Serina. "She upended everything. Got some of the crews to work together, to fight back. We won."

"I don't understand," Maris said, a rough edge to her voice, as if she were close to tears. "They made you kill each other?"

"Serina was sent here for *reading*," Nomi added. "How could—how—"

"How could death be the punishment for that?" Anika finished for her. Her black eyes narrowed. "This prison is not only for murderers and conspirators, don't you see? It's for any woman who challenges the way Viridia works, in even the smallest ways. It's for the *disobedient*."

And Nomi did see, at last. She thought of the queens of Viridia, the way they'd been erased from history. The way the Superiors, then and now, had tried to destroy every wisp of independence and rebellion from the women in this country.

"How did you disobey?" she asked, glancing at Anika's strong-jawed face.

The girl's lips twitched into a grim smile. "Ah well. I *was* one of the murderers."

Maris made a choked noise.

"Can't defend yourself in this country either, if you're a girl." Anika's expression changed, went dark and deep.

Into the silence, Malachi groaned.

THREE

SERINA

Serina knew she had to deal with Malachi, but she couldn't concentrate on anything but her sister's presence. She took in Nomi's bedraggled hair, half-fallen from its pins. Her smooth, clear skin, her delicate amber eyes. Her newly graceful bearing.

Nomi was *here*. It didn't matter why or how it had happened. Serina didn't care. All that mattered was that she was here. Serina's baby sister was here. They were *both* free. Hope sprang to life in Serina's heart, fed by this strange, impossible miracle. If her ribs didn't scream with every breath, she'd think it was a dream.

Serina couldn't imagine what Nomi saw when she returned her gaze. In fact, it might have brought her shame, the knowledge that she was dirty and wild and un-Grace-like, if she didn't know what her newly strong arms had accomplished. What her sweat-stained body had withstood.

Malachi groaned again.

"Please help him," Nomi pleaded.

Val pushed through the crowd, carrying a large leather bag. "I've got some extra medical supplies."

Serina glanced at Anika. With a nod, the girl raised her voice above the grumblings and questions. "Give him some room. Who's helping with the other injured? We've got wounds to stitch and food to distribute. Let's get on with it."

Before Serina turned her full attention to Malachi, she paused to watch the women scatter. Most she didn't know by name, but she saw Doll's tall frame and Claw's hunched shoulders. She wondered how Ember was doing; Oracle's death had leveled her. Since they'd returned from committing Oracle and the other dead women to the volcano, Ember had kept to herself, refusing to engage in any of the planning.

Serina needed to assess for herself how many were wounded, whether the move to Hotel Misery was going smoothly and the extra rations distributed fairly. And the captured guards—she still needed to check on them. She and Val had abandoned that task when the boat had arrived.

So much to do, and Serina was so tired.

Maris, the other Grace, paced awkwardly across the marble floor, her eyes never leaving Malachi's still form. Serina wondered what part she had played in all of this. Why had Asa sent *her* here?

"Serina, what can we do for him?" Nomi asked, kneeling again at Malachi's side.

Serina crouched down, despite her sore body's protests, and carefully pulled his wet jacket up to expose his stomach. He moaned weakly. A small hole marred his unnaturally pale skin. "He's still bleeding, but there's no pus or fluids leaking," Serina said. "That's good."

Nomi made a noise in the back of her throat, as if she were choking. Serina wondered why she cared so much about Malachi's fate. Was it just because she felt guilty for trusting the wrong brother, or had she developed actual affection for him? That was hard to imagine. Serina remembered Nomi's horror at being chosen as a Grace.

But people could change. Serina certainly had.

Still, if Nomi had felt something for Malachi, surely she would never have betrayed him. Serina didn't have all the details yet, but she had the sense there was more to the story than Nomi had had a chance to share. As there was more to Serina's.

"Let's move him to the infirmary," Val said. He gestured to a couple of the women loitering in the open walkways, and they helped him lift Malachi's limp form. Serina was grateful; her own injuries still ached from carrying Oracle up the mountain.

When they'd gotten Malachi settled on a pallet in a shadowy corner of the ballroom, away from the injured women, Val handed Serina a glass bottle of disinfectant and clean dressings. Nomi and Maris watched, eyes wide.

Serina dabbed at the rim of the wound, gently prodding at the skin. She found a needle and thread in the leather bag, careful not to jostle her patient, and sewed up the wound.

Behind her, Nomi swallowed loudly. "You—you can—"

"I was always good at embroidery," Serina said wryly. She wrapped thick pressure dressings around Malachi's torso. He shifted, his handsome face twisting into a grimace, but he didn't open his eyes.

"There's a slash on his arm too," Val said softly. He cut the jacket away from the ragged skin.

Serina worked quickly, smoothing salve over the ridge of stitches when she was done. "That one's not so deep."

Nomi was curled into herself, her olive skin ashen.

Serina couldn't tell if her sister was about to vomit or faint. She wiped her hands clean on an extra dressing and put an arm around her. Her own stitches pulled, and her arm and ribs ached, but she ignored the pain.

Nomi didn't relax. "Is he going to be okay?"

Serina glanced at Malachi again. He was breathing steadily and she'd felt a strong pulse in his wrist, but he still looked awful. "I don't know," she said honestly.

She sat with Nomi and Maris for a few minutes, holding vigil over the rise and fall of the Heir's chest. Holding her sister's hand.

Val went to see if anyone else needed the extra medical supplies. When he returned, he said softly, "We should check on the guards."

Serina nodded. With a groan, she stood up, her wounds flaring to life. Nomi's grip on her hand tightened. "Where are you going?"

Serina nearly cried at the thought of this small parting, after wishing to see her sister for so long. "Some of the guards survived the uprising. We need to check on them. I'll be back soon. I promise."

Nomi looked up, and even though fear and exhaustion lurked in her eyes, she smiled and, for Serina, it was everything.

Buoyed, Serina headed for the main archway. Outside, Anika was directing women from the other crews to their new rooms. Serina noticed a girl standing in the shadows beneath the trees a few yards away, watching the influx with hands fisted at her sides. Something about her looked familiar, the halo of dark hair, the glare . . .

Serina's chest tightened. The girl who'd killed Petrel. Who'd raised her bloody fist in the air and shouted in triumph.

It was difficult, suddenly, to remember Serina's own diplomatic words about the Commander forcing women to fight. Petrel's killer had . . . well, she'd seemed to enjoy it.

"What's that girl's name?" Serina asked, tilting her head.

Val glanced in the direction she indicated. "Oh. I think she's called Scorpion."

Serina suppressed a shiver.

"She's ruthless," she said, remembering Petrel's face as Scorpion's hidden knife had sliced her throat. "We should put her on rotation to watch the guards."

"That's a good idea," Val said.

As long as she's not on watch with me, Serina added silently.

They hiked up the narrow path toward the prison, retracing their steps from the morning. The back of Val's hand brushed hers as they walked. Each time it happened, her attention focused with precision to that one spot of contact, that brief pinpoint of connection. It was distracting.

"It's incredible that your sister was on that boat," he said, his voice full of wonder. "You must be so happy. Well, relieved. She's here, she's safe, and now we can all go to Azura together."

Happy. Serina thought about that word.

"Yes, it's a huge relief," she said.

They reached the prison complex. She wrinkled her nose at the stale scent of the dank, airless hall. Val led her up a set of stairs to a heavy steel door. This door didn't require a key, but the long row of barred doors inside did. She closed her hand around the cool weight of the keys again. Midway down the hall, two women sat on the floor facing each other.

Angry voices enveloped them.

One of the girls stood up. Gia, from Cave crew. Her normally golden-brown cheeks were flushed, her short hair standing up in sun-bleached whorls.

"Is it time to switch out?" she asked eagerly.

As Serina approached, the voices of the guards became clearer.

"I'm going to strangle you."

"I'm going to make you beg."

"You don't even know what I'm going to do to you. Open this door. Let me show you."

And worse.

Gia's impatience suddenly made sense.

As Serina came up next to the girls, one of the guards reached out, grabbed her braid, and yanked savagely. Serina's head knocked sickeningly against the steel bars of his cell.

Panic exploded in her chest. She fought the guard's grip as he ground her ear against the cold metal.

"*Stop*, Diego!" Val shouted. He reached through the bars and clamped his hand around the guard's neck. "Let. Her. Go."

Diego let out a choked laugh of defiance. His grip didn't loosen.

Serina reached back and dug her fingernails into his hand at the same time she braced her injured foot against the cell door and *shoved*. With a catlike yowl, Diego let go.

Serina stumbled back, into Gia. They tumbled to the hard floor, cracking elbows and hips. Belatedly, she became aware of the din; the other guards were cheering Diego on.

Val squeezed Diego tighter, until he squirmed and his face went purple. At last, when the guard's eyes were on the verge of rolling, Val let him go.

Diego slumped against the bars, coughing and sputtering. His ruddy cheeks stayed an ugly purplish red, clashing with the tan of his bald head. He was maybe forty, with the kind of muscle made for violence.

Another of the guards shouted, "Come on, Val. Let us out. We'll give you a good fight before we kill your treasonous ass."

Val's face was flushed, his glare murderous. It took him a while to compose himself enough to answer. "You're lucky no one's killing yours, Carlo."

Serina's legs shook. There were seven guards locked in their own small rooms. All but one of them dangled their arms through the bars and stared at her, their expressions eager, like ravenous dogs.

Slowly, she untangled herself from Gia, and together they stood up, careful to stay well away from Diego's reach. The other girl who'd been on guard duty had escaped down the hallway to the door. Serina didn't blame her. She sent Gia after her, with a whispered "I'm okay" to the girl's raised brow.

Then Serina drew Val in the opposite direction, toward the storage rooms. He moved sluggishly, probably resisting the urge to beat Diego senseless.

"Is it safe here?" Serina asked quietly. Her scalp burned.

Val ran a hand through his hair. His cheeks were still an angry red. "It should be," he answered. "We took anything they could use as weapons. They can't get out of the cells. You've got all the keys to the doors. I made sure there weren't copies anywhere."

"We should remind everyone to stay back from the cells," Serina said, shivering.

"Yes." Val ran a hand down her arm. "Are you okay?"

"Just shaken." Serina glanced back at the men, who were still yelling insults. "I guess we have to feed them." This was meant as a joke, but it didn't quite come out that way. It seemed a shame to waste their precious rations on men who wanted to kill them.

"If we run out of rations, they can be the first to starve," Val said mildly.

Serina glanced at him. His betrayal of the other guards didn't appear to weigh on him; in fact, he seemed lighter now, more at ease, than she'd ever seen him.

"Did you want this to happen?" she asked softly. "You seem so comfortable with rebellion."

Val paused before an unlocked cell housing the rest of the burlap bags of rations.

He took her hand, gently, and stepped into the small patch of bare floor in the cell, where they were out of sight of the guards. "Did I want a rebellion?" he murmured. "Yes. I hated this job, this life. Every day felt like penance for not getting here in time to save my mother. Every day was agony, watching more girls die."

"And now that's all over," Serina murmured. "No one else will die."

"No one else," he agreed.

She drifted closer, until only a breath separated them. Adrenaline still rocketed through her body, but the signals it was sending had changed. Their hands shifted, separated. She moved hers to his shoulders, ignoring the pinch of her injured ribs. His slid to her waist.

Her pulse fluttered in her throat.

"Serin . . ."

"You said you thought there was something between us," she said, her voice thick. "I said I needed time to sort it out."

"Yes, that's true," he murmured, and his eyes darkened, and he stared at her mouth.

"What if I told you that things are different now? Now that you're not a guard, and I'm not a prisoner?"

His fingers drifted to her bruised cheek. The lightest touch but somehow it still stoked a fire. Only, it wasn't the fiery pain she'd been managing for hours now. It was something else. A fire that burned without hurting at all.

Their first kiss had been impulsive. Fleeting.

Serina had begun that one, and she began this one now, leaning forward until their lips just touched.

Val's answer to her question came as a gentle pressure, an affirmation. He kissed her back slowly, sweetly, and let her take her time.

Serina's belly filled with heat. She wanted this moment to last forever, to block out all the horrors of the night before, all the blood and death and pain. To block out the guards' harsh voices, the memory of Diego yanking on her hair.

And for a few precious seconds, it did.

When she drew back, Val opened his eyes, and they were soft and lazy, as if he awoke from a dream. "I'm glad you sorted it out," he said.

She kissed him again, a quick, laughing kiss, because he had been right the first time. *Happy*. As implausible as it seemed, she *was* happy, despite Diego's attempts to derail her. She had Nomi. And she had Val.

"Come on," she said, moving to the door without picking up a bag. "The guards can go without rations until the morning. Won't kill 'em, right?"

Val nodded decisively. "Right."

Bolstered by their kiss and anxious to see Nomi again, Serina found it easy enough to ignore the guards as they headed back down the hall. The shouts of "I'm going to kill you" and "You're dead, flower" had lost their power to frighten her.

FOUR

NOMI

"I can't stand it in here any longer," Maris said as she paced their corner of the infirmary. She stared at the women lying prone at the other end of the makeshift infirmary. One of them was moaning incessantly. Hopelessly.

Nomi squeezed Malachi's limp hand. He was still too pale. Too still. "I'm afraid to leave him. What if . . . what if the others don't listen to Serina? What if they try to hurt him?"

"I know you're worried." Maris ran both of her hands through her hair, obsessively finger-combing out the tangles. "But what if we stand just outside? For a moment, for some fresh air? We'll keep him in view."

She had always kept her agitation deeply hidden. But now she looked as if her very skin were a restraint she wanted to tear free from.

Nomi hated to leave Malachi alone, but she couldn't bear to see Maris so distressed. She stood up, her gaze still pinned to the movement of Malachi's chest. Up and down, up and down. Almost steadily. The moaning bothered her too, and the coppery smell of blood. Fresh air would do both Maris *and* Nomi good. "Just for a moment."

Maris led the way to the door, almost running in her haste. Nomi kept her eyes on the golden square of daylight and away from the shifting, miserable women trying to live through their wounds.

Daylight broke upon her, and the scent of plumeria and a lit match, like a scented candle just blown out. The burnt smell came from the volcano, she assumed. Maris stopped near the crumbled fountain, tipped her head back, and closed her eyes.

Nomi stayed closer to the doorway, but she took deep breaths of the fresh, fragrant air.

Women filed through the courtyard, directed by Anika and others. Nomi looked for Serina but didn't see her. Instead, strangers passed, women dressed in ragged, sleeveless shirts, in boots or flimsy slippers, with spears and makeshift knives in their hands. Some carried handfuls of citrus fruit pressed into their chests. One woman, tall and sturdy, carried some kind of carcass over her shoulder.

Suddenly, a flash of blue cut through the gathered women like an arrow. A girl threw herself at Maris, so hard they both tumbled to the ground.

Nomi put her arms up, to protect herself or hide from whatever carnage befell her friend. A coward's reaction.

Maris screamed breathlessly. "Helena!"

Nomi dropped her arms.

Helena? As in, the girl Maris was in love with?

Helena's sunburned, freckled hands framed Maris's face as she kissed Maris's cheeks, her forehead, her mouth. The two girls melted into each other, their bodies twining like vines along the dusty ground.

Nomi blushed and shifted her gaze to the worn marble woman in the fountain, giving them what privacy she could.

41

Maris had told Nomi about Helena, about how they'd had a plan to bring Helena to the palazzo as Maris's handmaiden so they could be together. But Maris's father had discovered them and forbade it, sending Maris to the palazzo alone. Maris hadn't known what had happened to Helena, had assumed she'd never see her again.

Nomi's chest filled with unexpected joy. Maris and Helena had actually found each other.

And that wasn't the only miracle. Serina was free. Malachi still breathed.

For now.

Nomi glanced toward the doorway of the infirmary, but she couldn't bear to return to its dim, blood-choked air just yet.

Maris and Helena surfaced from their embrace, pink-cheeked and grinning.

Nomi had never seen Maris happy, not really, not like this. Not with the kind of brilliant, joyful smile that reached her eyes. She looked like a different person, or the same person washed clean.

Asa had never made Nomi smile like that, she realized, and the thought brought her comfort. She'd cared for him, trusted him when she shouldn't have, but she hadn't *loved* him. Not the way Maris loved Helena. That made it easier to hate him now.

"I didn't know you were here," Maris said to Helena, her voice still breathless. She stood up and brushed off her dusty dress, her gaze never leaving Helena's. "I thought you'd be married off, that your parents—"

"It doesn't matter," Helena said, tucking a strand of Maris's hair behind her ear. Her own hair was a ragged sandy-blond mop. "I can't believe you're here. I thought I'd never see you again, and you're *here*." She touched Maris's face, as if reassuring herself that she was not a dream.

"My father turned you in, didn't he?" Maris asked, the breathlessness gone. "He turned you in, even after I did everything he demanded. Didn't he?"

Helena raised one shoulder and let it drop. "I don't know *who* did. They came for me in the middle of the night. *My* father didn't try to stop them."

Maris buried her face in Helena's shoulder. They wrapped their arms around each other.

Nomi's heart ached. Helena's own father had let her be taken?

She didn't want to think about what her parents would have done if they'd known she could read and write.

Serina appeared at the head of the path, speeding up when she noticed the commotion.

"Are you well?" she asked when she reached Nomi's side. She glanced at Maris and Helena, who still stood within each other's arms.

"Fine," Nomi said, smiling. "We've had another reunion."

Serina relaxed. "And how is Malachi?"

"He hasn't woken up yet," Nomi said. "Maybe you can see if there's anything more we can do?"

"Of course," Serina replied.

Nomi and Serina ducked into the infirmary, leaving Maris and Helena in the sunlight.

——

Nomi stood in the center of a ballroom. Lights glimmered. Colors flashed. She was the only point of stillness in the room; dancers surrounded her, twisting and twirling. She noticed, with growing unease, their masks—not the sparkling masks of the masquerade, but heavy black ones with slits for eyes. Executioner masks.

Her gown was the color of old blood. Heavy. Constricting. She tried to move, but it held her fast.

Her breath caught in her throat.

Before her, the Superior sat on a raised dais. He, unlike his guests, wore no mask. His thin, ill face stared straight forward. Straight at her.

Three figures sat beside him.

Malachi.

Renzo.

Serina.

They wore black. No masks. Blank, dead eyes.

Nomi gasped. She pulled against the cage of her dress. Couldn't move.

The dancers didn't slow. They twirled around her, oblivious, their black masks turned toward their partners, expressionless and eerie.

Through the crowd, one figure moved with purpose. *He* noticed the people on the dais. *He* noticed her. As he reached the Superior, Asa turned and met her panicked gaze. He moved to stand behind his father. Then he drew his dagger and slit his father's throat.

Nomi tried to scream.

No sound came out. The musicians didn't falter. The dancers didn't deviate.

Asa moved down the line. His mild expression didn't change. And he never looked anywhere but straight at her.

Nomi felt the pressure of a sob building in her chest, but it had no outlet. She couldn't move, couldn't scream, couldn't save them.

Asa calmly slit Malachi's throat.

In silence, the Superior and his son bled across the dance floor. Their blood eddied like a river; it stained the delicate slippers and fine leather boots of the dancers. It rippled toward Nomi's red dress and her dirty bare feet.

Her heart pounded frantically; her muscles strained.

Asa smiled.

The dagger slid across Renzo's tan skin. His blood flowed red. Nomi lunged uselessly, railed uselessly, screamed silently as her soul churned in anguish.

Asa raised his knife to Serina's smooth throat. Nomi went blank with rage.

And somehow her scream broke through.

She could hear it, echoing. Broken with despair.

Hands shook her.

Darkness swallowed Asa's glinting smile.

"Nomi. Nomi! Wake up!"

She shot up, her lungs gasping in gulps of air. Her arms flung outward, as if they were tearing off restraints.

"Nomi, it's okay. You're safe."

Nomi opened her eyes, and Serina was there, lamplight flickering across her face. Slowly the ruined ballroom, half-eaten by swirls of blackened lava, coalesced around her.

Serina held her shoulders. Val stood behind her, his expression haunted. Malachi slept a couple of feet away.

"You were screaming," Serina murmured.

Nomi's gaze found Malachi's haggard face. "He didn't wake," she whispered.

"Don't worry," Serina said, and they were the words of an older sister, offering comfort for comfort's sake. It was a gesture of love, not an assurance that there was nothing to worry about.

"I saw him," Nomi mumbled, rubbing at her face. "I saw Asa. I saw him in my dream."

"Nightmare," Serina corrected. "That's all it was."

Nomi's throat ached, as if she'd been screaming for hours. At the other end of the ballroom, figures shifted and sighed on pallets. She noticed a couple of the injured women staring at her.

"I'm sorry," she said. "I didn't mean to wake anyone."

Reaction was setting in. Nomi could feel the burn of tears, the thickening in her throat.

Serina tugged gently on her arm. "Come on. Let's get some air. Val will keep an eye on Malachi."

Nomi pulled herself up and shuffled after her sister. Before they'd bedded down for the night in the far corner of the infirmary, Serina had given Nomi and Maris some threadbare shirts and pants so they could change out of their dirty gowns. Nomi appreciated the ease of movement, but she couldn't shake off the heaviness of the dress in her dream, the paralysis it had forced upon her.

Maris had found a room in the hotel with Helena; Nomi wondered if she was sleeping soundly or fighting her own dark dreams.

Serina led Nomi through the moonlit dark to a spot at the edge of a cliff, where the wind blew their hair back and the waves crashed in rhythmic percussion below. Serina dangled her feet off the cliff. Nomi didn't feel so brave.

She curled up next to Serina, close enough that she could lean into her side. Serina wrapped an arm around her.

"I had trouble sleeping my first night here too," Serina said. "I was so terrified . . ."

She told Nomi about the fight that first night, how shocking it had been. She told her about the lava tube, the way the rock weighed down on her.

"I imagined you in a cell," Nomi confessed, turning a small rock in her hand, its rough edges scraping the pads of her fingers. "You were confined, and angry at me, but you were safe enough. I had no—I had no idea you were fighting for your life. I felt so guilty, but *this* . . . Serina, I—"

Her sister cuddled her closer, easing the stiffness from Nomi's limbs.

"None of us knew the danger in being a woman with a book," she said softly. "And if you had known, would it have mattered? Could you have changed?"

Nomi burrowed into Serina's shoulder, ashamed. "I don't know."

I don't think so.

Nomi heaved a breath. "But if I'd known you would pay for my crime, I never would have taken that book. I never would have touched *any* book. You must believe me, Serina, I wanted to tell the truth. I wanted to tell them it was me. But Ines said it wouldn't make a difference, that you would have been punished for lying instead." Her voice shook. "All the plotting with Asa, it was all to get you out of here."

"I think it's time for you to tell me what happened," Serina said. To her credit, she never moved away from Nomi. Her voice didn't harden. Nomi still couldn't understand how Serina didn't hate her.

Her stomach twisted. She didn't know where to start. "There's so much. Asa, and Malachi ... he gave me a book, except I thought it was Asa who had. Malachi wondered if I could read. It was a little mystery he tried to solve. And he did figure it out. He tempted me with a book of Viridia's true history—"

"I don't understand," Serina interrupted. "Slow down, Nomi. You're not making sense. What does Viridia's history have to do with this?"

Nomi's lip quirked sadly. "More than you'd think. We had queens once. Viridia had *queens*. Our first came from Azura. She was a woman, a warrior, who overthrew the corrupt ruling cardinal by seducing and poisoning him. She and her daughters ruled for two generations before their own advisors betrayed them. Erased them."

Serina shook her head. "Of *course* they erased them," she said. "They are still erasing us, every day. But I don't know what this has to do with how you came to be here."

"I thought Asa had given me the book. I thought he wanted me to be his queen, just like those women. I thought I would have the power to save you from this place." Nomi took a deep breath. "But it was all a lie. He never meant to release you. He lied about wanting a queen and giving women rights. I didn't realize until it was too late."

Heart aching, the words sucking slowly through the guilt and grief, Nomi told Serina about Renzo. About how she had written to him, asked him to be part of the plot. How she'd changed her mind at the last moment and begged him to run.

"I don't know where he went or if he got away," Nomi said, tightening her fingers around the rough stone until it hurt. "I used Luca's address for the letter, but Asa met Renzo himself. Renzo might have told him his real name, where he really lives. I don't know."

"You involved *Renzo*?" Serina's voice rose over the crash of the waves. "You—you asked him to *kill the Superior*?"

"No!"

Nomi explained exactly how the scheme was supposed to work, how Renzo was just supposed to pretend, just enough to throw suspicion onto Malachi. "He wanted to help, Serina. We were trying to save you."

Serina's mouth twisted into a horrified frown. "And now Asa is after him."

Nomi's tears fell. "I have to go back for him. I have to help him."

Serina's head dropped forward into her hands, as if it were suddenly too heavy to lift. "Yes, you do."

"I'm sorry," Nomi whispered, her nightmare blooming in her mind. What if Asa had already killed Renzo? Self-loathing poured through her. Her poor judgment had put both her sister and brother in danger. "I'm so sorry for everything. This is all my fault."

FIVE

SERINA

Renzo is in danger. Her whole family was.

Serina could feel a familiar anger bubbling up, the same words she'd said to Nomi so many times before rising to her tongue: *How could you be so careless?*

But she didn't say them, not this time. How could she lecture Nomi when it was for Serina's own salvation Nomi had been fighting? And who else could Nomi have asked? Of course Renzo would have wanted to help. He was as much a rebel as Nomi.

As me.

"None of this is your fault," Serina said, conviction coating every word. Her anger wasn't for Nomi anyway. Not anymore. "It is *Viridia's* fault. Sending women to their deaths for reading, for wanting to make their own choices . . . This country is sick, Nomi, rotten to its core."

Her sister looked at her, the whites of her eyes gleaming in the moonlight. "But if I hadn't stolen that book—"

"You should never have *had* to steal it. You should have always been allowed to read."

"S-Serina . . ." Nomi stuttered, obviously shocked.

It was true that Serina hadn't always supported her sister's secret. But now she knew better.

"Now then," Serina said, clearing her throat. "We need to figure out what to do about Renzo."

"And our parents," Nomi said. "As long as Asa is in power, they're in danger."

Serina's mind spun. What could they do? "The plan is to wait for the next prison ship," she said. "Overpower the guards and escape to Azura. Once the women are safe and on their way, Val and I were going to take a small boat back to Bellaqua to find you. We can use it to find Renzo instead. We'll get him and our parents to Azura. We should all be safe there."

Nomi picked at a small hole in the knee of her pants. "How long until the ship arrives?"

"A week. Maybe two." Serina, thinking of Renzo trying to evade the new Superior's clutches, found that her own hands were restless.

"That's too long," Nomi replied, her back stiffening. "Asa will be looking for him. He'll kill Renzo if he finds him. We have to go soon. *Now*."

"And how will *we* find him?"

Nomi shifted. "I don't know. He won't go home. I suppose . . . I don't know how we find him. But we have to, Serina. Before Asa does."

Serina wanted to help Renzo, desperately, but she'd made a promise to these women. She'd made a promise to herself . . .

"We need to think, plan," she said, hating that it felt like stalling, even as it was true. They *did* need a plan. "And we need to wait for Malachi to wake up. Asa thinks he's dead; that makes the knowledge that he's alive powerful. We need to make sure he *will* live before we return to Bellaqua."

Nomi sighed.

Serina stared out at the endless darkness of the ocean, the enduring glint of the stars, and the faint twinkle of Bellaqua. She pointed. "See that? I came here so often to sit and stare at those lights, trying to imagine what you were doing. If you were happy. If you were scared." She turned to Nomi's shadowy profile. "I'm sorry I didn't understand why that world would be so unwelcome to you. I understand now."

"It was just as I expected, and yet different as well," Nomi said. "Malachi, he . . . well, I didn't realize it at first, but he was different too. You're right about him. I can't leave until I know he'll live. That he'll be all right."

Serina remembered the intensity in Nomi's face when she'd pleaded for his life. "Why are you so protective of him? Did you . . . I mean, do you care for him?"

Nomi didn't answer right away. A glow along the horizon hinted at dawn, but it wasn't enough light to reveal her expression.

"It's not so simple as whether I care for him," she said at last. "It's that I owe him. I misjudged him from the moment I met him, and I destroyed his life. He didn't deserve that." She trapped her windblown hair and twisted it around her hand. "Two nights ago, at his birthday ball, Malachi told me he would not force me to be his Grace. That it had been unfair to choose me, unwilling as I was."

Serina's brows rose. "He said that?"

Nomi nodded. "It's why I tried to call off the scheme to frame him. But it was too late. Asa took matters into his own hands." Her voice cracked.

53

Serina couldn't mistake the naked misery in her sister's voice. "He . . . he must care for you, to let you go."

Nomi's face crumpled.

Understanding dawned. "But you cared for Asa."

Nomi's voice hardened. "I thought I did. I trusted him, and he used me. He used my affection for him, my love for you, for his own ends. He killed his father and tried to kill his brother, and he shipped me off to prison . . . but before all of that he kissed me and told me he wanted me to be queen, and I believed him."

Serina put her arms around Nomi, aching for her sister. She sat in silence, holding Nomi as she cried, just as she'd done when they were children. The moment was bittersweet; Serina hated that Nomi was hurting, but she was also grateful to be able to comfort her. Not long ago, she'd been certain she'd never get this chance again.

After a while, she murmured, "Asa will pay for what he's done. I am certain."

Nomi cleaned her face on the edge of her shirt. "I hope so."

They curled into each other's arms and listened to the surf and let the wind whip through their hair, and soon enough, dawn found them.

———

A shout stirred Serina from her exhausted haze. She straightened, her back stiff, her broken rib pulsing. She'd only gotten a few hours of sleep in the infirmary before Nomi had woken up screaming, and every ache and sore spot told her that it wasn't enough.

But Nomi's soft cheek snuggled into her shoulder was worth the pain.

They both turned to see Val jogging toward them.

Nomi scrambled to her feet; it took Serina a few extra moments to coax her battered body to do the same.

Val stopped in front of them. His chest rose and fell quickly, straining against his gray shirt. He must have run the whole way.

"I thought you might be here," he said, by way of greeting.

"What is it?" Serina asked, worry unfurling in her chest. His hair twisted in every direction, as usual, and his bright blue eyes were alert, but there was no pinch of concern to his mouth or furrow between his brows.

"Malachi woke up," he said simply. He cast a glance at Nomi. "I thought you'd want to know as soon as possible."

Nomi's eyes widened. "Oh, thank you," she said. Her hands grabbed for phantom skirts, an ingrained instinct, before she caught herself and hurried down the path.

Serina turned and followed, Val at her side. His hand brushed hers. With a little intake of breath for courage, she slid her palm against his and linked their fingers. His grip tightened without hesitation. He shot her a smile.

They walked the rest of the way back to Hotel Misery holding hands.

When they entered the makeshift infirmary a few steps behind Nomi, Serina had to pause to let her eyes adjust to the dimness. The smell crept up on her, sharp and sickening: the scent of blood. And then the sounds: quiet weeping, a pain-filled groan, whispered voices.

In the far corner, Malachi sat propped up against the wall, staring straight ahead.

Nomi shot a nervous glance back at Serina before approaching him. Serina and Val followed more slowly, but they were close enough to hear Nomi say the Heir's name.

He looked up at her. Serina studied his handsome face, with its sharp cheekbones and jaw, its rough stubble and full lips. She searched for a softening around his eyes or a smile at the sight of Nomi. She was sure he must have affection for her sister, to free her from her position as his Grace. But his face remained expressionless.

"Nomi," he said, and Serina could read nothing in his voice. A thread of ice knit itself into her spine.

"I'm so happy you're awake." Nomi knelt before him. Serina hated the way she bowed her head, the way her voice cracked. "I'm so sorry. About everything. I—I didn't realize . . . I'm sorry."

The Heir licked his chapped lips. "Nomi," he said again, and Serina saw the shift, saw the anger begin to creep through. He didn't care about her sister's obvious regret. "How could you?"

Nomi's shoulders shook. Serina stepped forward, intending to comfort her—or maybe say something rude to the Heir—but Val's hand tightened around hers. "Give them a moment," he whispered. Reluctantly, Serina paused. She could only guess at the weight Nomi carried.

Malachi's gaze never left Nomi as she told him everything—the plot, how she'd involved Renzo, even how she'd used Renzo's friend's address to send him a message. And she told him that she'd come to realize Asa was wrong, and she'd sent Renzo away. Malachi's stony expression never changed. Neither did he acknowledge Serina and Val standing right behind her nor ask who they were.

"I'm so sorry," Nomi said again, her voice vibrating with emotion. "I just wanted to help Serina and the women of Viridia. I shouldn't have trusted Asa. I didn't know—"

"You should have trusted *me*," Malachi interrupted, his voice sharp as a whip. "If you'd talked to me, if you'd told me you wanted to save your sister—"

Nomi made a noise in her throat and raised her head. There was a new strength in her voice when she said, "Of course I wanted to save my sister. I didn't have to tell Asa this. He already knew. He spoke to me about her, not the other way around."

"He was using you," Malachi snapped.

"Yes, but how could I trust you instead? Your brother told me you were volatile. Cruel. He fed into my own prejudices. You chose me for a Grace without ever considering my wishes, remember? And you said nothing of my sister. How could I speak to you of letting her go?"

He frowned but, to Serina's surprise, didn't snap back.

Nomi glanced over her shoulder at Serina, but her words were for the Heir. "Did you know the guards here forced the women to kill each other over food? *Kill each other*, Malachi."

His eyes widened. Serina thought the shock on his face was genuine, but she wasn't sure.

"They fought back," Nomi continued, still looking at Serina, with something like pride in her eyes. After a pause, she turned her gaze back to the Heir. "They didn't want to have to keep killing each other. My sister was sent here to *die* for being able to read. And you did nothing."

"I didn't *know*. If I had—"

Serina couldn't hold her tongue any longer. "You knew," she snapped, stepping closer until she towered over him. "Maybe not about the fights, but you knew women sent here never came back." She put her hand on Nomi's shoulder. "You knew I would die here, one way or another. And for what? For reading? There are women here who've done nothing more than displease your father. And *you knew*. Your brother may be a monster, Malachi, but you are still part of the problem."

He stared up at her, eyes glittering, and for a split second, Serina was back in the library of the palazzo, and the Superior was glaring at her, peeling back her mask of serenity with a single piercing gaze. Serina had known then that her sentence was coming, just as she knew it now. She reminded herself, forcefully, that this was *her* domain. His future was the one in question, not hers.

"Fine," Malachi said, his expression hard as steel. "Then help me be the solution. Help me take back Viridia. Help *me* fight back."

Serina's jaw went slack.

SIX

NOMI

It was the last thing Nomi expected Malachi to say. For a moment, she couldn't speak.

He tried to shift—to stand up or maybe just sit taller—and winced, putting a hand to his stomach. His face, to which a small amount of color had returned, still looked haggard, with dark circles beneath his eyes and a sunken quality to his cheeks.

Serina knelt on the floor beside Nomi and leaned over Malachi to check his bandages.

"Is he feverish?" Nomi put a tentative hand to his forehead. A little clammy, but not unnaturally warm.

He turned away from her hand.

"I'm not ill," he growled. "I'm angry. I've lost my father and my birthright. I want my country back. With your forces—"

"*Forces?*" Serina let out an ugly laugh. "We are not an army. And even if we were, we would not be *your* army."

Nomi rubbed her hands against her thighs. Malachi was here because of her. And she knew how dangerous Asa was. *And Renzo . . .* If Malachi regained the throne, Renzo would be safe. He wouldn't have to run. But only if . . .

"Serina," she began. "Maybe—"

"No." Serina stood up. She glared down at them both. "I will not watch these women die in the service of a country that will happily destroy them. That has *already* destroyed them."

"So, don't." Nomi stood up too, her chest tight with a wish—a hope—Asa hadn't quite burned to ash. "Don't fight for the old world. Fight for a new one."

She looked down at Malachi, at the sharp planes of his face, the pallor of his skin, the purse of his full lips. His gaze latched onto hers and maybe there was a warning in his eyes, but she didn't care.

"The rightful Heir must make concessions," she said, and she didn't recognize her own voice. It sounded like Serina's: certain and self-assured. "If he wants our help, he must *change* the laws upon our victory."

Malachi didn't blink. "What laws?"

Nomi's heart pummeled her ribs, stealing her breath. "A woman who reads does not deserve a death sentence."

"Nor any punishment, I agree," he returned. "I will revoke all laws barring women from an education."

Beside Nomi, Serina made a small noise, maybe a gasp. But Nomi didn't break her hold on Malachi's gaze to glance at her sister. The moment had a vulnerability to it, like a thin sheet of ice on a pail of water. One breath, one small movement, and it could shatter.

Nomi took a deep breath. "No woman shall be sold like cattle by her father," she stated. "No forced marriage, no forced service. If a woman takes employment, her wages are her own. And Graces will give their consent. Willingly. Freely. No one will force them." She didn't move, not even to breathe. Surely he knew it would have to go this far.

60

Malachi looked down. Just for a split second, but it was enough. Something in Nomi broke. "It will take time," he said. "Those changes, they are larger than one law ... Our whole society is informed by—"

"You will have one year," Serina interrupted. "One year to give women a place at the table. You will have advisors: me, my sister, anyone else here who wants a voice." She turned to face Nomi. "If he doesn't listen to us, if he turns on us, the women of Mount Ruin will rise up against him, just like we did to Commander Ricci. We'll burn it all down."

A shiver raced down Nomi's spine. She heard the promise, the conviction in Serina's voice. And she heard the warning. Serina expected Nomi to choose a side.

Nomi nodded. She was with her sister, her family, first and foremost. Forever.

"Renzo is in danger," she added hurriedly, trying to keep her voice steady. "Asa is hunting him down because he knows the truth about what happened the night of the ball. You must swear our brother will be safe. Protected from Asa, and from you."

There was a long, painful silence. Nomi could hear her own quickened breaths and the groan of a woman at the other end of the room. She couldn't look at Malachi. Behind Serina, Val shifted, but he didn't speak either.

"I can agree to your conditions," Malachi said at last, but there was a strangled quality to his voice.

Nomi realized belatedly that she'd clenched her fists, as if expecting a fight. With an effort, she forced her hands to relax.

"Do you trust his word, Nomi?" Serina asked.

Asa's kind smile flashed through Nomi's mind. Her sister didn't know how difficult a question that was for Nomi to answer. She studied Malachi's face, tried to stave off the memories of his brother. But it wasn't just Asa who haunted her. She wasn't sure she trusted *any* man in this. They were asking for so much.

"I trust his intent." It was the most she could offer.

"You can trust *me*," Malachi said, surprising her with his vehemence.

He held out a hand. After a brief pause, Nomi shook it, biting back a gasp as his large warm palm enveloped hers. His grip was strong, stronger than she'd expected for a man recovering from a murder attempt.

Then Malachi turned to Serina and shook her hand as well.

"I'll write it all down," Nomi said suddenly, with the sense that somehow this would make it more official. That the words, written by own her hand, might quiet her unquiet fears of betrayal.

"There's paper and ink in the Commander's room," Val offered, the first thing he'd said since they'd entered the infirmary. Nomi had forgotten him almost entirely, in fact. She glanced his way, surprised he hadn't inserted himself into the negotiations.

Serina said, "We'll get the paper, and Nomi will write down our agreement. Then it will be up to the women of Mount Ruin to decide."

"What do you mean?" Malachi asked, his brows drawing together. "I thought *we* had just decided."

Serina lifted her chin. "I am not Commander Ricci. I will not force these women to fight. This isn't just about your future, Your Eminence. It's about theirs too. I'll put it to them, and they'll vote."

Malachi's jaw clenched. "Fine."

It wasn't as if he could argue. Here, Serina held the power. It was afterward, if they won, that Nomi worried about.

Serina squeezed Nomi's shoulder again. "I'll get some food for you too."

With a last thoughtful look at Nomi, Serina turned and headed for the bright rectangle of light at the other end of the room. Val followed.

Nomi sat down beside Malachi and leaned against the wall. Not too close. Her mind still whirled. Would it happen? If the women of Mount Ruin took the palazzo, took back Malachi's throne, would he really change the laws? What would it be like for women to have the freedom to learn to read, to choose their own employment, their own husbands? To choose their own futures?

And Renzo . . . with this plan, they were counting on him hiding, keeping himself safe, for as long as it took the ship to come and for them to attack the palazzo. Was that too long?

It didn't matter, not really. Even if they knew exactly where Renzo was, how could she and Serina leave now in their little boat, when Malachi had promised the women of Viridia a new world?

"*Damn.*" Malachi swore, but with more fatigue than

anger. He shifted uncomfortably, disrupting her line of thought.

"Are you in pain?" she asked.

"Of course I'm in pain!" he snapped.

Nomi moved to stand up.

He put out a hand toward her. "I'm sorry," he said more calmly. "Don't go. Please. I am ... frustrated by my own weakness."

"Your body will heal. Already you're so much stronger," she said, her guilt slithering back to choke her.

"It's not just my injuries," he admitted. "I was not prepared for that conversation, for your demands. You have a talent for negotiation."

"And my sister for threats," Nomi returned.

The corner of Malachi's lip quirked. "True. Mount Ruin has changed her."

"How could it not?" Nomi thought she heard disapproval in his voice, but she was in awe. Serina had spoken to Malachi as if they were equals. No, as if *she* held the power. Serina, Nomi's sweet, submissive sister.

Nomi had never been more proud.

For a while, they sat in silence. But it wasn't long before Nomi's questions bubbled up.

"Why did you try to give me my freedom? Back at the ball, I mean." She didn't know what to think of Malachi. One moment he was volatile, just as Asa had described him. And other times, he seemed thoughtful, considerate even. She couldn't puzzle him out, and that made her nervous. For this plan to work, he had to be deserving of her trust.

And she just wasn't sure if he was. In truth, he was probably wondering the same about her. She'd already betrayed him once.

He stared down at his hands, still as marble in his lap. Through the ripped sleeve of his shirt, she could see the ridge of stitches along his forearm. "The more time we spent together, the more it pained me, thinking of how I chose you without warning, without your knowledge or consent. It became untenable, knowing you hadn't prepared for the life of a Grace. That I was forcing you."

"So why *did* you choose me? Was it a mistake? You meant to choose Serina?" She'd always wondered. He'd seemed so unhappy with Nomi at first.

When he didn't answer, she added, "Back in the palazzo, you said I was defiant and different from the others. But you never said why that appealed to you."

She glanced at him. To her surprise, his cheeks had reddened. He focused all his attention on the cracked marble floor between them, picking at it with a finger.

He cleared his throat. "Well. The truth is, it *didn't* appeal at first. But you, um, served a purpose."

"A purpose?" What a callous way to regard a human life.

"When I met you the first time in the hallway, do you remember?" When she nodded, he continued. "I was angry. I'd just left a meeting with my father and his magistrates. I'd assumed *I* was the one to pick my Graces, and I was prepared to do my duty. But I'd been informed in that meeting that the *magistrates* choose. Well, they lobby. It's an honor for them, a way to curry favor. If their girls are chosen, it often means increased access to the Superior. It can be very good for a province. That night, Father decreed I would select the prospects from Lanos, Golden Isle, and Sola."

"Serina, Maris, and Cassia," Nomi said softly. She'd had no idea the magistrates had so much power. That Signor Pietro, Lanos's representative, could prevail upon the Superior to choose her sister.

Malachi nodded. "I was furious. I thought it was this sacred *duty* or something . . . at the least I thought it was *my life*. I hated being told what to do."

Nomi rolled her eyes at the irony, but he was staring at the floor and didn't see.

"When I met you, I had this brilliant flash of inspiration . . . I thought I could choose you to spite my father. It wouldn't interfere with the politics of it all—you were still from Lanos—but I'd be my own man, making my own decision. I just, well . . . I didn't consider what *you'd* think."

This was the least surprising bit of the entire story. Of course he hadn't considered what she thought. She was a woman, after all.

"I wondered why you'd chosen two girls who obviously didn't want to be there," Nomi said, thinking of how angry she'd been and how hopeless Maris had seemed. "Asa said it was because you wanted to break us. The Superior said it too. I think . . . I think he liked the unwilling ones."

Malachi skimmed a hand along the row of stitches on his arm. "I thought I was being rebellious. I didn't want to break you . . . I didn't want anything to do with you, at first. You were only there to annoy my father. But then your sister was accused of reading and I was intrigued. I wanted to know if you could read too. I wanted to know all about you. You didn't simper like Cassia or brood like Maris. And you were, well, you were *mine*. The only girl I actually chose. And while I did it for the wrong reasons, I found myself glad. I started feeling, caring—"

"But you told me that I could go," Nomi broke in, an unexpected restlessness filling her. "You released me from my position as your Grace."

Nomi didn't know what to think. She'd come to suspect he cared for her, but to have it laid out like that, and to know he'd been rebellious in his own way . . .

If I'd trusted him, if I'd let myself care for him, would he have found a way to help Serina? She thought back to all their interactions and how much of those were influenced by what Asa had told her about him.

Malachi looked up at last, his mouth quirking sadly. "I told you you could go. But if you'll recall, I also asked you to stay. I *wanted* you, Nomi. I was hoping you might want me back."

For a moment, she was caught in his eyes, and he held her captive, just as he had in the hallway that first night. Except this time, anger and fear weren't the emotions that drew color to her cheeks.

Malachi turned his attention back to the marble. "But you wanted my brother."

It was on the tip of Nomi's tongue to say *I don't anymore*, but she couldn't. She didn't know if Malachi still cared for her after everything she'd done, but she couldn't risk her own heart. It was still broken.

She was still broken.

SEVEN

SERINA

Serina sat with her back against the bars of an empty cell, legs stretched out in front of her, and ignored Diego's vitriol.

"You're going to die here, just like all the rest," he said, spitting the words. A vein pulsed along the side of his bald head.

"I am going to slit you open." Carlo stuck his narrow, pimpled face through the bars and leered.

"I'm going to bury you," Hector growled. He was the largest of the guards, as big as Commander Ricci, with close-set eyes and rotting, broken teeth.

Serina knew the names of five of the seven guards now, from them egging each other on. One, down at the end, kept his mouth shut. But he watched her and the other girls, his eyes gleaming, and she knew he was no less a threat.

Not a single guard begged for his life or tried to weasel his way into their good opinion. They didn't pretend to feel as Val did, or admit to a single regret. They didn't care one bit that they'd been responsible for hundreds of women dying. They *reveled* in it.

Beside her, Mirror crossed her arms over her chest. "I wish they'd be quiet," she murmured.

"That's why they do it," Serina replied.

Every shift watching the prisoners was more draining than the last. But it seemed more dangerous to leave them unsupervised. Val had been taking more than his fair share, just to give the women a break, but Anika always insisted on standing watch with him. She didn't trust that he wouldn't betray them.

It had been four days since Nomi had arrived. Serina had given the women time to heal, and Malachi time as well. She'd made sure every woman knew the options—escape to Azura or stage a coup—and what each would mean. Malachi had broken down for all of them how they could take the palazzo—the hidden passages they would use to breach the canal so they could attack without warning, the number of guards and soldiers they would have to face. He made the gambit sound reasonable.

Val had started training the women how to shoot the guards' firearms. He'd also answered what questions he could about Azura.

Nomi had explained the concessions Malachi had made, what he'd promised to change if they were successful and he became Superior. She'd shown them the pages where she'd written the terms and where he'd signed it. One of the girls had asked Nomi to write out a promise that they would not be persecuted if they returned to Viridia, and Malachi had signed that as well.

It was all the women spoke of, whether to flee to Azura or return to Bellaqua and fight.

The vote was today.

The prison ship would be here in a week, maybe even less. It was time to commit to a plan. The more Serina thought about it, the harder her heart pounded. This was the best chance to protect Renzo. And she *wanted* to fight. She'd promised herself she would try to change Viridia. This was her chance.

She just hoped the others felt the same way.

Serina tapped on Mirror's arm. "Let's go. We need to be in the amphitheater soon."

"Going back to your baser natures, are you?" Hector said, with a grotesque, gap-toothed grin. "Can't live without the fights. Without the *blood*."

The other guards cackled.

"I could live without *you* just fine," Serina muttered.

No women arrived to relieve them—the guards would have to insult each other for a while. Everyone deserved a vote.

"I've never voted for anything in my life," Mirror said as if she were reading Serina's mind, as they hiked down the path.

"Me neither," Serina said. The only votes *anyone* cast in Viridia were in province-wide elections of minor government administrators, and only the men did that. Every other position, like the magistrates—and the Graces—the Superior decided.

"I wish I could go back to Viridia, to be with my sister," Mirror said. She'd told Serina once her sister was her mirror image, down to her many freckles. It was how she'd earned her name. "But that's what got me put here to begin with. I ran away to be with her and her new husband, thought I could be her maid or something, but he turned me in because my father had not given me leave to go. The authorities didn't even bother sending me home. They just sent me here. If I go back now, he'll just do it again."

"No, he won't," Serina replied. "The Heir will put an end to all of that. You'll be able to choose where you want to go, what you want to do."

"I'm voting to go to Azura," Mirror said, her voice hardening. "Why would the Heir actually change the laws? Once he has what he wants, his promises are worth nothing."

"I don't believe that," Serina said firmly. But deep in her heart, she had her own doubts. Still, she trusted Nomi. And she would never choose to leave her family behind.

By the time they reached the amphitheater, most of the women had already gathered. Val waited on the dais with Malachi and Nomi.

Serina studied the crowd as she headed down to meet them. The women weren't divided by crew anymore. Cliff and Ember sat together where Serina and the other Cave freshies had, but a couple of girls from the Beach sat next to them. Maris and Helena sat with them too. Helena was from Jungle Camp. Everyone called her Serpent; even Serina had heard the story of how she'd caught and cooked a large snake when Jungle Camp had gone weeks without rations.

Val said both Maris and Helena were doing well with firearms training. Serina wondered if they imagined their targets as the men who'd forced them apart.

When Serina reached the dais and turned to face her audience, her pulse leapt. She hadn't been to the amphitheater since the morning after the uprising.

72

Everything suddenly felt too familiar, and the memories, the horrors, rose to choke her.

She wiped her sweaty hands on her pants. Fought with every breath not to look behind her at the guard's booth. There were no men training firearms at her back. The Commander wasn't standing on the edge of the balcony, preparing to throw a box of spiders or bricks to the ground. This was a safe place now.

This is our *place.*

And Nomi was standing with her. Nomi, and Val, and Malachi. They stood *together.* Serina held up her hands. "Quiet, please," she said. Voices faded to silence. Everyone turned to her.

Val sidled a little closer and Serina channeled his support as she addressed the crowd of nearly a hundred fifty women.

"I know we're all still adjusting to our new reality," she began. "This place is *ours* for the first time. But soon the next prison boat will come and with it, more guards and men who wish to harm us. We will take that boat. We will defend our freedom." She glanced at Malachi. Even in his hand-me-down guard uniform, he held his head high. He still looked like the Heir. "Tonight we decide what we'll do afterward. Seek asylum in Azura, or go back to Bellaqua and fight."

She nodded to Val, who repeated all he knew about Azura. "I believe we will be safe there," he concluded. "But it will mean leaving friends and family in Viridia behind."

"Or we fight back," Serina said, taking a step closer to the edge of the stage. She gestured to Malachi. "We have the true Superior here on this island. As you all know, he has agreed that if we help him attack the palazzo, he will enact change in Viridia. He will give women more rights. He will help us reunite with our families. If we help him take back Viridia, we can change it forever." As she spoke, Serina saw the battle unfold in her mind . . . female warriors swarming the golden beaches of the Superior's palazzo, the roar of gunfire echoing down its delicate halls.

Asa would fall, and the women of Viridia would rise.

"Asa cannot be allowed to rule," Nomi added, her voice shaking. "He is even worse than his father, even more capricious. He has no qualms about destroying all those in his way. He killed his own father, tried to kill his brother . . . but his real danger is in his smile. He will convince the magistrates, his generals, and courtiers that he is kind and thoughtful, that he has the country's best interests at heart." Her voice hardened. "But he only cares for himself. He is a danger to everyone."

"But how can we trust *him*?" Fox shouted, pointing to Malachi. "What stops him from using us to get what he wants and then running this country just like his father did?"

Malachi cleared his throat. "You have my word, here and in writing. I know this may be difficult to believe, but I also want change for Viridia. I've come to see how cruel it is to deny women—you—the right to choose your own path." He cut a glance to Nomi.

Serina tried to read the emotion that flitted across his face.

"So fight or run. Those are the only options we've been talking about," Blaze said from a spot near the stage. "But what about staying here? To some of us, this island is home."

"We could try," Serina said. She'd heard similar rumblings over the past couple of days. "But we have limited resources and only one guard to preserve the illusion of the island running as usual. The prison boats *will* come, and it will be increasingly difficult not to arouse suspicion. Still, it is an option. We'll add it to the vote."

"What if we just want to return to our families? Without fighting?" someone yelled.

"What if our families are the ones who turned us in?" someone else countered.

The rumble of voices built as the women discussed among themselves.

Serina held up her hands, but before she could say anything, Anika's voice rang out. "No solution is perfect. Some of us have family we are desperate to return to. Some of us want to take down the men who put us here. Some of us want to run. But we can't do it all. We can't split our focus. No matter *what* we do, we'll have to deal with the prison boat. We'll have to survive here until it comes. If we don't find common ground, if we don't work toward a unified goal, none of us will make it."

Serina watched the crowd as Anika gave her speech. A couple of the women shook their heads, and a few looked scared, but everyone was listening. Even Fox. They all heard what Anika was saying.

"We've come here tonight to vote," Serina announced. "You can vote to stay, to go to Azura, or to fight. Anika is right—we can't split our focus. There will only be one boat, so whatever the majority decides, all of us must commit to it."

Serina sent up a little prayer.

"Who wants to stay on Mount Ruin?" Nomi asked.

Serina counted hands. Only a few were raised, mostly the older women and the ones who'd been here the longest. She was surprised to see Ember's hand go up. Serina had expected her to want to fight, to get revenge for Oracle's death.

"Fourteen," she stated.

"Who wants to go to Azura?" Val called.

A new set of hands went up. Maris and Helena. Fox and most of Jungle Camp. There were a lot of hands, more than Serina had expected. It took her a long time to count.

Her stomach turned over. She glanced at Nomi; her sister was frowning, her own hands balled into fists at her sides. Malachi's face was blank.

"Eighty-two," she said, her heart pounding. She paused for a moment to steady her nerves. "Now, who wants to fight back?"

This was it.

To Serina's surprise, Mirror raised her hand. She must have changed her mind. Cliff raised her hand too, and Anika. Many of the women voted to fight.

"Sixty."

But not enough.

A numb disbelief crept through Serina. She felt Nomi sag beside her. Her own shoulders wanted to slump, but she held herself rigidly upright. The whole point had been to give these women a choice.

"The vote is clear. When the boat comes, we'll commandeer it and seek asylum in Azura." Serina tried to hold her voice steady, even as her hopes for Renzo's safety, for a new future for the women of Viridia, died.

EIGHT

NOMI

Nomi paced to the edge of the dais and back, her jaw aching from the force with which she clenched her teeth. Her future, Renzo's future, crumbled to dust before her. For four days, she'd let herself believe that it was possible to have all that she wanted—freedom, Renzo's safety, her family back together.

She couldn't bear to look at Malachi. Everything he wanted, everything he deserved, was beyond his grasp now too.

The amphitheater filled with a clatter of voices. Arguments broke out.

"I'm tired of fighting."

"You're tired? I'm *angry*. Those bastards deserve our wrath."

"I don't trust the Heir. He'll break every promise he makes. What man do *you* know who's ever kept one?"

"My father. He promised to send me here if I refused to work at the factory. And here I am. If we don't fight back, nothing will ever change."

"I don't care about change. All I want is a soft bed and fresh food. I don't care if I ever see Viridia again."

Nomi couldn't stand it.

Just beyond the stage, Anika pounded her fist on her thigh. "We should go to Bellaqua. This is ridiculous. Fleeing our own country. Our families. *Ridiculous*."

"The vote was fair," Serina told her softly, her own disappointment showing in her furrowed brow. "We have to honor the results."

Nomi pulled her sister away from the crowd, noting Val and Malachi's heads tipped close together in their own private conversation.

"Nomi, there's nothing I can do. I'm sorry," Serina said. She was wearing her stoic big-sister face, but Nomi could see through to the dejection beneath.

"What about Renzo?" Nomi asked. "We can't go to Azura and leave him behind."

Her stomach churned. She couldn't tell if she was about to retch or scream. She'd supported the vote, of course she had. She'd wanted to give these women a choice. But she'd been so *sure* they would vote to go back to Viridia and stop Asa.

Serina pressed her fingers to her temples and massaged in small circles. "We'll have to take Val's boat, I suppose. But there will be others who want it . . . Anika wants to return to her family . . . We'll have to be quiet about it, I don't know how."

"Serina, you can't leave," Nomi said. She clutched at her belly, willing her twisted nerves to relax. "Not now. You're the leader here. These women are trusting you to get them to Azura safely."

"We could all go to Azura," Serina offered. "Then go back for Renzo from there. Take a small crew maybe, people like Anika who want to go back."

With regret, Nomi shook her head. "No. It'll take too long. We can't do that. But you can't leave them."

Serina shrugged miserably. "And you can't take Val's boat alone."

"No. She can't. Because I will be," Malachi said shortly, approaching them. Nomi stared up at him, shock widening her eyes.

He was healing well from his wounds, but he was in no shape to be walking around. His face had lost most of its color and he moved stiffly, as if every joint hurt. He needed to rest. "I'm going to Porto Rosa, to a regiment that might be loyal to me."

"That is not your boat to take," Serina snapped. "You've no—"

"Serina, he's the rightful Superior," Val said gently, coming up beside them. "He's worried he'll find little support in Azura if he comes with us. But if he can find troops loyal to him in Viridia, he may be able to stage a rebellion after all. We can't deny him that chance."

"Yes, we can," Serina countered obstinately. "It's *your* boat. You can do what you like with it. He can't just come in here and *demand* things, like every other—"

"I'll go with him," Nomi broke in, without giving herself time to think. "I'll make sure Renzo is okay."

Malachi immediately shook his head. "Absolutely not. I mean to wage war, Nomi."

"You can barely walk," she retorted, her voice—and resolve—strengthening. "You can't sail a boat on your own, not in your condition. I'll help you get to Porto Rosa, and in return, you'll help me save Renzo. You must promise to protect him should your gambit succeed, just as we discussed before."

80

His lips thinned. "I don't need—"

"What?" she interrupted, her own hackles rising. "You don't need help? You were willing to accept the aid of the women of Mount Ruin only moments ago. I may not be useful in a war, but I can help you survive long enough to fight one."

"It's dangerous, Nomi," he said, something changing in his expression. His brows drew together. "*Too* dangerous."

"And *that* is a result of my error in judgment," she said, refusing to back down. "My brother's life is at risk because of me. Your predicament is my fault as well. These are my wrongs to right, Malachi. You must let me accompany you. You *must*."

He looked at her for a long moment.

Nomi's throat slowly closed. The truth was, she wanted to go to Azura with Serina. She wanted to get as far from Asa—and from Malachi's piercing gaze—as she could. But she would not leave her family behind.

"As you wish," he said at last, and all the breath left her body. "But we must leave soon. Tomorrow."

———

That night, Nomi fell asleep with her hand curled into Serina's braid, both of them huddled close together on a pallet in the far corner of the infirmary, near Malachi and Val.

Long after Serina's breath had deepened into sleep, Nomi finally drifted off herself. And dreamed of Asa, his smile dripping blood and his hands clenched at her waist, pulling her closer. Closer. Bending to kiss her with blood-soaked lips—

"Nomi! Nomi!"

Nomi woke to Serina shaking her.

"You were screaming again," Serina said.

"S-sorry," Nomi mumbled, trying the shake the image of Asa's ghoulish grin from her mind.

Soon dawn brightened the doorway, and they all rose, bleary-eyed and quiet.

Val disappeared for a few minutes, returning with the news that the tide would be out in a few hours. "We need to leave soon. It's a long hike to the boat."

Nomi's heart seized. She'd thought she'd have more of the day with Serina. Unbidden, her brain grasped for excuses to hold off their departure. But she knew Malachi would not consent to waiting.

Serina met her eyes, staring as if memorizing her features. Nomi felt the shape of a similar expression on her own face. They'd only just found each other—this new parting threatened to tear apart every shred of Nomi's resolve.

But she couldn't love Serina without loving Renzo. She couldn't forget the rest of her family just because she'd found her sister.

"I should come with you," Serina said again, for maybe the hundredth time.

"But you can't," Nomi reminded her again. "We've gone through it. You and Val must negotiate with Azura for the safety of all the women here. And if Malachi and I fail, you'll

82

be Renzo's only hope. I'll send a letter to Papa for Renzo. I'll tell him to go to Azura and find you. It won't work if you're not there, you know that."

Serina stared down at the burlap sack—an old rations bag—they were packing together. "We spent so long apart, and now . . ."

And now it was more time, more distance.

Nomi's heart shuddered. She wanted to hold on to Serina and never let her go. She wanted to tell her that she should come. Or that they should both stay here and wait for the prison boat. But Nomi had spent her life watching Serina do her duty. Her sister had always faced her fate with serenity. Now it was Nomi's turn.

"You need more water," Serina said, her voice thick with tears. "I'll get another flagon."

"Thank you." Nomi watched her leave the infirmary, her stomach tight.

Nomi glanced over at Malachi, automatically noting his color, whether he winced when he moved.

"Do you feel up for the hike?" she asked.

"Of course." His sharp jaw tightened. Dark circles still clung beneath his eyes, but his intensity was back, as vibrant and terrifying as ever.

"Of course," she echoed sarcastically under her breath. He still thought he could accomplish this task without her, yet he could hardly bend over without whimpering.

"Nomi . . ." he started, his expression softening, but at that moment Maris arrived, and he turned away to focus on his own burlap sack.

"Your sister said you're about to leave," Maris said. Helena was a few steps behind her. Nomi hadn't seen the two apart since their reunion.

Nomi nodded.

"Good. We wanted to walk with you to the boat." Maris had trimmed her long black hair to her shoulders and kept it tucked neatly behind her ears. She was so at ease now, more so than she'd ever looked in the palazzo. Helena smiled calmly, her blue eyes brightening every time her gaze shifted to Maris. There was no need for them to hide their feelings here, no sneaking around as they'd done before Maris had been selected as a Grace. This was the one place in all of Viridia that Maris and Helena could be themselves.

Serina returned with several extra flagons, and Val with a pair of boots for Malachi. Serina had already found boots for a lot of the women, including Nomi. They were too big, but Nomi had stuffed scraps of fabric in the toes so she could walk.

She readjusted the burlap sack over her shoulder. Her stomach churned with nerves. She was scared to leave Serina. Scared to get on a small boat with Malachi. Scared of what would happen when Malachi challenged Asa. Scared Renzo was already dead.

And what about Serina, when the prison boat came? What if their plan to overpower the guards didn't work? Nomi took a deep breath and tried to calm her mind.

Their little group—Val, Malachi, Serina, Maris, and Helena—snaked up the path to the north, along the rim of the island.

"Do you think there will ever come a time when I'm not juggling a hundred different fears at once?" Nomi asked Serina quietly as they walked.

"I hope so. But in the meantime, maybe this will help with a few of them." Serina paused to draw a small but wicked homemade knife from her boot.

Tentatively, Nomi took it. It was thin and sharp and felt like holding violence in her hand. "What am I supposed to do with this?"

"Whatever you must," Serina said simply.

They walked in silence for a while. The hike gave Nomi blisters and a savage headache, but she didn't hate the physical effort. It felt more productive, at least, than the endless dance lessons and statuesque poses in the palazzo.

Clouds swept across the sky, providing welcome patches of shade, and the wind this close to the coast helped cool Nomi's heated cheeks. She could see the wink of the ocean through the trees, and the smoky haze of the volcano in the distance.

She glanced back often to assess Malachi's progress; so far he was keeping up, though his face looked haggard and sweat-slicked and he kept a hand on his injured side.

She thought about asking him if he was okay, but assumed she'd only get a gruff *of course*. He held on to his pride as tightly as he did his wound.

But she did check on Maris and Helena, who brought up the rear.

"You didn't have to come," she said. "It's a long hike."

Maris shrugged.

Helena said, "I thought we'd collect some pox berries on the way back. We can tip our blades with their poison—it might give us an advantage in our fight for the boat."

Nomi rubbed away the sudden chill from her arms.

"Will you be okay here?" Nomi asked Maris. They scrambled over a rock fall, using their hands to push themselves up. Maris wasn't trained for battle, not like these girls.

"I'll be fine," Maris said. "I'm happier here than I ever was at the palazzo." But a shadow passed across her face.

"What is it?" Nomi asked.

Maris brushed the dirt off her hands. "It's nothing. I just . . . I keep thinking about Cassia. All the Graces, really. Rosario said that if a Superior dies, the Heir decides their fate. That means Asa decides for them."

A new chain of guilt wrapped itself around Nomi's chest. She hadn't even *thought* about Cassia and the others. About Angeline, the sweet handmaiden who'd helped her after Serina was taken away. "Surely he'll send them home. And I . . . I suppose choose his own." He'd told her he didn't *want* Graces, that he wanted a queen. Just another of his lies to ensnare her. He was probably thrilled at the prospect of his own Graces.

"The poor girls," Maris said, her face a storm cloud.

Nomi thought about the way Asa had charmed her. Disarmed her.

Used her.

"Yes."

At the head of the line, Val stopped. They all gathered in the shade of a scrubby stand of trees. "Short break," he said. He didn't look at Malachi, but Nomi did. The Heir was struggling. But he was still upright, and he took the water Val offered gratefully.

They arrived at the north beach a short time later. Val passed the broken husk of a grounded ship Serina said Beach crew used as their home; it was empty, truly abandoned, now that the crew had moved down to Hotel Misery.

They picked their way across the black sand to a spot where old lava poured out in a frozen outcropping, artificially extending the shoreline. Val clambered across the rock to a crevice that would be hidden at high tide. Deep inside, his small sailboat waited.

Serina and Helena helped him drag it out. Malachi went through his supplies one more time. Nomi hugged Maris, her heart thudding painfully.

Then the boat was bobbing on the water, Malachi had boarded and hoisted the sail, and Serina stood on the sand before Nomi.

It was time to say goodbye.

NINE

SERINA

Serina couldn't bear it. Her baby sister was putting herself in danger, and the only thing Serina could do for her was give her a knife she didn't know how to use.

She hugged Nomi tightly, ignoring the searing pain of her broken rib. Within the circle of her arms, her sister felt too small, too delicate for this journey. And Malachi, big, hulking Malachi . . . Would he keep her safe? What if he betrayed her just like his brother had?

Serina had studied him over the past few days, had watched how he spoke to Nomi. He was gruff and short with everyone, but sometimes she caught him looking at Nomi and his face changed. The tension eased. It was that expression . . . that softening . . . she was choosing to trust.

"Journey well, little sister," she murmured into Nomi's hair. "Take care of yourself."

"You too," Nomi replied, her voice thick with tears. "Don't take risks, Serina, you understand? I need you to make it to Azura. I'll send word as soon as it's safe for you to return. Or . . . or Renzo and I will come to you. But you must *be there*. You must be safe."

Serina nodded, but she couldn't speak.

This moment was harder than the last time they'd been pulled apart. They hadn't known what it meant then. But

Serina knew what this meant. It meant her whole family would be out there, the object of the new Superior's wrath, and Serina still had to let Nomi go.

With a wrenching pain too near her heart, Serina pulled herself out of Nomi's embrace.

"I love you," she said hoarsely. The harsh sunshine made her squint, surrounding her last view of Nomi with sparks of light.

Tears streamed down Nomi's cheeks. "I love you too."

Then, before either of them could change their minds, she turned and climbed aboard Val's boat.

Serina watched the small boat catch the wind in its sail and slide toward the horizon. She couldn't keep tears from slipping down her cheeks. It was too much.

Maris patted her shoulder, then let Helena show her how to collect clams from beneath the wet sand. They both seemed to understand Serina needed a moment before heading back.

Val stayed close to Serina. He watched the boat too. She wondered if he was thinking about his mother and the reason he'd brought it here to begin with.

At last, when the sailboat was almost out of sight and her tears had slackened, Serina turned to go.

Anika appeared at the edge of the trail, her bronze skin glistening with sweat.

"You let them take the boat, didn't you?" she yelled. "Without a word, without a *vote*."

Serina wiped at her face and tried to pull herself together. "I had to. I—"

"You should have *told* me," Anika snapped, and it wasn't anger that lined the words but desperation. "I could have gone too. My family, Serina. They *need* me."

"I'm sorry, Anika," Serina said, her heart aching anew. "I couldn't risk saying anything. The Heir took the boat . . . There are some soldiers who might still be loyal to him. He needed to return. *We* need him to return . . . if there's any chance of breaking Viridia free from the new Superior's rule."

"Nomi is with him," Anika said. "I could have gone too."

"He needed Nomi's help to sail the boat. But it's small . . . too small for everyone who wanted to go back. I couldn't tell you . . . I couldn't tell anyone. We made a promise, Anika," Serina said, almost pleading now. "That we'd honor the vote."

Anika stared at the horizon, her shoulders sagging. "I know."

"I'm sorry," Serina said again, at a loss. "I still have hope that we can help your family. The people of Azura can help us. We fought for our freedom. We'll find a way to fight for our families too. Maybe, once Malachi regains the throne, he'll—"

Anika made a noise in her throat. "That ship has *sailed*. He owes us nothing now." She turned back toward the path. "The women want to train more with the firearms. We're nowhere near ready for the prison boat to arrive." She didn't wait for Serina to respond, turning on her heel and heading back down the path.

Serina hugged herself, a numb emptiness filling her. Anika was right. If Malachi *was* successful in regaining his throne, he'd be doing it with his own soldiers. All the promises—concessions—he'd made to the women of Mount Ruin would mean nothing.

———

Val lined up four girls at a time, with the half wall of a destroyed building as their target. Serina took her turn with the rest, but she hated the kick of the weapon in her hands, and the noise of it. She was happy to relinquish the firearm until it was her turn again.

Val helped with aim and showed everyone how to load the weapons. The boom and ding of bullets put Serina on edge.

"They're terrible," Anika said, crossing her arms over her chest as she stared at the women training.

"We're all new at this," Serina reminded her. "It will take time. We'll get there."

"We don't *have* time," Anika replied. "A week at most."

"That's not our only problem," Val said, approaching them. "There's only so much ammunition . . . if we want to have enough to subdue the guards on the prison boat, we can only train like this once or twice more."

"But no one is hitting the targets!" Anika exclaimed. Her words were punctuated by the percussion of gunfire.

"How many guns do we have?" Serina watched the women shooting. The concrete wall was quite pockmarked by now, but the circles Val had drawn on it had alarmingly few dings inside them. Maris hit the target a couple of times. Val was right—she was doing well.

"These four, plus forty or so more in the compound," Val said. "But we've only got enough ammunition for three or four rounds if we use them all at once. Doesn't leave much for training."

Serina didn't say anything for a moment. She pictured herself back on the cliff watching Nomi's boat arrive, its steam engines slowing, the shriek as it ran along the concrete pier. The two guards jumped out. How many guards had there been when she herself arrived? Four or five on the boat? And then a couple on the dock to meet them.

"This doesn't have to be a large battle," she mused, playing it out in her mind. "There are four or five guards, and they're expecting a couple of island guards to meet them. Right, Val?"

He nodded. "Four or five guards, plus two sailors. Six men, maybe as many as eight, if there are a lot of women to transport."

"If there are no guards waiting on the pier when the boat docks, what would the men do?" Serina asked, trying to work through the possible scenarios.

Val scuffed his boot against the rough volcanic ground as he thought. "They'd disembark maybe, try to figure out what's wrong."

"So they wouldn't assume they were under attack right away? They wouldn't use the prisoners as shields or anything like that?" Serina waited while he considered. The day had turned hot and dry, the screaming winds blowing the sulfuric smoke of the volcano in their direction. It was giving her a headache.

"I don't think so. Not at first, anyway," he said at last.

"What are you getting at?" Anika asked.

"Well, we don't have to plan for a war, do we?" Serina said. "And we can save our ammunition too. If we choose the ten best girls, the ones who've picked it up really quickly and won't need as much practice to hone their aim, and we station them along the ridges above the pier, hidden where the boat guards can't see them, we can pick off the guards as they wander the pier trying to figure out what happened."

"Or I could go down to the pier like I did with Nomi's boat. Play the part until we get the new girls out of sight, and then we could overwhelm the guards and lock them into cells." Val glanced over at Serina.

She knew what he wanted. He saw himself in the men transporting the female prisoners; he wondered if there was one man, even just one, who ached for the women in pain. He wanted to save them, those hypothetical guards, just in case.

She took his hand. "We have hardly enough food for ourselves. We've already committed to releasing the surviving guards with any remaining supplies on the island and letting them fend for themselves, most likely sentencing them to a slow death by starvation. We can't spare the boat guards, just to make them suffer the same fate. And there are so many more things that could go wrong." She squeezed his hand. It wasn't as if she reveled in the thought of killing anyone, even these men. "Remember, these guards will know the protocols. They'll know something is wrong."

Val sighed. "I know. I just hate picking them off, not giving them a chance to defend themselves."

Anika made a derisive noise.

Serina could guess what the girl was thinking. But she merely said, "It's safer this way. And it'll save our ammunition. We should take the firearms with us to Azura. We don't know for certain that they're as friendly as you say . . . and if they are, the weapons may be useful to trade or sell."

Val nodded reluctantly. "It's a good plan. I'll pay attention in the next round of training, try to pick out the girls with the most potential."

Serina nodded.

The four markswomen were handing their firearms to the next women in line, when a ragged scream echoed through the clear afternoon air. Serina's head snapped around.

"What was that?" she yelled, already moving toward the sound.

A handful of women ran up the path. Serina and Anika took off after them.

Another scream.

Serina pushed through the crowd. A woman lay on the path, arms and legs akimbo, her neck at an unnatural angle. Serina knelt beside her, panic coursing through her body. What had happened?

The woman's eyes were still open but unseeing. Serina recognized her as one of the older women from Hotel

Misery, who liked to wander just off the paths surrounding the hotel collecting any edible plants she could find.

"What happened?" Anika asked loudly, taking a spot next to Serina.

"Did anyone see what happened?" Anika yelled again when no one answered her.

Serina felt a sinking horror fill her chest. None of the other women would have done this, surely. What motive could they have? But there was no one else—

That wasn't true. There were *several* people on the island who would do this, if given the chance. Serina took off running toward the prison compound.

Her feet slammed onto the stairs, vaulting her up to the guards' cells.

Three of the doors were ajar.

The remaining guards howled.

Doll lay on the ground, her arms limp, as if their marionette strings had been cut. Scorpion, Petrel's killer, lay beside her. Their eyes stared upward, their necks an ugly purplish red.

TEN

NOMI

"Tighten the jib—no, the other rope. Yes, that one." Malachi's endless commands sent Nomi scrambling across the small bow of the boat, and in a short time, she found herself half-wishing she could throw him overboard, just as those sailors had. But it wasn't his fault she didn't know what she was doing.

"The sail is flapping, you've got to—"

"I know!" She tightened the rope and collapsed onto the deck, cradling her blistered hands to her cheeks. "I'm sorry. This is all so new. I don't know what I'm *doing*."

Malachi heaved himself up to a sitting position. "I would do it myself. Believe me, I wish I could. But that hike . . . it wore me out. I'm sorry—"

Nomi threw up her hands. "Please don't apologize. That's why I'm here. I'm supposed to be a *help*. But I can't seem to do any of this properly."

More gently, he said, "You're doing fine." He glanced up at the rigging, where the sail pulled taut. "See? We've got it now."

She sagged forward, head in hands, and took a moment to breathe in the briny air. She liked the way it rushed through her hair—that meant they were moving forward.

To her surprise, she heard him chuckle.

"What?" she asked, looking up.

Malachi met her gaze steadily. A small smile played across his mouth, partially hidden by the scruff darkening his jaw. "I find it amusing that you expected this to be easy. Have you ever even been in a sailboat?"

A small bobbing sailboat surrounded by endless ocean. She swallowed. No. She had never been on a sailboat. "I didn't expect it to be easy, exactly. I just . . . expected that I would be up to the task."

"That's not a sentiment I've ever heard from a woman."

"That's because it's difficult to expect much of yourself when the rest of the world doesn't bother," Nomi returned, staring out at the waves curling toward them.

"I can see that," Malachi said, surprising her again. "But *you* believe yourself capable of, well, just about anything as far as I can tell. Why?"

Nomi leaned back against the gunwale and sighed. She thought about his question for a moment. Why *had* she expected she could sail a boat? Or read?

"I think it's because of Renzo," she mused. "My brother and I are twins, and I saw him treated differently . . . saw him go to school, leave the house and play with the boys down the street, come home dusty and happy and free. He never needed an escort. He was permitted to speak his own mind. And yet, it wasn't because he was bigger, or smarter, or older. I could do everything he could do. I just wasn't allowed. I felt the injustice early and often." She brushed her hair from her face. "That's what I've always wanted. The chance to speak, to choose, to control my own future, like Renzo does."

Malachi was silent. She didn't look at him.

More confessions, inexplicably, found their way to her lips. "I was so angry. All the time." Asa's boyish grin rose to her mind, unbidden. "Your brother promised me a future where I would have power, where I could give some of that power to all the women of Viridia. For me, it was a seductive dream."

"That's why he used it," Malachi said softly.

"I know that now," she snapped. She was *still* angry. So angry. Angry at her naiveté. Angry at Asa's betrayal. "I would kill him, I think. If I could."

She glanced back at Malachi. Her words hadn't shocked him. He held tightly to the tiller and stared at the boards of the deck, his brow furrowed.

"That's exactly what I plan to do," he said grimly.

Nomi hissed a startled breath.

"Can you tighten that rope over there?" Malachi pointed.

Nomi did as he asked, and the boat surged forward, wind filling the sail. Beyond the tip of the bow, land was coming into view as a smudge along the horizon.

"How long do you think it will take to get to Porto Rosa?" she asked.

"Three days, maybe four," he replied. "We'll stay near shore in case we need more provisions."

Three days on a tiny boat in the boundless ocean. Alone, with him.

———

Nomi stared at the great dome of stars above her, her jaw slack. In Lanos, the haze of industry dulled the sky, and the palazzo was always lit with endless strings of lights. She'd never seen so many stars in her entire life, and so bright.

Lying on her back, tears trickled down the sides of her face, wetting her hair.

"Are you crying?" Malachi's voice broke through the silence like a thunderclap.

"No. I was ... The wind ..." Nomi stuttered. She sat up and swiped at her face. She'd been lying on a scrap of blanket near the stern, Malachi a few feet behind her, propped against the hull with his hand on the tiller.

"I didn't mean to startle you," he said, more quietly. "Are you well?"

There were so many things Nomi could have been crying about. Leaving her sister, fear for her brother and parents. Heartache at the thought of Asa's betrayal.

And she'd been crying over the beauty of the stars.

She couldn't tell Malachi that.

"I'm fine," she said, cursing the hoarseness of her voice. She cleared her throat.

The stars still pressed close, so close she imagined she could pluck one out of the sky, if only she stood up and reached.

"Since you're awake, I could teach you how to steer," Malachi offered.

Nomi scooted over to sit on the other side of the tiller, her own back pressed against the wooden hull. "So . . ."

"So." He gestured that she should put her hand on the tiller.

Together they held on to the rough wood, their hands a few inches apart. Immediately, Nomi could feel the tension running through the handle. She followed the movements Malachi made, saw the sail tighten. The constant rush of water against the hull filled her ears. Running to their right, Viridia was a hulk of black that swallowed the stars.

"Keep her into the wind, like this," Malachi said. "Slight adjustments, that's all."

Slowly, he removed his hand. Nomi tightened her grip as the tension in the tiller increased. She concentrated on keeping her hand steady.

Beside her, Malachi sighed and slumped back.

"You should have told me you were tired," Nomi said. She watched the sail, waiting for the small shifts of wind that she'd have to adjust for.

"I've never been so tired in all my life," he admitted.

"Rest," Nomi said. "Your wounds are still healing."

"Was that a command or a suggestion?" he asked, shooting her a glance.

For a split second, the familiar contrition swirled through Nomi, tightening her chest. But, with an effort, she forced it away. She wouldn't apologize for being forthright. How would the world change if she didn't *make* it change?

"It was the truth," she said.

He let it go without commenting further. When he pulled a couple chunks of jerky from their bag of food, he offered one to her.

Nomi chewed at the tough meat and tried to keep the boat steady.

"Follow the wind," Malachi said at one point. "If it takes you farther away from shore, or closer, follow it. Sailboats travel by zig and zag. It's all about using the wind to our advantage."

"It's a shame that's the only advantage we have," Nomi muttered. That, and the ugly knife in her boot. But she hadn't told Malachi about that.

"We have more advantages than you think," he replied. In the starlight, the circles under his eyes looked like black holes, but his skin wasn't quite so deathly pale as it had been. And Nomi could hear his steady, strong breathing. It echoed the pulse of water sluicing along the sides. "A boat, food. The element of surprise. My brother thinks I'm dead and you're as good as. Once we've connected with Dante, we'll head to Bellaqua with his regiment. Asa will not expect us."

Nomi made a small adjustment with the tiller. A burning ache already captured her arm, but she held firm. Malachi needed the break.

"And," he said, a new, hesitant tone creeping in, "we have each other. Surely that can be seen as a positive, in this case?"

"I hope so," Nomi replied, but she couldn't keep a certain grimness from her voice and expression. Malachi had done a fair job convincing her they were chasing the same goals. But she'd thought the same of Asa. She wasn't ready to trust anything but her own hands, her own mind, and her own resources, limited as they were.

She held on tightly to the tiller and said nothing more. At some point, she glanced at Malachi and found him asleep, slumped on his side, his head pillowed by their burlap sacks. She spent the rest of the night alone with the stars.

ELEVEN

SERINA

Serina screamed to keep from sobbing. She'd told these girls they were *safe*. She'd *promised them*. Doll—Doll had come to the island the same day as Serina. She'd been in her crew. They'd shared meals together, her and Gia and Jacana. And now only Serina and Gia were left. Doll had died on Serina's watch. This was on *her*.

The four remaining guards shouted and laughed at her, chaotic as jackals. In a haze, she noted the missing guards: Nero, the quiet one, and Hector, the one with rotting teeth who called all the girls *flower*. Diego, bald and big as a house, the one who'd grabbed her hair. Was that what he'd done to Scorpion, whose cloud of dark hair looked twisted and disheveled? Had he grabbed her, strangled her, made her open the cell? But he couldn't have . . . none of the girls had the keys. Only Serina did. These guards got out some other way.

Val thundered up the stairs and took in the scene. While Serina was still frozen, he ran to the weapons cache at the end of the hall.

"Still locked," he reported back. "They couldn't get in."

"Did anyone see where the men went?" Serina asked him.

He shrugged. "I don't know."

"We know where they went," Carlo mocked, his pimpled face red with excitement.

"Come closer and I'll whisper it in your ear." Tiberius's smile was cruel. His beckoning finger sent ice down Serina's spine. She hardened herself to the feral grins, the vulgar suggestions.

"They didn't have keys. How did they escape?" she asked Val, forcing her voice not to shake through sheer will. "Could they come back for the others?"

"If Diego hadn't gotten jumpy, Nero would've sprung us all." Carlo winked grotesquely at Serina.

Val shook his head, his expression troubled. "Nero must have picked the locks. We searched their rooms, but we must have missed something. Nero's a real piece of work. Quiet, sly . . . always has been. Women sometimes turned up dead during his shifts, and he had a way of watching you, squirreling things away . . ."

Carlo and the others whooped and roared.

"Should we move the other guards?" Serina asked, trying to ignore the noise. Her pulse pounded in her throat. She couldn't bring herself to look at Doll, and yet it felt like an additional betrayal to pretend she wasn't there.

"There's nowhere else we can reasonably secure them," Val said, frowning. "Maybe the in-processing room, if we cleared it out and jammed the door somehow . . ."

"That would take too long," Serina said. "We need to find Diego, Hector, and Nero now. They could try to contact Bellaqua, or signal the boat."

With a rumble of footsteps, Anika, Ember, and several other women arrived. They stopped in the doorway at the sight of the bodies.

"Val, let's move the firearms and the rest of the food to Hotel Misery," Serina said.

He nodded.

Serina unlocked the armory and handed one of the weapons out to Ember. "If they bother you, or the others come back, shoot them."

Ember leaned against the wall opposite Carlo's cell and stared him into silence. Her strip of red hair caught the dim light and shone like fresh blood.

Anika and the others helped Serina and Val carry the weapons and bodies. By the time they emerged from the compound, night had fallen with a great, garish splash of red. The sulfuric haze of the volcano had intensified. Serina choked on the darkness and the memories; the industrial weight of Lanos's air had been like this, thick and strangling.

They laid Doll and Scorpion gently in the clearing before Hotel Misery, next to the other woman who'd been killed. Serina felt their deaths, even Scorpion's, like stones on her chest, suffocating her.

Women milled uneasily around the broken fountain and the dead women, murmuring to themselves and glancing into the darkness nervously. More torches than usual were burning.

Serina sent twenty women back to the compound to relieve Ember. "You see those rogue guards, you put them down, understand? Station yourselves in the hallway itself, and at the entrances to the building. Hide in the woods. If they come back for the others, we'll get them."

The women nodded and disappeared into the night.

"I need another twenty of you to stay here," Serina continued, glancing around the gathering. "Protect our injured and the women too weak to fight. Hotel Misery is our home. Do *not* let them in."

Val locked the firearms in a room in the hotel, distributing several to the girls who'd done the best in training. Maris, Helena, and Anika were among them.

Serina wished there was time to take the dead to the volcano, but they had to find the guards first. She couldn't let them run loose on the island. They could cause far too much damage.

"Where would they go?" Serina asked Val.

"We should kill the guards still in the compound," Anika said before he could answer. "They're a threat to us. We—"

"We said we'd leave them on the island when we escape," Serina interrupted. Maybe it wasn't such a large difference, shooting them now or leaving them to starve. But there was a *chance* they could survive that way. That was the difference. That's what made the women of Mount Ruin different from the men. She'd made herself a promise that they wouldn't kill anyone unless they absolutely had to. And as long as those men stayed locked up, they weren't a threat.

Serina didn't want anyone haunted by these guards. And executing someone—staring into their eyes and pulling the trigger—that would haunt you.

Val stared at the shadowy swirl of rock beneath his feet as he thought. "I don't think Diego, Hector, and Nero will go back for the other guards. At least not right away.

They've no supplies, no weapons. They would have gone for the stream first, for water. Maybe they'll aim for one of the guard towers to give themselves a vantage point. Some of the towers have a few supplies, some food, maybe some water."

"Weapons?"

"No. No weapons. Commander Ricci didn't want any caches in the guard towers, in case a guard missed his shift or left the tower unprotected. He didn't trust you lot."

"A reasonable instinct, as it turned out." Anika glanced over her shoulder. Serina wondered if she was imagining the escaped guards staring out at her from the darkness. That was what Serina was doing. She shivered, even though the night was warm and thick with humidity and volcanic haze.

"Let's get them." Serina bounced on the balls of her feet, nervous energy making her restless. "Before they can hurt anyone else."

They hurriedly split the rest of the fighters into search parties, each with someone who could use a firearm.

Serina joined a group with Maris, Helena, and Tremor, whose arm Serina had once stitched up after a boar attack.

"But I don't know how to fight," Maris told Val when he handed her a firearm.

"Maybe not. But you know how to shoot," Val explained. "You've done well in training."

Helena put her arm around Maris's shoulder. "*I* know how to fight. I'll be with you the whole time."

Maris took a deep breath, glanced at Helena for reassurance, and nodded.

Val teamed up with two of Blaze's lieutenants and a Jungle Camp girl, Shard, who knew the quickest, quietest way to the stream that ran through the heart of Mount Ruin.

Anika joined a group with Mirror and three of Hotel Misery's girls.

Once firearms and unlit torches had been distributed, Val addressed the small parties, giving them each an area to search. "When you get close to your target area, douse your torches. Stay as silent as you can. If you see the guards, fire a warning shot so the rest of us can come to your aid. Or shoot to kill—these men can't be allowed to wander free."

"Be careful," Serina added. "Be methodical."

She shared a last look with Val. His hair had fallen into his eyes, and she fought the urge to brush it back. She wanted to feel the skin of his cheek beneath her hand, remind herself that he was here, that he was real, that he wouldn't be swallowed by the darkness of Mount Ruin.

"See you soon," she said softly, and prayed that it was true.

Three men without weapons or food shouldn't feel as looming a threat, but they did. Maybe it was the heavy, humid night pressing close, or the red glow of the volcano pulsing in the distance.

Serina set out with her team along the western cliff path. Their destination was the guard tower northwest of Cave crew's former home. The same tower Bruno had been overseeing when he'd propositioned Serina, where Petrel had told her to always fight back.

Serina could see the faint flicker of the other groups' torches through the trees. Val was heading for the stream, Anika the guard tower closest to Hotel Misery. Cliff's team had the longest hike ahead of them, to the northeast guard tower.

Serina led the way, a lit torch in her hand. She peered out beyond its wobbly glow into the night, and wished she could shake the feeling that the night stared back.

The constant crash of waves to her left made it impossible to listen for the furtive scurry of footfalls or breaking twigs as bodies moved through the forest. Her imagination supplied the sounds, twisting them up with the real noise of the waves and her companions and the snapping torch until she'd almost convinced herself she *was* hearing footsteps, that the guards were pacing them.

"What if I can't do it?" Maris asked, and even though she kept her voice low, Serina still jumped at the sound.

"Do what?" Helena asked.

"Shoot someone." Maris's hands gripped the firearm so tightly her knuckles had gone white.

Helena rubbed a hand down her back. "Then you shoot in the air to signal the others, and we'll take care of the guards." She glanced at Serina, who nodded agreement, and added, "We've been fighting without firearms for a long time. We know what to do."

Maris heaved a sigh. "This is so strange. I feel like I'm in another world."

Serina grimaced. "You are. *Our* world."

The path arced away from the cliffs and into the trees not far from the entrance to the cave. It was strange to think of it now, empty and abandoned, nothing but a few rusted chairs and the remains of the cook fire to show that it had once been inhabited. Serina hadn't been back since the night of the fight with the Commander.

"Hey, Tremor," she said, a thought niggling at her. "When Cave crew moved down to Hotel Misery, you brought all the supplies and weapons, right?"

"Most of it, I think," Tremor responded after a moment. "Cliff sent the girls up to grab their pallets and personal belongings. I think they collected the food and weapons too."

"But you're not sure." A heavy weight settled in Serina's stomach. Probably the guards had gone to one of the watchtowers or the stream. They'd have gone somewhere familiar. But what if they'd decided to raid the abandoned camps? What discarded weapons or food might they find?

"I think we better go by the cave first," she decided. "If there's anything left we'll take it with us. The last thing we need is Nero or Diego getting their hands on a boar spear or someone's dropped knife."

As Serina left the path for a small trail that passed through the forest to the cave, her heart beat faster. The thought that the guards might have found their way to her former home, that they could even now be huddled in the dark cavern where so many of the women they terrorized had slept, made her ill.

And yet, part of her hoped they *were* there.

It seemed a fitting place to remind them they had no dominion here.

Oracle would have approved.

But as the trees opened and the yawning black mouth of the cave came into view, it wasn't Oracle who haunted Serina, but Jacana. She felt the girl's presence all around her. She and Jacana had stood just here on that first terrifying night, staring into the dark maw of the lava tube as Cliff and the others disappeared inside. Jacana had been Serina's first friend on Mount Ruin—her first friend ever, if she didn't include her siblings. Jacana was gone now; maybe if she hadn't been friends with Serina, if she hadn't been on the stage that last night, maybe she wouldn't have died. Her small, pointed face and sad eyes wouldn't leave Serina.

"We should douse the light," Serina said softly.

"You want us—we have to go in *there*? In the *dark*?" Maris asked. In the flickering torchlight, the whites of her wide eyes gleamed like those of a panicked horse.

"If the guards *are* inside, the light will warn them we're coming. It'll give them a target to attack."

"Stay behind me," Helena said.

Maris grabbed a handful of Helena's shirt in one hand and held the firearm tightly in the other.

With a deep breath and a silent prayer, Serina doused the torch and led the way into the tunnel.

Almost immediately, the space shrank around her, until the stone hemmed close. Behind her, she could hear the steady footfalls of Tremor, who was used to the tunnel, and the tentative shuffle of Maris and Helena.

Serina had lived within these walls for weeks, and still the air sucked from her lungs and her hands trembled the deeper she went. She walked blind, feeling her way along the walls of rock. The closer she got to the main cavern, the more she strained for any hint of light. If the guards had lit a fire, there'd be a glow along the lava tube; there'd be some warning.

But no light appeared, even as the air changed, and the space opened up. They'd reached the cavern.

She stopped, and the girls behind her stopped too. Silence filled the darkness. Serina held her breath.

One, two, three . . .

Still no sound.

She'd relight the torch and have Helena and Maris block the tunnel while she and Tremor searched the cave properly. If the men were hiding in the shadows, they'd find them.

Serina was fumbling for her flint when she heard a faint bang. Behind her, Tremor flinched. The distant gunshot echoed strangely in the cave; it was impossible to know which of the other search parties it came from.

But it meant the guards had been found elsewhere.

"Did you hear that?" Helena murmured.

Serina turned around. "Let's—"

Someone grabbed her from behind. She screamed, and the sound ricocheted back at her from the walls and the other girls. She went limp, becoming deadweight as Petrel had taught her, and the man grunted at the unexpected burden. Serina drove her elbow into his groin and tried to twist away, but his hands clawed up her body, ripping her shirt, toward her throat. She twisted again and ducked, slashing at his arms with her ragged nails.

Somehow, she managed to get away.

The darkness was heavy as a blanket, filled with the screams of the other girls. Beneath the chaos, if she concentrated, she could hear the man panting. She thought it was just the one; maybe the three had split up.

She backed away, bumping into Tremor, but she wasn't fast enough. The guard's hand snaked out and grabbed her arm. She kicked outward, connecting with flesh. He grunted again.

Tremor pushed around Serina and threw her weight at their attacker, sending them both stumbling into the echoing space of the cavern.

Behind her, the screams had stopped, but Maris was sobbing.

Helena murmured, her voice low and urgent.

Serina went after Tremor. The thuds and grunts of the fight were the only guidance she had, until a body flew into her, knocking her to the ground. She struggled, trying to free herself. Was it Tremor who'd fallen on her? Or the guard?

The thought of Nero's calculating gaze, his hands creeping around her throat—

"Tremor?" Serina whispered shakily.

"Yeah," the woman murmured. Slowly, the two untangled themselves, moving as quietly as they could. The darkness was a challenge for the guard as well. He couldn't attack them if he couldn't find them.

Suddenly, a deep voice filled the black. "You're all going to die here, flowers. Surely you know that?" Serina recognized Hector's voice. He let out a cold chuckle. "No one escapes Mount Ruin. *No—*"

A flash exploded to Serina's left, followed by the concussion of a gunshot that made her ears ring. A hollow groan, and then a thud.

Hector didn't speak again.

"Did I get him?" Maris whispered. "I—I aimed toward his voice . . . Did I get him? Serina? I—I didn't hit you, did I?" Her voice rose to a wail.

"I'm here, I'm fine," Serina mumbled. She scrambled for her flint and crawled across the uneven rock until she found the torch. With shaking hands, she lit the oiled rags.

Maris was slumped near the entrance to the tunnel, firearm gripped tightly in her hands, her eyes wide. Helena hovered over her. Tremor sat a couple yards away, clutching her elbow. Shadows jumped wildly across their faces. Serina slowly turned. Near the dead dregs of the cook fire, Hector lay on the hard ground, staring up at the rock above his head. His mouth opened and closed without a sound. From beneath him, a rusty stain spread across the stone.

She stepped carefully up to him. The torch threw sickly orange light across his sunken cheeks. He blinked at her, silently, as his life bled out at her feet.

"We're going to escape, Hector," Serina promised, her heart still pounding heavily in her throat. "But you never will. Mount Ruin will never let *you* go."

TWELVE

NOMI

Over the next couple of days, Nomi and Malachi found a kind of rhythm. They took turns at the tiller, and Malachi kept up his lessons on how to sail, until Nomi no longer got so frustrated and was reasonably confident she knew when it was time to tighten a rope or change course to better find the wind.

They slept in short intervals through the days and nights, covered their faces and ears when the other needed to relieve themselves over the side, and spoke, haltingly, of their plans to connect with Malachi's friend Dante. Nomi thought of Renzo often and hoped they weren't already too late.

They didn't talk about Asa, but Nomi saw him frequently in her dreams.

Not dreams. Nightmares.

Nomi thought often of Serina as well.

Had the prison boat arrived on Mount Ruin yet? Was her sister even now on her way to safety in Azura? Nomi's thoughts spun from Renzo to Serina, from fear to doubt to hope.

On the morning of their third day at sea, Nomi woke to find, in the distance, a fleet of large flat-bottom boats roped together and anchored. She stared in disbelief as the floating village slowly grew before them. Mazes of rigging ran between the vessels. Tiny as ants from this distance, men ran along the ropes.

Nomi had heard of these communities, families who lived just offshore in their boats, some of them strapped together to create whole floating cities, but she'd never imagined she'd see one.

"We'll give them a wide berth," Malachi said, adjusting the sail to take them farther out to sea. "The fewer people see us, the better."

He'd gained strength steadily in the last couple of days. Nomi didn't find herself checking his pallor anymore; then again, they'd both browned up in the sun.

Nomi leaned on the tiller. The movement didn't feel natural, exactly, but she no longer feared the boat would capsize at any moment.

They were nearly beyond the floating city when a shouted "Ahoy!" startled them both.

Nomi twisted to see a slick sailboat approaching. Several men lined its deck.

Malachi swore under his breath.

"Can we outrun them?" Nomi asked, panic bringing beads of sweat to the back of her neck.

"They're too fast," Malachi said. "Bigger sail, better skill. And trying to run would make us even more intriguing. We're going to have to bluff it out." With a sigh, he slackened the ropes, letting the sail flap. The boat slowed.

"What if they recognize you?" Nomi asked, her pulse racing. If these men figured out Malachi was the rightful Heir, surely word would get back to the palazzo. And then

Malachi would lose the advantage of Asa thinking he was dead.

Malachi rubbed a hand over the short black whiskers on his chin. "Would *you* recognize me?"

Nomi studied him. The stubble hadn't quite grown into a beard yet, but it masked the unexpected fullness of his mouth and softened the sharpness of his jaw. Dark circles beneath his eyes spoke of a recent illness and his normally short, orderly hair was spiky and disheveled. His eyes, bright as polished wood, *she* would recognize, but she'd spent a lot of time staring into them.

"You're right," she said slowly, taking in his hand-me-down guard uniform and ill-fitting shoes. "You don't look like yourself."

Malachi quirked a little grin. "I'm a ruffian now. The Heir died, remember?"

As he took the tiller from her and directed her to the bow, Nomi wondered at the strange spark in his eyes as he'd said this last.

"What do we say?" she asked as the small sailboat approached. "What if they ask what we're doing out here? I don't look—my clothes . . ." She gestured to the worn blue pants and shirt of her prison clothes.

Malachi glanced at her again; she hadn't seen *this* look, the intense, frightening one, in days. "*You* don't say anything."

Nomi's throat closed.

"Sailboat ahoy!" the sailors shouted. The boat slowed, drawing up alongside. It was larger but not by much. Four men, all with heavy beards and sun-weathered skin, lashed the boats together without asking permission first.

One man, obviously the leader, hopped between decks, his leather boots landing with a thud. He was a big man about Nomi's father's age, shirtless and scorched deep brown by the sun.

Nomi lowered her gaze, a new fear bursting to life in her chest. What if these men wanted their boat? What if they stole it? Would they throw her and Malachi overboard? How long would it take to drown?

A shiver sluiced down her back, as chilling as a splash of seawater.

She smoothed her hands down the front of her threadbare pants, painfully aware of her own appearance. Women didn't usually wear trousers in Viridia, or their hair in a tangled mass down their backs. Would this man recognize her garb as prison clothes? Would he wonder why she was so untidy, so . . . wild?

Nomi snuck a glance at the man, and sure enough he was staring straight at her, his attention fixed.

"And what are you folks running from?" he asked bluntly, crossing his arms over his chest. "Or running to? Are ye smugglers?"

"I'm taking my wife to Corrado to help care for my ailing parents," Malachi said without hesitation, his gruff, authoritative delivery masking the lie. "Nothing nearly so thrilling as running or smuggling. Though I'm open to barter. We were thrown off course by a storm a few nights ago and lost some of our gear and food." Malachi pulled a watch from his pants pocket. Its gold case caught the sunshine, and the man's attention.

"Whatcha want for that trinket?" he asked Malachi, his gaze returning to Nomi.

"A few fish, some bread if you have it, and a dress for my wife. Can't have my parents see her like this. Her finer clothes were ruined in the rain."

The man sniffed and pursed his lips. "Haven't had storms here in a week or so. Where'd you say you're coming from?"

Nomi twisted her hands behind her back, trying to look demure, but the constant rocking of the boat threw her off balance. She widened her stance. Now she looked like a soldier at attention. Too confident. She released her hands, letting her arms fall to her sides. Her palms were damp.

"We're up from Bellaqua," Malachi said smoothly. "Doubt you would have gotten the storm. It blew from the south and went inland."

"Long way to travel in such a small boat." The man glanced over at his companions, who were silently following the exchange. Then he pointed at the handle for the storage space under the bow. "Not a good sailor, are you? To lose all your belongings when you have a perfectly good lazarette to store 'em in . . ."

Malachi glanced at Nomi for a split second with an unreadable expression. Then he turned to the man and straightened his shoulders. When he spoke again, the gruffness of his voice had turned ugly. "Truth is, the girl's a handful. Bought her off her father, who'd spoiled her something fierce. She tossed our things in a rage when I told her I'd be leaving her to care for my parents alone. Got some work to do to tame her before we get to Corrado."

Nomi's jaw clenched, and she stared fixedly at the worn deck, heat climbing her neck to her cheeks. *You know it's a lie. You know he's doing this to protect us.* She told herself this over and over, but his tone of voice, the ease with which he spoke, as if she were a dog he'd purchased and must now bend to his will . . . it dug inside her chest and hollowed her out.

"Ah," the sailor said, and in that one small word, Nomi could hear his suspicion dissipate. He shifted, rocking back on his heels. At ease, now that it all made sense to him. Now that he knew her place. "Well, now. I think we can work with ye."

Nomi had thought the palazzo was stifling. She'd wanted to escape the tight corsets and heavy dresses, the endless lessons and twisted politics of being a Grace. But the luxury had shielded her, just as Serina had once tried to convince her it would. And Asa had too. He'd given her the illusion she had some choice, some agency.

But Viridia was still twisted, its queens still buried deep.

Nomi stared at the scuffed tips of her too-big boots. She drifted, their voices losing meaning as they haggled over price, as they commiserated over the uselessness of women. She didn't want to hear Malachi speak of his plans to tame her. She didn't want to hear his voice turn him into a stranger.

The big sun-browned man hopped back to his boat and unlashed the two, retying Malachi and Nomi's boat behind to tow it back to the flotilla of boats. Once docked, the man in charge disappeared for a spell, but Nomi didn't move. She didn't meet Malachi's eyes, even when he cleared his throat and softly said her name.

When the man returned with their goods, Malachi thanked him and his companions and navigated the small sailboat north, away from the men lining the deck of the massive network of ships. Nomi sat down, moving carefully, precisely. Holding herself together with an iron grip. She kept her gaze fixed to her toes and her mouth shut tight.

"Nomi. *Nomi.*"

Nomi lifted her chin and stared at Malachi, a challenge in her eyes.

"He was suspicious," Malachi said.

"I know." She tried to keep her voice level, tried to ignore the pressure building in her chest.

"I told him what he needed to hear." He looked at her, all earnest and reasonable. He didn't understand.

"I know," she said again. *She* understood. She understood everything.

It was good Serina was escaping to Azura. Nomi wasn't sure that she believed anything would, or could, change. The truth was all around her, had always been. It didn't matter if she fought against it or accepted it. Each small interaction, each small moment reminded her.

Malachi rubbed the back of his neck, burnt now by the sun, his expression cracking. "Then why are you looking at me like that? Why are you angry?"

Sea air swept across her cheeks, cooling the heated skin. But it didn't cool the fist of flame in her chest. She tried to contain it, tried to think of a polite response, but she couldn't do it.

"You called me a handful. You said you would tame me. You said you *bought* me!" she exploded, and the wind stole the words.

"But you know—"

"What? That it's a lie?" She shook her head. "Maybe this time. But *those* are the words that allayed that man's suspicion. Knowing I was your property made me safe, made me make sense in his world. It was okay that I was a 'handful' because you had me under control." She wanted to get up and pace, but the little sailboat had caught a strong breeze and was bobbing violently up and down as it strained forward through open water, leaving the village of boats far behind. "Malachi, you didn't blink. You didn't have to think about it. You *knew* what would reassure him, and it was treating me like an unbroken horse."

Tears were streaking down her cheeks now, and she felt so *stupid*. She knew she was overreacting, that he'd done what he had to do to protect them. She *knew* this was the way her world worked. She even knew he didn't mean those words. He'd proved it the night of his birthday, when he'd tried to give her her freedom.

But she couldn't forget that man's expression; it built in her head, multiplied by the thousands of times she'd been dismissed so easily, erased from every decision that concerned her. She'd only spent a few days with Serina, in a place where women made choices for themselves, where women had a voice and a vote. But that was enough to make anything less untenable.

Malachi said nothing for a long, awkward moment. He concentrated on steering the boat and stared past her to the faint hump of coastline in the distance. Behind him, the sun sank toward the horizon.

"What should I have done instead?" he asked at last.

"I don't know," Nomi said, dipping her damp cheeks into her hands. What *had* she expected? Frustration boiled up inside her, scorching her to the core. "You can't change the world in the space of a single conversation, can you?"

A new Viridia. *That's* what Nomi wanted, and she knew now that even if he wanted to, Malachi couldn't give it to her.

She watched the sun slowly drown itself along the watery horizon and pined for a new world.

THIRTEEN

SERINA

"Are you sure?" Ember asked. She held up a knife made from an old curved piece of metal, its edge newly sharpened.

Serina took a deep breath and nodded.

With her other hand, Ember held Serina's long braid taut. Then she began sawing.

Serina closed her eyes. Her hair had been a nuisance since she'd arrived, but now it played a part in her nightmares. In her dreams, Diego used it to grab her, he used it to bind her, he used it to choke her.

She refused to give this power to him.

The cutting took longer than she expected. She had time to remember the hours her mother and sister had spent brushing her hair, all the time they'd spent together, laughing and gossiping, while they twisted it into one elaborate style after another. Homesickness punched her in the gut.

"Are you all right?" Ember asked when it was done. Her own hair was shaved close to her skull, with a longer strip of red down the center.

Serina glanced at her and then quickly away—the braid hung over Ember's hand like a dead snake.

What would her mother think of her if she could see her now?

Serina ran her callused hands through her ragged, shoulder-length hair.

She would be ashamed.

"I'm fine," Serina said. It was just hair, a silly thing to become attached to. She was still Grace, still the person Mount Ruin had made her—helped her—become.

Ember slipped her knife into her boot and headed into the woods to dump the hair, her purposeful stride scattering a group of younger women who loitered by the broken fountain.

Hotel Misery had once seemed hollow and frightening to Serina. Now it was a hub of semicontrolled chaos. Previously empty rooms teemed with women from the Beach, Southern Cliffs, the Cave, and Jungle Camp. The ballroom remained an infirmary, the half-destroyed lobby had become a gathering place, and the walkway that lined the stinking canal rang with voices.

At the moment, the shouting was louder than usual.

Serina jogged out to meet the returning search party, her heart sinking when she saw the body they carried.

It was not one of the missing guards.

"What happened?" she asked. The night of the first search, Maris had shot and killed Hector. But the other gunshot they'd heard had come to nothing. Diego had evaded the group that had come upon him at the stream near Jungle Camp. And no one had seen Nero, that night or since. Three days, and the two guards were still terrorizing and killing the women of Mount Ruin.

"One of the girls guarding the southern entrance to the prison building was killed," Fox reported. Her pale swoop of hair hid one eye, but her glare came through just fine.

"She walked a couple yards into the woods to relieve herself. Never came back. We found her on our search along the southern cliffs. No sign of the guards, though. The girls on watch with her didn't see anything either. Didn't even hear her scream."

Serina's skin crawled. They'd lost two women the day before in the same area.

"Nero and Diego are testing our defenses along the southern gate to the prison. Probably trying to get to the other guards. *No one* goes off alone, even for a moment," she ordered. "I want more women down there tonight. I'll find Val, see if we can spare one of our markswomen."

The firearm training was going well, but their supplies of ammunition were dwindling.

Fox slammed the end of her spear into the dirt. "The women are spread thin," she growled. "Too many search parties, too many places to guard. And our food is almost gone."

Behind her, the three women carrying the body set it gently on the ground. They'd started taking their dead to the volcano first thing in the morning; it was too dangerous at night with Nero and Diego out there, ready to pick them off.

Twig, leader of Beach crew and by far the tallest person on the island, even taller than Val, approached them. "Have you cut off the guards in the prison yet? Why should they be fed when we've barely enough for ourselves?"

"We've reduced their rations, but we're still feeding them. For now," Serina replied. "The boat will be here in three more days at most. We have enough."

Serina held herself tall and smiled at the woman, yanking up her Grace training from the depths. She'd never felt the weight of anything but her parents' expectations on her shoulders before. She'd never been responsible for anyone's life. The fact that most of the people who looked to her for answers also seemed to hate her didn't help. She was exhausted.

You're determined. She gave herself a little mental push. *You can handle this.*

Twig shook her head in disgust and walked off.

"Take a break," Serina said to Fox and the rest of the search party. "Your share of the midday meal is in the infirmary."

The women headed into the shadowy ballroom. Serina crouched by the murdered woman. Black hair, cut to her shoulders, just like Serina's. She wasn't someone Serina recognized, but the purple ligature marks around her neck were familiar. *Just like Doll and Scorpion.* Just like all the victims.

Anger boiled in Serina's chest, as violent as it was useless.

Val and Anika came looking for her while she was still holding vigil over the body.

Serina told them what had happened. "She was killed down by the southern gate, near where the women were found yesterday. I think they're trying to get the rest of the guards out."

"Did you order more search parties?" Anika asked. "We can't let them keep killing us. We've got to find them." There was little animation in her face; she'd been subdued since the vote. Serina ached for her. She understood, better than most, the agony Anika felt knowing she had to leave her family behind.

Serina shook her head. "No new search parties . . . but I want more women on the southern gate tonight. Val, can we spare the ammunition for a markswoman to help patrol?"

Serina glanced at Val. He stood near the fountain, splitting his attention between the conversation and the shadows beyond the clearing. He'd been like that ever since Nero and Diego had evaded them—watchful.

They were *all* on edge.

"I'll check our ammunition after our markswomen finish today's training," he said, without commenting on whether he thought it was a good idea. Aside from logistical questions and suggestions on where to search for Nero and Diego, he kept his opinions to himself. She appreciated that, even as she found herself occasionally wishing he would tell her what he thought she should do.

She'd never made so many decisions as she had over the past week. She'd been raised to believe men were the decision makers of her world. Her job was to look pretty and keep her mouth shut. Oracle had fought a lot of that training out of her, but Serina couldn't erase it all. She couldn't erase her history, any more than she could reveal Viridia's.

The fact that this country had once been ruled by women

didn't make it easier for her to lead now. Her instincts were to defer. To submit.

She took a deep breath. With enough practice, her instincts would change.

"Anika, I need you to join the southern patrol," she said with one of her placating Grace smiles. "I trust you to keep everyone safe."

"Fine." Anika turned to Val. "I'm taking a firearm. If I see either of those monsters, I'm shooting them." She stalked off without giving him a chance to answer.

Serina and Val moved the dead girl into the corner of the ruined lobby with the body of a woman who'd died of an infection that morning. They would take them both to the volcano at dawn.

By implicit agreement, they headed into the hotel, to the room where the rations were kept, where they could have a few moments alone.

"You cut your hair," Val said. He slipped a hand through the ends, and his smile was so kind and sweet Serina forgot to feel self-conscious.

As easily as a breath, she moved into the circle of his arms. She rested her head against his chest and closed her eyes.

"How are you?" he asked.

"Tired. Worried."

Gently, he ran his hands down her back. "You keep going, even when I expect you to stop. Ever since we met. It's my favorite thing about you, the way you keep getting up, keep moving forward."

"And smile in the faces of people who hate me?" She buried herself in the worn softness of his shirt. The rumble of his laugh vibrated against her cheek.

"Yes, exactly. It's *hard* to smile at someone who hates you," he returned. "But I don't think Anika hates you. Twig might."

She gave him a little push.

His hands glided up to her shoulders and then her cheeks, cupping her face. She put a little distance between them so she could look up at him.

"A year ago, you were learning how to be a Grace." He brushed his thumb across her cheek. "Your whole world revolved around submitting to someone else's needs. Now you're leading a hundred fifty women to freedom. *You're* the one in charge. And you're succeeding, Serina. I know you have doubts, but you are helping everyone on Mount Ruin."

His words sent heat through her. It surprised her when he spoke like this. She had never imagined she'd see a man joyfully watch a woman claim power. She never thought she'd see a man stand back and support, rather than assert his will. She'd once thought the Heir was handsome. But she'd never seen anything so attractive as the respect in Val's eyes.

She pressed her face into his hands, tilting her head back, and he accepted her invitation, bending to kiss her. Their lips met and made their own small universe of sunlight and dizzying stars. Serina's hands slid up his chest, around his shoulders and into the soft hair at the nape of his neck. She pulled him closer, down into her darkness, into the sweet heat of her mouth. His hands moved too, abandoning her face for the curve of her waist. Serina sighed into him, their breath mingling, sparking new flames low in her belly.

Running footsteps drew them apart.

Serina turned in time to see Anika skid into the room.

"We found another body," she panted.

All the warmth drained out of Serina, leaving an icy wind in its wake. *Not another. Not so soon.*

"What happened?" she asked, already following Anika out of the room and down the rock-splashed staircase. Val hurried behind her, his hand on his firearm.

"Lion, a girl from Beach Camp. She was one of our sentries on the north side, near the amphitheater." Anika glanced over her shoulder long enough to add, "She was strangled, just like the others."

Serina pounded her fist into her thigh. "Any sign of Nero or Diego?"

Anika shook her head. "The girls out with her saw nothing. One moment she was there and the next, gone. Her knife's gone too, and her water."

Serina swore under her breath.

They came to the hotel's open-air lobby, still framed by a couple of cracked urns, the decorative plants they'd once housed long dead. A group of women surrounded Lion's still form. Serina felt tears build behind her eyes.

Twig bent and picked up the girl's body, cradling her protectively against her chest. Lion's legs dangled bonelessly, and Serina's stomach turned over.

131

Anika said quietly, "The other sentries picked up a trail for a while before they lost the track near the stream. They can't figure out how the guard managed to double back without them seeing him."

Serina's heart sank. "All right, bring everyone in, except for the women guarding the prison compound. We'll stick close to the hotel tonight, tighten up our defenses here, and pray the boat comes tomorrow." They were already stretched too thin. No one was getting enough sleep. "Make sure no one goes out alone. Everyone gets a weapon. But no firearms. I don't want to risk Nero and Diego getting their hands on one. Except you, Anika. You take one to the southern gate like you planned."

Anika nodded. "That boat *better* come soon. We need to get off this rock."

Serina went to find Ember. The older woman had been helping in the infirmary when she wasn't leading combat training. She didn't sleep much or stop moving, as far as Serina could tell. Val walked with Serina, and she couldn't decide if it was comforting or concerning, the way he scanned the scrubby trees with narrowed eyes.

"I want to be part of the next watch at the prison," she told him. "Ember, you, me, Cliff if I can find her. I can't shake the thought that Nero and Diego are going to go for the other guards."

"Or they're just trying to pick us off, one by one," Val said grimly. "They got Lion near the amphitheater."

"What about firearm training? Are we ready if the boat

does come tomorrow?" she asked. They were still trying to get ten girls who could use the firearms reliably.

Val shrugged. "It's going. Maris hasn't wanted to train, so I picked another girl to fill her place. She's not as good, but she's getting better. The rest are picking it up."

Daylight was fading, and the infirmary teemed with shadows. Most of the wounded were recovering, though a girl had died that morning and one more would likely follow. A third woman, from Beach crew, had lost feeling in her legs. Val had told Serina privately that he suspected she would never regain it.

Serina was surprised to see Maris in the corner, huddled with Helena. She headed over to them, her pulse dancing a little faster. "Are you all right? I heard you haven't been training."

Maris looked up at the sound of her voice, and Serina was shocked at her haggard appearance. Dark half moons sat beneath her eyes, and her hair hung dirty and tangled around her face. If Serina hadn't known, she never would have guessed Maris had once been a Grace.

"Are you well?" Serina asked again.

Maris dropped her head into her hands. "I just keep hearing it," she mumbled. "The gunshot . . . it echoes and echoes without end. And the blood . . ."

"She's been having nightmares," Helena said softly. "Ever since that night in the cave. She's scared to fall asleep now . . ." She rubbed Maris's back, over and over.

Serina sank to the cracked marble floor before the two

girls and reached for Maris's hands. "You saved our lives. Your quick thinking saved Helena."

Maris looked up. Serina's heart clenched at her haunted expression.

"Hector wasn't going to stop," Serina continued, pitching her voice low and soothing. "He wanted to hurt us. He would have killed us without a thought. If you hadn't shot him, he could have ripped the firearm from your hands. He could have shot you and Helena and all of us in that cave. You did what you had to do, Maris. Helena is here now—she's safe, because of what you did. So if you're going to carry the memory of his death, make sure you're carrying joy that she's alive too."

"I didn't want to kill anyone," Maris whispered.

Helena put an arm around her and drew her close. "None of us ever did." She looked up, meeting Serina's eyes. "I wish I'd had the firearm. It would have made me happy to kill him. What does that say about me?"

Tears spilled down Helena's cheeks.

"It says you want to survive. We all do." Serina stood up. "It won't always be this way. Soon, we'll leave Mount Ruin—all of this—behind."

Helena ran her hand over Maris's hair and cradled the girl against her shoulder. "Will we?"

"You saved Helena's life, Maris," Serina said firmly. She remembered the shock of watching her first fight, of knowing she'd have to fight one day herself. She knew how horrifying it was, coming from the palazzo. "Try to focus on that."

With a last look at the two women, Serina turned and made her way to Val. He'd collected Ember from the women caring for the injured.

"I want to relieve the watch at the prison," Serina said to Ember. "Are you up for it?"

Ember nodded. "Of course."

They snagged Cliff from a quiet spot near the hotel, where she was whittling branches into spears. "Bring your knife," Serina said.

They hiked to the prison compound in silence, searching every shadow.

Night had fallen in earnest by the time they arrived, and Serina was grateful for Ember's torch and Val's firearm. She didn't like the way the darkness crowded around them.

Ten women guarded the entrance nearest the path. They nodded solemnly as Serina's group filed inside. The dim, musty stairwell was as narrow and shadowed as the cave's entrance. Serina filled her mind with images of tall ceilings and sparkling chandeliers. She drew in a breath and imagined it as a clean sea breeze, without the smell of sulfur, or ash, or blood.

Blood?

They'd reached the top of the stairs. The thick iron door stood open.

Val raised his weapon. Serina fitted her knife to her hand.

Slowly, they stepped into the long hall. For the first time, Serina could hear the buzz of the lights. Belatedly, she realized why.

The guards weren't shouting threats and insults.

Serina stared at Anika, Mirror, and Fox. They all held firearms. It wasn't their turn on watch.

"Anika," Serina said softly, and then she could see into the shadows of the cells: the arms splayed, the blood spatters. "What have you done?"

FOURTEEN

NOMI

Nomi woke with her head pillowed on her arm, curled up in the bow of the boat. Faint streaks of dawn illuminated Malachi's face. He was asleep next to the tiller, head back against the gunwale, his mouth slack.

If they'd both been asleep—

Nomi sat up fast, belatedly noting other details: the sails, slack; the lights of a village glowing at the edge of shore, a dozen yards away.

Shore, just a dozen yards away.

She scuttled to the stern of the boat.

"Malachi!" she said, shaking his shoulder.

With an un-Heir-like snort, his head fell forward and he woke, sputtering like she'd dropped him in the water. "What? What is it?"

She pointed wordlessly at the village, so close.

He slumped back and rubbed at his eyes. "I know."

"You . . . what—" It was Nomi's turn to sputter.

"You were asleep. I didn't want to wake you, and I knew we needed to wait until sunrise to dock anyway. So I took down the sails and threw the anchor." He yawned. "I'm glad. I got some sleep too."

Nomi stared across the water to the houses climbing spiderlike into the hills. "That's Porto Rosa?"

He nodded. "It is."

She craned over the gunwale, looking for the anchor line. "Then let's go."

"Not yet," Malachi said. "We need to eat. And you need to change."

Nomi looked down at herself, at her threadbare shirt and baggy prison pants.

"I know it will be painful, but we'll need to play the part," he added, almost gently.

"You mean the part of quiet, obedient girl following her husband with her head down." The familiar urge to scream rose in her chest.

"You are *not* a quiet, obedient girl." He put a finger on her chin, startling her, and tipped her head up so she'd look him in the eyes. He gave her a sharp smile. "You are dangerous."

Unbidden, her mind returned to the night of the storm, when he'd first told her she was dangerous and then kissed her, their faces flushed and wet with rain. It had been different from kissing Asa, in ways she'd never let herself examine.

She was certainly not going to examine those feelings now.

She turned away from him, toward the lazarette and the stash of goods they'd traded for. "Fine," she said, with forced calm. "I'll wear the dress."

Nomi didn't have a brush so she finger-combed her hair and braided it down her back. She had nothing to replace her boots, but the dress was long enough that they wouldn't be obvious. Hopefully. Even though she had no idea how to use it, she was comforted by Serina's knife hidden in the leather along her ankle.

Once she was clothed, Malachi left his post staring out over the stern and hoisted the sail.

"How are you feeling?" she asked, gesturing to his stomach. He'd hidden his pain well the past few days, but she'd seen the blood-flecked dressings and the occasional wince when he pulled a rope tight.

Malachi put a hand to the wound. "I'm fine."

She raised a brow.

"I'm healing," he amended. "I'll survive."

"Good," Nomi replied. "I . . . I'm nervous," she found herself admitting. "What if Dante doesn't want to join you? What if he's loyal to Asa?"

"He was my best friend from the time we were children," he said. "He knows who Asa is."

Nomi moved to the bow and watched the port approach, trying to focus her mind.

A long golden beach curled beneath houses with vermilion roofs that climbed into the hills. Beyond the city, a green, tree-covered hill shouldered up to the sky. To the north, a long pier extended into the sea, the squat concrete and steel of the port at its base a blemish in contrast to the rest of the city's charm. Malachi navigated to this pier, where several dockworkers ran to help him tie up.

Nomi took a deep breath.

You can do this.

She cast her eyes downward and became a woman of Viridia again.

Malachi helped her off the sailboat with a hand under her elbow. For a few moments, her legs wobbled sickeningly, unused to the unmovable ground beneath her feet.

"How can I help you, sir?" A man walked out to meet them, sharp and weasel-faced in his navy brocade waistcoat and gold breeches.

"I'd like to store my boat here for a few days," Malachi said. He slipped a few coins from the pack, spoils from his trade with the men on the floating village. "That'll cover it, I should think."

The boatyard foreman counted the money and appraised Malachi with a quick look. "You're two silvers short," he said, raising a brow. His hair was thin, a nondescript brown with wisps at the top, not long enough to hide his bald spot.

Malachi handed him one silver. "I'll pay the other when I come to retrieve my boat."

The foreman opened his mouth to protest, but he wilted under the intensity of Malachi's gaze. As Malachi urged Nomi forward, she almost felt sorry for the weasel-faced man.

Dawn had broken upon Porto Rosa, and the streets were full of men pushing carts toward the central piazza. Some had wives and daughters following them—women could be put to work selling wares as long as they didn't handle the money themselves.

We do the grunt work, the backbreaking tasks, Nomi thought, staring at a thin girl carrying a heavy basket of bread on her hip, her back bowed with the strain. It made Nomi think of her own mother, hunched over her sewing machine, working for decades while her husband collected her wages. Nomi's father was kind, but he'd never questioned the fairness of the system. He'd never asked Nomi's mother what *she* thought about anything.

But Renzo . . . Nomi had *made* Renzo listen to what she thought. Her radical views had wormed their way into him, whether he liked it or not. She didn't know if her persistence had made him different, or if it had to do with them being twins, or maybe he was just the kind of person who saw value in everyone.

His smile shone in her mind like a candle flame, drawing her forward.

Malachi marched through the cobbled streets with his shoulders back and his intense glare threatening to burn anyone who challenged him. A new beard and tattered clothes couldn't hide the haughty confidence he'd inherited from his father. How could he *not* be recognized?

Nomi's heart seized every time someone passed them and gave him a second look.

"Can you tone it down a bit?" Nomi whispered, feigning fear of a passing dog to squeeze herself a little closer to him.

"Tone what down?" he muttered in response.

Nomi came very close to rolling her eyes. "Your . . . Superior-ness. You're walking down the lane as if you own it. Someone is going to recognize you."

Malachi kept walking, but gradually his demeanor shifted. He stopped glaring at everyone they passed. He let his shoulders slump a little. And he slowed down.

A loud burst of laughter made them both jump. Two men stood on the corner, their backs to Malachi and Nomi.

Nomi followed Malachi through a narrow alleyway. Above them, women hung laundry on wires strung between the two buildings. Nomi remembered completing this same task, the wire burning against her fingertips, already raw from the hot water and harsh soap of the wash.

Every street they walked along, Nomi looked for signs the country was in mourning for the Superior. Black curtains in windows, or black ribbons hanging from light posts and the twisted iron gates that protected the nicer homes.

There was nothing.

"The whole country should be hung in black for your father," she murmured. "Do they not know the Superior is dead?"

"I saw a portrait of Asa hanging in a shop. They know my father is dead." Malachi's jaw tightened. "It seems Asa did not declare a mourning period upon his ascension."

Nomi shifted closer, pressing herself into his side. She didn't know what else to do to show that she was sorry. It didn't matter that the Superior had been cruel and capricious. He'd been Malachi's father. And maybe Nomi wasn't sad that Viridia did not mourn such a man. But Asa had made the choice not to, and that tainted it.

"Almost there," Malachi muttered.

Here, it was quieter. Nomi guessed they were moving away from the central piazza and the day's business. The houses on this street were larger, with tall wrought-iron fences and bright green foliage. Aside from an elderly woman sweeping a stoop and a child playing with a small wooden ball on the corner, no one was around.

They had traveled a good distance from the pier, up into the hills, but the air still smelled of fish and brine. It reminded Nomi of her first day in Bellaqua, when she'd seen the city's fairy-tale bridges and canals for the first time and smelled the city's rot.

She hoped this excursion would have a more positive outcome.

Malachi turned right, and they came upon a grassy training field with a squat building at its corner. He paused.

"What's wrong?" Nomi asked.

Malachi shook his head slowly. "I don't know. Maybe nothing. But it's curious that no one is training. Every unit trains in the morning."

"Let's go see," she said. She pulled against his grip on her elbow, drawing him forward.

They approached cautiously, though Nomi couldn't say why. Maybe it had to do with the birdsong in the trees, and the peaceful quiet.

She imagined training grounds and garrisons were not often peaceful, quiet places.

"You'll have to stay out here," Malachi said when they reached the building's heavy front door. "Women aren't allowed."

Of course they weren't. But she didn't like it. What if Dante was not as loyal as Malachi supposed he was?

And if that's the case, what would you *do?*

So Nomi nodded meekly, playing her part, and remained on the walkway as he entered the garrison.

She studied the large, thick-trunked trees across the street, noticing the boy standing on the corner, his ball forgotten as he stared unabashedly at her. She gave him a tentative smile, which he didn't return.

Malachi was back much more quickly than she expected, no Dante in tow.

"What happened?" she asked.

"No one is there," he replied, confusion tightening his mouth. "No one in the whole building. They're gone."

A shiver slithered down Nomi's spine. "Gone? But how is that possible?"

Malachi shook his head. "I don't know. There's no reason for them to leave, nowhere they would go. Unless . . ."

"Unless what?" Nomi asked. Suddenly, the quiet and birdsong didn't seem peaceful so much as ominous.

Malachi looked around as if he might find the soldiers hiding in the shadows. His gaze stopped on the little boy pretending to play with his ball. "Unless Asa is amassing troops somewhere, for some purpose."

Nomi hugged herself, her stomach churning. Why would Asa need to amass troops?

"Wait here for another moment." Malachi jogged back to the corner and crouched before the boy. Nomi couldn't hear what he said.

The boy shrugged. Shook his head. Scuffed his toe against the cobbles.

Malachi returned, passing Nomi and disappearing into the garrison. When he emerged, he was carrying a small, folded piece of paper. She stood silently, hands clasped demurely, as he handed the paper to the boy and ruffled his hair.

The boy grabbed his ball and took off, disappearing down the street.

"What was that?" Nomi asked when Malachi rejoined her.

He shrugged. "The child said he didn't know where the soldiers went, but I think he was lying. I gave him a message for Dante, just in case."

Nomi couldn't ward off the crush of disappointment. "What do we do now? Wait in case they come back? Or will you go to Bellaqua and fight Asa alone?"

What would *she* do? Perhaps try to look for Renzo?

Their plan had hinged on Dante; without him, they had nothing.

Malachi glanced around the empty street, as if he might find the answer there. When he refocused his attention on her, his look was piercing.

"Lanos is not so far. We should visit your parents. Maybe Renzo has sent them a message revealing his whereabouts."

"But—" Her brain stuttered to a halt. "But what about Asa?"

"I would like to wait a day or two for Dante, in case the boy delivers my message." His voice softened. "And you've come so far. If your brother is nearby or your family is in danger, we should try to help them."

Sudden tears pricked Nomi's eyes. An odd feeling came over her, a strange twinge near her heart. "Thank you. I'm supposed to be helping you fix all of this. I don't know why you want to help me."

He gave her a long look. "You don't?"

Heat rose to her cheeks. She couldn't answer.

FIFTEEN

SERINA

Serina couldn't sleep, so she spent the night standing watch outside Hotel Misery, with Ember's silent presence and the quiet crackle of the torch they'd driven into the ground. All around the building, other women waited. Watched.

How could you murder them?

The argument replayed in Serina's mind, again and again.

Your whole plan was to murder them. Or is it not murder if they starve to death?

Anika hadn't backed down from her decision, not for a split second. Serina had watched closely, and the girl had never once faltered.

"These guards were a risk," Anika had said when Serina confronted her. "They were eating our food; they were drawing more and more of our fighters to keep watch over their worthless lives. If Nero and Diego had gotten the chance to let them loose, they would have surely killed more of us, maybe found a way to signal the boat. They were a *threat*. And your plan was for them to die anyway. At least they went fast at my hands. I don't think *they* would have preferred to starve."

"No," Serina had argued, her heart pounding in her temples. "I was giving them a chance. Leaving them here on the island to fend for themselves is not the same thing as

147

murder. I was giving them more than Commander Ricci ever gave *us*. And I was saving *you*." She gestured to the women holding the firearms. "I was trying to save you from this moment, when you have to face the knowledge that you stared an unarmed man in the eyes and ended his life. This wasn't a fight for survival. It was a calculation. It was murder."

Anika put her hand on Serina's shoulder, turning her so they met eye-to-eye. "I didn't need you to save me from this. You needed *me*. This wasn't a call you were ever going to make." Her gaze flicked to Val. "And it needed to be made."

She patted Serina's shoulder. "We'll take care of the bodies. If you want to use the prison as a trap for Nero and Diego, we can. Or we can close it down and regroup at the Hotel. Up to you."

Serina had stood there as Anika asked her for the keys, as the women had unlocked the cells and dragged the bodies of the guards into the hall. She'd stood in silence when Mirror said quietly, in passing, "These were not good men, Serina."

When Val and Serina were alone, she'd turned to him.

"I wanted to give them a chance at survival," Val said softly.

She remembered Diego grabbing her hair, Carlo and Hector gleefully threatening to kill her. The guards sitting above the fights, betting on which girls would die. Bruno trying to violate her and, later, trying to kill her.

She remembered the boat Nomi had arrived on, with only two guards and how Val had chosen not to kill them and take the boat.

148

Anika had wanted to kill the guards from the beginning, but Serina had stopped her. She'd said it was because they might need them for leverage or information. But how much had been because of Val?

Had Serina failed the women of Mount Ruin because Val was *her* blind spot? Doll and a handful of other women were dead. If Serina had allowed the guards to be executed right away, those women would still be alive. There would have been no threat, no fear on the island while they waited for the ship.

Now Nero and Diego were out there stalking them.

"Mirror was right," she said slowly. "The guards hurt so many of the women here. And Anika was right too. They were your blind spot, so they were mine as well. Nero and Diego have killed so many girls . . ." She trailed off. "Their blood is on our hands."

"I'm so tired of all the blood" was all Val said. And then he went to help with the bodies.

Now Serina stood watch as dawn bled up from the horizon.

"The ship could come as early as today," she said to Ember, trying to shift her thoughts to a more productive task. Reliving last night wouldn't help anyone. "Are we ready?"

Ember cracked her knuckles as she mentally took stock. "Don't know about the girls with firearms, but physical training has been going well. Shouldn't be much of a fight, I hope."

"If it's a normal prison boat with the normal number of sailors and guards, it *should* be easy." Serina glanced down the path. In the morning, she'd send lookouts to keep watch for the boat. She'd send many. Not so much for the boat, but to protect themselves from Nero and Diego.

If the guards killed their lookouts, they wouldn't know when a boat was on its way.

"We should practice at the pier. We need to figure out how to get everyone in position fast enough." *Today, maybe tomorrow. This nightmare will be over soon.*

Unless Asa had changed the whole system somehow. Unless he'd stopped sending women to Mount Ruin. It was a possibility Serina had never entertained.

———

When dawn had broken fully over the island, Serina and Ember left the prison compound and gathered everyone not on watch in the run-down lobby of Hotel Misery.

"We need to shift from training to preparations for our travel," Serina said, loud enough so all could hear her. "No more hunting, target practice, or search parties. I want you to bring all your belongings, food stores, everything you can down to the infirmary. It'll make it easier to access. When that boat comes, we're going. We can't give Nero and Diego a chance to stop us."

A flurry of activity answered her announcement. She sent a team to take Lion and the others to the volcano. Then she pulled Anika aside. "Get all the markswomen together. I want to head to the pier and practice our approach."

Anika nodded and hurried away. When she returned, Serina was surprised to see Maris among the markswomen.

"Are you sure?" Serina asked her.

Maris raised her chin, and as her hair fell away from her face, so did the shadows; her eyes no longer looked so haunted. "I'm ready to do my part."

Serina smiled. "I'm glad to hear it."

She tracked down Val in the infirmary. He gave her a small, sad smile when he saw her, but neither of them acknowledged their conversation from the night before.

"Can you pull a couple of groups together to collect water?" she asked. "We need to fill every flagon we have. Water will be our most precious cargo on that ship."

He nodded. "There are some empty barrels in the compound we can use as well."

"Good," she said. "We need everything ready. We can resupply as needed if the boat is late."

He turned to go, but she called out to him. He paused.

"Don't go out on your own," she said. "To Diego and Nero, you'll be a desirable target."

He gave her hand a quick squeeze. "I'll be careful."

She watched him for a moment as he walked away, then she returned to the markswomen. "When we get the signal from our lookouts, we'll have a very small window to take position without being spotted by the men on the boat. So we're going to practice getting into location right now, for as long as it takes."

A few of the girls nodded.

Serina and Ember led them down toward the pier.

"Feels like the boat is taking a long time," Ember said. "Maybe a magic has trapped all of us here, and we'll walk these same paths and worry about these same guards forever."

Serina glanced sidelong at the older woman. Ember never talked much except to bark out commands during her training sessions. She wasn't prone to flights of fancy.

"It does feel like it's been a long time. Almost two weeks, I think," Serina replied.

"They seemed to come one on top of another before," Ember said. "When we knew they meant food and death."

"How long have you been here?" Serina asked, wondering how many fights Ember had seen. How many she'd won. The woman's face and body bore a map of scars, some faint, others thick silvery ridges. Ember was a force, and Serina couldn't deny she was still vastly afraid of her.

"I don't know how long," Ember said, her strong legs taking giant strides down the path. Serina struggled to keep up. "After the second year, I stopped keeping track. I've won in the ring six times."

"Six . . ." Serina breathed in disbelief. Sometimes it hit her all over again how many women had died here. For every one of Ember's victories, four other women had died. Twenty-four women, just in those six fights. Eleven women in the fights since Serina had come to Mount Ruin. The numbers were staggering.

"Oracle was here longer. She was the first person I met on Mount Ruin." Ember's voice thickened slightly, but her stony expression never changed. "She won ten fights. One of them was for me. I was sick on the day of my fight— bad boar or something—and she volunteered to fight in my placc. She wasn't leader yet, back then. Afterward, she spent three days nursing me back to health, hoarding my portion of the rations so I would have something to eat when I felt better."

It was the most Ember had ever said to Serina. And it broke her apart. By the time Serina had come to Mount Ruin, Oracle had been hard, all iron and barbed wire. But she obviously hadn't started that way. And maybe she'd never been as ruthless as she'd seemed. She'd yielded when Petrel had made a similar request to help Serina. She'd told Serina of her history as a Grace. Oracle had kept so many of the women here alive. She'd saved Serina's life.

She'd deserved to escape more than any of them. Oracle should not have died on Mount Ruin.

"You and Oracle saved my life," Serina said softly, those final moments playing over in her mind. "You made all of this possible."

Ember shifted her shoulders uncomfortably. "I told Oracle we should fight. I convinced her. And then she died."

All the air left Serina's lungs.

"I thought maybe she and I could be free of all of this. I dreamed of escaping together." Ember slowed as they approached the cliffs above the pier. She looked out over the water, and her voice bottomed out. "Now I'm not sure I want to leave." She turned to Serina. "If I don't die here, if my body doesn't get committed to the volcano, do you think Oracle and I will be able to find each other?"

Serina felt Ember's agony like a sword to her chest. "Yes, yes I do" was all she could say.

As the rest of the women gathered behind her, the cracks in Ember's armor disappeared. Her jaw hardened, and her eyes turned to flint.

Serina had a hard time putting the conversation from her mind, even as she and Ember worked out where each markswoman should stand. Some they ranged along the cliff, in the deep shadows where the sailors wouldn't see them. They asked a couple to hide among the scrubby trees above the pier as lookouts for Nero and Diego. Then they had the girls on the cliff fire a few shots toward the pier to check range and aim.

"The escaped guards will hear those gunshots," Ember said.

"Good," Serina said. "We want them to know we've got weapons and know how to use them."

Serina surveyed their trap. She ran it through her mind. *Boat arrives; no guards come to meet it. The sailors come on shore, look around a little. Our markswomen take them out.*

And if Nero and Diego make a move, the girls will shoot them too.

She walked the pier, turned to look up at the cliffs. Could she see the women hiding there? The glint of weaponry. One pink-cheeked face stood out.

She made a mental note to tell them to use mud or dirt to darken their skin.

Even with the morning sun shining against the rocks, it was difficult to make out the figures. That was good. Usually the boats came in the afternoon, when the sun had passed over the cliffs. There'd be more shadows then.

"All right, I'd like you all to head back to the compound and wait there. I'll sound the alarm. Let's see how long it takes to get into position."

Serina ran the women through their paces until late afternoon. The signal of an approaching boat—three loud shouts of *aiee, aiee, aiee*—carried well, but if the wind picked up, it might be harder to hear. So she set Anika and another of the girls as lookouts.

"Instead of shouting, I want two gunshots if you see a boat," Serina said shortly. "One if you see the guards. Preferably in one of their hearts."

"I won't let them ruin this for us," Anika said. Her dark eyes drilled into Serina's. "We are getting off this island."

Serina nodded. She didn't always like Anika's methods, but she did appreciate the girl's determination.

Serina, Ember, and the other markswomen hiked back up the path. The air was more humid than it had been the past few days, and the breeze was picking up, whipping Serina's hair against her cheeks.

She wondered if Nomi had made it to Porto Rosa yet. Had she and Malachi found the regiment loyal, as Malachi had hoped? Was Renzo keeping himself alive?

The air thickened gradually, clinging in her throat. The volcano would be active today.

Serina's nose wrinkled. No. The smell was wrong. The air didn't burn with sulfur and iron; it smelled more like a campfire, like woodsmoke.

"Do you smell that?" she asked Ember. Had one of the girls built the cook fire early, and too big?

Wordlessly, Ember pointed.

Serina craned her neck in the direction Ember indicated, toward the heart of the island. A strange glow permeated the area. It was larger, closer than the caldera.

Serina quickened her pace. The prison compound was quiet. Without the guards or weapons there, they'd shut up the building. No one guarded it anymore. Still, it was eerie to see it this way, its blank, barred windows staring.

The smell of burning wood got stronger.

Serina began to run.

She, Ember, and the markswomen thundered into the clearing before Hotel Misery. Here, all was not quiet, though it still had an element of the macabre. Women were running everywhere.

"What's going on?" Serina shouted, securing the attention of Mirror, who was hauling a half-empty bag of food out of the infirmary.

Mirror's face was pale beneath her blanket of freckles. Fear had tensed her muscles, made her jerky and awkward. She didn't have time to answer before Serina saw it.

Flames climbing to the sky. A crackle and *whoosh*, like a million birds flooding the air.

Fire. A wall of it, a wave, roaring down through the forest toward Hotel Misery.

SIXTEEN

NOMI

The hired carriage bumped bruisingly along the rough country road. Nomi's palms sweat through the fabric of her dress as she gripped her thighs to keep them from jiggling impatiently. An elderly woman with a large basket sat beside her, squishing her into the side of the carriage. On the woman's other side sat her middle-aged daughter, who constantly jostled for more space. Nomi barely had room to breathe. Across from them, Malachi and the old woman's husband sat, their knees spread comfortably. Malachi had a straw hat tipped low over his eyes and pretended to nap, discouraging the other gentleman from speaking to him. No one tried to speak to Nomi.

She kept her chin down. She stared at the woman's basket until she'd examined every thread of the red-gold-and-green towel that hid what smelled like fresh bread. She ignored the ache of her empty stomach.

She'd wanted to take the train directly to Lanos City, but Malachi had suggested they conserve their limited funds and travel by public coach. They'd counted on the resources and protection of Dante and his garrison for the trek to Bellaqua; now they had little but the clothes on their backs, a few coins, and one misshapen loaf of bread, left from the trade with the men on the boat. Nomi wasn't sure whether she should stay with her family in Lanos, push them to escape to Azura with her, or travel to Bellaqua with Malachi. Much would depend on whether her parents had heard from Renzo and knew where he was.

The rest depended on her courage.

The carriage moved as slowly as a pour of molasses. It stopped often. The family disembarked, and two big, loud, smoke-soaked men stepped on. Then another family, with two small sons. After the stop at Vesta, for a brief time the carriage was empty save for Nomi and Malachi.

She relaxed enough to catch her breath, but it was almost dark and they still had another two hours to Lanos City. Two hours to wonder and worry. Maybe Malachi really was sleeping. He didn't tip his hat back or try to speak to her.

So her mind filled the silence, reliving every minute that had passed since she'd told Renzo to run. She tried to imagine what he'd done with the time, while she was chained to a prison ship and nursing Malachi to health and traveling up the coast. Had her brother actually run? Had Asa sent men to track him down?

What if Renzo had been captured that same night? What if all this time she'd been hoping, the worst had already happened? If Renzo were dead, would she feel it deep in her bones, their connection as twins spanning the distance? Was that what she felt now, in the sinking in her stomach, the aching and pervasive dread?

"You look distressed," Malachi said.

She started. He was sitting up, the straw hat abandoned on the seat beside him.

Nomi glanced out the warped glass of the window. "I was wondering what I'll do if Asa's already found Renzo. How I'll feel if we're already too late." Tears built behind her eyes. "I don't know why it's affecting me so much now, when we're so close to the truth."

"Maybe that *is* why," he said. "When you don't know, there's always hope."

Nomi dropped her head to her hands. She wasn't ready to give up hope, and yet not knowing tore her to shreds. Maybe they should have stayed in Porto Rosa. What were the odds Renzo had actually sent her parents a message?

When Nomi returned to the home she'd never expected to see again, how many heartbeats would it take for her to break down and run into her mother's arms?

She wondered what her parents would say when they saw her. When she'd left Lanos, she'd been Serina's frumpy, forgettable handmaiden. Her hands had been red and cracked from the endless washing up, her hair in disarray. She'd held her secret—that she could read—like a flame in her heart, a candle she kept burning where they couldn't see. What had they thought when she'd been chosen instead of Serina? They would have been shocked, of course. Would they have wondered *why*?

The carriage rumbled into what felt like a giant pothole and wobbled, throwing Nomi against its musty fabric-lined walls. Outside, the driver shouted something at his horse. With a shriek, the carriage strained forward, only to list to the side, an ominous crack sounding below.

Malachi's cheeks flushed. "The imbecile's broken his

wheel," he muttered as he wrenched open the door and dropped to the ground.

Nomi listened to the raised voices and angry retorts of the men and wished she could add her own. She wanted to fill up the whole dome of air above, the whole world, with her scream.

Malachi popped his head into the carriage a few minutes later. "There's an inn a fifteen-minute walk away. We can stay there tonight; the driver says another hired carriage to Lanos will come through at daybreak."

"Daybreak?" Nomi echoed in dismay. "We can't wait that long."

He shrugged helplessly. "I wish we didn't have to. But I've only enough money for a room and the public carriage fare back to Porto Rosa. It's not enough for the train or a private carriage." He made a disgusted noise. "I'm sorry, Nomi."

With a frustrated sigh, Nomi let him help her to the ground.

The driver was untying his horse, probably getting ready to ride for help with his wheel. Nomi kept her head down as she followed Malachi. She wanted to steal the man's horse and head for Lanos City as fast as she could. But she breathed deep, angry breaths and kept walking.

They didn't talk. Nomi's ill-fitting boots rubbed blisters into her heels. The air held a chill she hadn't felt since leaving Lanos, and the trees that lined the road had begun showing their fall brilliance. In the distance, the mountains rose like rotting teeth.

They were so close. The delay held her hostage, twisted her stomach and her heart into knots. She tried to remind herself that going to Lanos had not been the plan as of this morning, but it didn't matter. Now that it *was*, the distance between her and her family was excruciating.

The inn took them longer than fifteen minutes to reach. Nomi would have expressed her anger, except that Malachi's grumbles and glares did the job nicely and her jaw had clenched itself so tightly her head ached.

"We'll have to share a room, pretend to be married," Malachi muttered, staring up at the inn's bright red door. "It wouldn't be safe otherwise."

Nomi might have felt nervous at the prospect, if he didn't look so vastly irritated about it himself.

Malachi left her just inside the door in the warmth of the barroom while he went to speak to the proprietor. Only a couple of men frequented the small smoky room, and they turned immediately to stare at her. This wasn't the sort of place where women were welcome; that was clear enough.

". . . don't go out, now that it's dark," a short, balding man said, crossing the room with Malachi in tow. He noticed Nomi by the door and frowned.

He handed Malachi a key and gestured toward the stairs. "Up one floor, second door on your left. Come on down when you're ready and I'll have dinner for you. Might want to bring something upstairs for the wife. As I said, keep her out of sight."

Nomi played her part and followed Malachi upstairs, her head tipped demurely. But unease wound through her.

It was true that unmarried daughters in the company of their families often ate out of sight when traveling—when she had traveled to Bellaqua on the train with Renzo and Serina, they'd eaten together in their sleep carriage and hotel room, never in the public restaurants—but a married woman? Married women always ate with their husbands. It was their duty to serve their husbands, even in public. Especially in public.

She waited until they were inside the bedroom, door closed, before she voiced her concern. "What was the innkeeper saying? Why am I supposed to stay out of sight?"

Malachi frowned. "He said the soldiers have been taking girls, but I'm not sure what he meant . . . It was very strange. I'll see if I can find out more."

"Oh no," Nomi said, straightening her travel-mussed hair. "I'm coming with you. We will eat supper together like a proper husband and wife. I want to know what's going on."

Malachi clasped his hands behind his back and rocked on his heels. "I don't know, Nomi. The proprietor seemed concerned for your safety. If it's dangerous—"

She grabbed his arm and steered him to the door. "How could it be dangerous? It's just supper. Let's go."

They headed back downstairs, avoiding the barroom for a small back parlor with tables and a roaring fire. Two men sat at a table near the small dirty window; an older woman with gray-streaked hair and a wrinkled dried-apple face set out two large plates of pasta before them. She looked up when Nomi and Malachi entered, her lips pursing.

162

Malachi chose a table near the fire. Nomi was grateful; her dress was too thin to keep her warm in the chilly evening air.

The woman shuffled to their table. "Did Sir not speak with you?" she asked, glancing worriedly at Nomi.

"Supper for two, please," Malachi requested firmly.

The servant bowed her head and disappeared through a side door.

Nomi stared at the knotted wood of the table. The men in the corner murmured quietly; she couldn't catch what they said.

Malachi drummed his fingers on the table. After a while, he stood and warmed himself by the fire. The woman returned, her hands empty, a new urgency in her movements. She scurried over to Nomi, just as a burst of laughter exploded in the hallway.

"Please, please," the woman said, picking at Nomi's shoulder. "Please go upstairs. Soldiers are here. Please go upstairs."

The voices outside got louder. Coarser.

"Why?" Nomi whispered, suddenly frightened. "What's happening?"

The woman urged her to stand. Malachi made his way back to them, annoyance washing across his face.

"The new Superior's collecting Graces," the woman said, so fast and quiet the words slurred together. "His soldiers pick up whatever pretty girls they see. Don't matter if they're too young, married, don't matter. They take them to the palazzo. If the Superior doesn't approve, they're sent home, but if he *likes* you . . ." Her mouth puckered in sorrow. "Please go." She pointed to a door. "Back staircase."

Eyes wide, Nomi motioned to Malachi to stay and let the servant sweep her up the stairs. Once alone in the bedroom, Nomi paced. She could hear the raucous laughter and occasional shout of the soldiers, the thudding boots and banging doors. She suspected her room was above the stables, because the sounds of horses whinnying and stomping filtered up to her as well.

She glanced out the small window. Lit the lamp on the bedside table. Tried not to think of what the woman had said.

Asa is collecting his own Graces.

Snatching women off the streets. Unwilling women.

Nomi shook her head, wishing this were a nightmare she could wake from. It was even worse than she'd feared. How many girls—and how many of their mothers and brothers and fathers and sisters—would despise her if they knew *she* was the reason for all of this? *She* was the reason Asa had come into power?

The doorknob rattled. She jumped.

But it was Malachi, returning with a tray of food.

He placed the tray on the small table in the corner, and they fell on their portions with urgency, even though the meat was tough, the noodles soft, and the sauce too salty.

"It's true," he said, sitting back and wiping his mouth. "Asa has ordered his soldiers to bring pretty girls to the palace. He's taking his own Graces, as many as he wants. He isn't going through the magistrates, and they're angry."

The food curdled in Nomi's stomach. "What about your father's Graces? And Cassia?"

Malachi bent forward, staring at his empty bowl. "No one seems to know what happened to them."

Nomi pushed the tray of food away, her appetite gone. What had happened to her handmaiden, Angeline? Was she still in the palazzo, helping one of these new Graces? What about Rosario? Ines?

Malachi grabbed the roll from the edge of her plate and stuffed it into their bag. He poured the jug of water into one of their flagons, and then set the dirty dishes outside their door.

Outside, the sun had disappeared, ushering in the dark. Inside, the lamplight flickered golden on his skin.

"The public carriage will be here at daybreak," Malachi said. "We should try to sleep."

Nomi excused herself to use the washroom at the end of the hall, hurrying back when she heard male voices eddying up the stairs.

When she returned to the room, she took off her boots and pointed her toes, stretching her tired calves. She paused beside the bed. Wrought-iron frame, pushed up against one wall. Suddenly, she had flashbacks to Malachi's chambers in the palazzo, to that big white bed. She blushed.

As if reading her mind, Malachi said, "You can have the bed. I'll sleep on the floor by the door." He bent to examine its lock. She stared at his back.

"You don't have to," she said softly, her heart hammering in her throat.

He turned around, his eyes a question.

"I just . . . I just mean the bed is big enough for us both." Her tongue stuck to the roof of her mouth, dry as sand, and a rash of red heated her cheeks. "You're still injured and we both need sleep."

He took a step closer, and Nomi fought the sudden, strange impulse to run her hands up his arms. Quickly, she turned away. "It's fine. Whatever you think is safest. I—I'm very tired. Good night."

She scrambled under the sheet and curled into herself, closing her eyes tightly.

A few moments later, the glow of lamplight disappeared, dousing her in darkness. Another pause. Despite herself, she craned to hear. Was he lying on the floor? Was he standing over her?

The bed creaked, the hard mattress giving. The sheets whispered as Malachi stretched out. He sighed. "Thank you," he murmured. "Compared to a ship's deck and a cracked marble floor, this bed is a dream."

Nomi didn't reply. He didn't touch her, but every nerve in her back was alert, waiting, straining through the darkness.

"You're safe with me," Malachi said, as softly as breathing. "You know that, right?"

For a long moment, Nomi didn't speak or move.

Then, slowly, she unfurled.

Her legs welcomed the stretch. Inch by awkward inch, she forced her body to relax. There was still space between them, a space he didn't attempt to breach. Neither did she.

He said, haltingly, "I want you to know . . . I never would have forced you. Grace or no Grace, I never would have, Nomi. And I never will."

Nomi thought of all the moments they'd shared at the palazzo—in the ocean, in his chambers, on the dance floor. How he'd never crossed the line. Even the night they'd kissed, in the center of the thunderstorm, she'd been surprised but . . . but eager, though she hadn't admitted it to herself.

"I believe you," she replied.

Nomi thought of Asa's girls, taken from their homes, taken to the palazzo, without their parents' consent. Without *their* consent.

"But . . ." His voice trailed off. The air thickened between them. She couldn't feel his skin against her own and yet the knowledge that his arm was there, inches from hers, made her dizzy. "But I still feel the same as I did the night of my birthday. I still wish—I wish we could be . . ." He trailed off again.

He still cared for her.

It wasn't a surprise, and yet it was. Nomi's pulse raced. She couldn't speak.

"Do you trust me?" Malachi asked when her silence filled the room. "Do you . . . do you want to be with me?"

Nomi took a few moments to answer. These were not simple questions. "I'm not sure it matters," she said at last. "When you stop Asa, you will be the Superior. You will have Graces." She let out a breath. Maybe, in a different life, a different world, her answer might have been different. "I can't be your Grace, Malachi. Not now."

"It wouldn't work anyway," he said, the ghost of a smile curling through his voice. "You've learned how to argue with me. You'd teach the other Graces to stand up for themselves, and there'd be a mutiny."

"I hope they stand up to Asa," Nomi blurted. She was worried for these women, these strangers. Now it seemed so inconceivable that she'd trusted Asa. That she'd believed him when he'd spouted all the things she'd wanted to hear. How strange that he'd poisoned her view of Malachi using the very qualities and dishonesty he himself possessed.

"I was so stupid," she whispered.

Nomi had almost drifted into sleep, when Malachi's voice spiraled into the darkness. "When I was eight or nine, Father gave me a carved statue of a horse. I loved it. It was so delicate . . . the legs were so thin they were practically matchsticks. It had a mane, eternally frozen in wild tangles. The carving was exquisite, as beautiful as anything I'd ever seen." He shifted, turning toward her. Nomi shifted too, because in the dark it was easier to be brave, and faced him. They lay, breath mingling, not quite close enough.

"One day, I was playing with my little horse, galloping it down the walls of the hallway near my room. Asa found me and wanted to play with it. I told him I didn't want to share, but he didn't listen. Eventually, we fought over the toy, and two of the horse's legs snapped clean off."

Nomi drew in a sigh. She could see little Malachi in her mind, so devastated at losing his favorite toy.

"Father wouldn't get me a new one. He said I had to learn to be more careful with my things."

"But it wasn't your fault," Nomi responded, feeling a pang in her belly. "It was Asa's."

"It didn't matter to Father," Malachi said.

"Your brother was rotten," Nomi said.

"My brother spent every waking moment he had over the next six months to learn to carve and make me a replacement," Malachi responded. "It was terrible, Nomi. Thick crooked legs, a chunky block for a tail, a misshapen head. It was the ugliest thing I'd ever seen. But all those hours and weeks and months Asa put into making it, just for me . . . I treasured it. Until I discovered the effort was for Father's benefit. He was so impressed at Asa's commitment, he gave him a real horse."

Nomi could think of nothing to say. "Why are you telling me this?"

He shifted. Sighed. "Because . . . I suppose I wanted you to know I thought he was kind once too. I was angry that you trusted him over me. But it was not so strange that you did. He has always found ways to use people to benefit himself. I wish I'd known. I would have warned you."

Nomi pressed her cheek into her pillow so hard the down pricked her and ached for lost chances.

With a sad sigh, she confessed, "I wouldn't have believed you."

SEVENTEEN

SERINA

The fire devoured Mount Ruin's distinctive golden grass. It ate the informal groves of citrus trees, the scrubby brush and jungle foliage. It ate and it roared and it raced toward Hotel Misery.

Around Serina, women were running, their arms full of extra clothes, extra food, whatever they could carry.

Where could they go? Serina needed to compose herself. She needed to give them a direction. Where would be safe from the fire?

Serina's body shook, fine tremors running up her arms and legs. She was shivering apart. She was breaking down.

No.

She closed her eyes. Straightened her shoulders. Took a deep, ashy breath.

You are poise. You are grace. You will never let your mask crack or your calm shatter. Do you hear me, Serina? You will be a Grace.

Her mother's voice filled her mind. Serina was the furthest thing from a Grace, but her training served her well in this moment, when she needed to be calm. She needed to *think*.

The hotel had survived the volcanic eruption so many years ago because the lava had only come so far . . . and because the building was made of marble and concrete.

When the lava poured through the ballroom and partway up the stairs, melting the stone beneath, the walls hadn't caught fire. They had withstood.

Could they again? Should Serina take the chance?

Some of the girls were carrying their belongings to the upper floors. Could they ride out the fire there? But what if they were trapped?

"Hey! Hey!" Serina screamed, opening her eyes. She grabbed an arm, dragging Mirror to a halt. "Tell everyone to gather their things and head to the prison compound. It's gated in iron and steel. It'll withstand fire. It'll be safer."

Mirror nodded, her face soot-stained and haunted.

"Head to the compound!" Serina shouted. She ran to the door of the infirmary. Some of the women with more serious injuries were still lying on their pallets, their eyes wide with fear. "We need to move all the injured to the compound. Come on! Help me!"

She ran to the nearest girl's side. "Can you walk?"

The girl had a ridge of stitches across her forehead, and her arm was tightly bandaged. "I get dizzy."

Serina helped her to her feet. "It's okay. I'll hold on to you. I won't let you fall."

They moved slowly through the doorway. Serina shouted orders, and somehow they cut through the panic. Doing something helped Serina tamp down her own.

She studied every figure appearing through the smoke, looking for Val. Who else had gone with him to get water? Had they made it back?

"Is it the volcano?" Ember asked, coming up beside

Serina. She took the injured girl's other arm and slung it across her shoulder. The girl groaned.

"I don't know," Serina said. "I don't think so. No lava. Just fire."

Ember looked up, toward the billows of black smoke and lick of flames. "Maybe the lava's coming."

"I'm so dizzy," the girl they were helping muttered, her head lolling forward.

"Hang on," Serina said. "We've got you."

All around them, other women were heading for the prison compound. To their right, the roar of the fire built, louder and louder. Smoke settled in a haze above them. It was getting closer.

Serina hadn't explored the prison compound fully. She didn't know if there was a meeting room or any large space beyond the terrifying processing room. So she hoisted the injured girl up the narrow staircase and helped her onto the nearest cot in the prison guards' rooms, one without any blood. A line of women followed.

"It'll be a tight fit," she said. "Anyone feeling intrepid should explore the building, see if there are any larger spaces we can use."

Then she pushed her way down the stairs and back into the choking air.

She ran back to Hotel Misery. The hike normally took fifteen minutes; she sprinted it in ten, stopping to cough every few yards. Panic beat in her chest. There were still women filing out of the hotel when she got there, even as the wall of fire raced toward them.

172

"Hurry!" she yelled. And, "Where are the firearms? Did someone move them?"

No one answered. They were too preoccupied with their own survival.

Serina raced to the room on the second floor where they'd stashed the weapons and ammunition.

They were still there.

She swore under her breath. Her fault for forgetting to tell the women to bring the weapons. And it was too much to move on her own. She grabbed what she could—two firearms and a couple bags of ammunition. If there was time, she'd find someone who hadn't left yet and ask them to grab more. She was scared the fire would ignite everything and they'd lose their one advantage—

A dark shadow filled the doorway, silent as a ghost, and even through the haze of smoke, Serina recognized him.

Nero.

Suddenly, she was sure no lava was coming.

"You set the fire. A distraction so you could steal our weapons." Her voice sounded thick, distorted, in the dirty air. Her hands shook. She couldn't shoot him with her arms full. She needed *one* firearm, held the right way—

She dumped all but one of the firearms onto the floor, the clatter and clank too loud.

"I wanted you scared," Nero said, and it was the first time she'd heard his quiet, mild voice, and it chilled her to the bone. "But the boat's coming soon, and I want *it* full of soldiers. That fire's shooting smoke a hundred feet in the air. The Superior will see it, and he'll know something is wrong. He'll send troops to investigate, and they will kill you all."

Serina's lungs collapsed in on themselves, her organs and bones cracking and falling inward, crushed by despair.

A smoke signal.

A hundred feet in the air. In full daylight.

"But yes. I'm taking the weapons," Nero added, stepping into the room. "And I'm going to kill *you* myself." His smile was a ballroom smile: polite and shallow. A mask, like so many of Serina's smiles. And still it couldn't to hide the evil underneath.

He lunged for her, and Serina did only thing she could. She raised the weapon and fired.

She had no way of knowing if it was loaded, but her ability to aim wasn't an issue. He was only a couple of feet away, his arms out to grab her. The bullet tore out of the weapon with a roar, kicking her backward, and buried itself in Nero's stomach. He stumbled back a step.

She fired again.

Half his neck disappeared.

Slowly, his body crumpled. Serina watched through a haze. She could feel every beat of her heart in her temples, and those little percussions weren't fast enough. *Beat, beat . . . beat.* Her vision went spotty. The smoke, the death . . . she was going to faint.

Diego stormed into the room.

Serina tried to will the darkness away. He'd get his hands on the firearms. He'd get his hands on her throat, choking her with his fingers instead of her hair. He'd—

174

But Diego never touched her.

Ember swooped in, long savage homemade knives in each hand, her face sharp and vengeful. She lunged and twisted, and Diego went down.

Serina's mouth opened, but no sound came out.

Calmly, Ember wiped her knives across Diego's shirt, cleaning off the blood. Nero's body twitched.

Ember didn't blink.

Serina's arms fell, but she held on to the firearm with her numb fingers.

"They started the fire," she said, her voice hoarse.

"We need to get out of here. It's nearly reached us" was all Ember said.

Serina piled the firearms she'd dropped into her arms. Ember grabbed as many as she could. It wasn't close to all of them. "I'll send someone up to get the rest."

"No time." Ember disappeared through the doorway.

Outside the smoke was heavy and thick, making it nearly impossible to breathe. Serina coughed, wishing she'd thought to pull her shirt up to cover her mouth and nose. Now it was too late; her hands were full of firearms and ammunition.

They thundered out of the stairwell to the ground floor, and Serina gasped.

The trees just beyond the hotel were aflame.

Hazy figures moved through the smoke. Hands grabbed her.

"Oh, *Val*." Tears streamed from Serina's eyes.

He pulled her around the back of the hotel, pushing through scrub in the direction of the compound, and grabbed half the weapons from her arms. "Come on. Hurry!"

"The rest of the guns," Serina tried to say, but a coughing fit overtook her. Darkness was falling, making the red snap and crackle of flame even more terrifying. There was no air left, only smoke and heat and confusion.

"We can't worry about the weapons," Val said, his voice moving through the air like a wagon wheel through mud. She could hardly hear him.

Serina stumbled. Val put a wet scrap of fabric over her face. It helped her draw a couple of breaths that didn't claw at her throat with burning fingers. The world shrank to the burn of ash in her nose, the heat of danger against her skin, the lion roar of the flames.

Serina wanted to turn to check on Ember, the other figures in the smoke. Did everyone get out? Was the compound safe?

What if she'd sent everyone to a death trap instead of a refuge?

At last, they reached the iron gate. Val bundled her through a door she'd never seen on the opposite side of the building, away from the worst of the fire. A line of women followed them in.

The air inside was stuffy and warm, but its haze was a far cry from the heavy blanket of smoke outside.

Serina bent over her knees, coughing, the firearms clutched to her chest. Ember had made it; she stood coughing beside Serina.

Val led the small group to a long open room, a dining

hall. A crowd of women filled the space to bursting, sitting on tables, pacing along the windowless walls.

Serina, Val, and Ember divested themselves of their burdens, placing the firearms and ammunition carefully on a table out of the way. Only seven weapons. That's all they'd been able to save.

Serina searched the crowd for Anika, spotting her in the far corner. Another girl was tending to the long gruesome burns on her forearms. Anika wasn't the only injured one either. Girls all over the room were crying, coughing, cradling arms or cheeks or hands.

Serina grabbed Val's arm and pulled him out into the hall.

"Is everyone here?" she asked, her voice still raspy and painful.

He cupped both her hands in his, caressing the soot-covered skin like he couldn't believe he was touching her, that she was here. She understood the impulse.

"We lost two girls," he said quietly. "We were trapped by the fire and had to get to the coast and use the beaches and cliffs. One of the girls fell. The other couldn't handle the smoke. She collapsed. Diego and Nero—they were clever. They waited for the wind to blow from the north. I think they set several fires, in a line straight across the island. They were aiming to destroy everything."

"Nero said it was meant to be a signal." Serina gripped his hands more tightly. "I don't know if everyone who was at the hotel made it. There was a lot of confusion . . . people running."

"When I got back, I looked around, but there wasn't much time," he said. "By the time I saw you and Ember, the fire was too close. We had to go."

"Most of the firearms are still back there. I don't know if we'll be able to salvage them." She was so tired. Her lungs labored, filled with ash.

"When the fire runs its course, we'll go see." Val ran his blackened hands over her hair. "I'm so glad you're okay," he murmured, leaning forward to press his lips to her forehead, the gesture as much a sigh as a kiss.

Serina struggled to take a deep breath. The truth sat in her chest, as black and choking as smoke. "Asa will see the smoke. He'll know something is wrong. He won't send a prison boat; he'll send an army. And we've lost most of our weapons. We've nothing to fight him with."

Val gently rubbed her back. "I know."

EIGHTEEN

NOMI

Nomi woke to a deep, velvet darkness and the silken heat of Malachi's body against hers. Somehow, in sleep, she had curled into him, tucking her head against his shoulder and her arms into his chest, their legs tangling. The smell of him—sea spray and sweat and peppery spice—surrounded her. She froze, every sense focused on the slow thud of his heart against her cheek. Malachi breathed steadily, heavily. He was still asleep.

Nomi was afraid to move, lest she wake him. And he was so warm, so solid and . . .

No. What was she doing?

She could never be with Malachi. She would never be his Grace. And Asa's betrayal still clung like a film to her heart, sticky and suffocating. It didn't matter how Malachi felt, or how *she* felt. This embrace was empty, a promise of nothing.

And yet, she couldn't bear to separate her limbs from his, and she couldn't fall back asleep. So she gave herself this one secret moment to breathe him in, to relax against him, to drink in each forbidden breath.

It was quiet, save for the *shush-shush* of Malachi's breath and the stamp and whinny of a horse down in the stables. Nomi thought of the soldiers slumbering in rooms of their own, thought of Renzo, of the public carriage that would arrive with the dawn. The horse whinnied again.

She moved softly, gently, trying to worm her way off the bed without waking Malachi. As careful as she was, he sighed, shifted, his arms tightening around her. She knew the exact moment he woke. His breath hitched, stopped, his body stiffened. One hand was splayed over the bare skin of her arm. She disentangled herself, happy he couldn't see her flushed cheeks in the dark.

"We need to go," she said softly, slipping her feet into her uncomfortable boots. She hissed when one of her blisters tore.

"It's still dark. Come back to bed," Malachi murmured, the soft, sleepy growl of his voice caressing her. "The carriage won't be here for hours."

"We're not waiting for the carriage," she said, tossing him his boots. "We're going to steal a horse."

———

They were flying.

Nomi wound her hands into the coarse mane that whipped at her face. Malachi's chest pressed into her back, and his arms framed her, his hands clutching the reins. So high above the ground, she still felt safe. Even though the morning was cool, the proximity of his body put heat in her cheeks and her fingertips.

The dark and the wind rushed past them. The soldier's horse they'd stolen ("It's not really stealing," she'd pointed out as they snuck down the back stairs. "You're the rightful Heir, so this horse, these soldiers, are yours") was big and fast. They galloped to meet the dawn like racers in the

180

Premio Belaria, and Nomi loved every moment. She'd always wondered what riding a horse would feel like. She'd never imagined it would be this dangerous, this exhilarating.

They thundered into the outskirts of Lanos City on the tail end of daybreak. Malachi pulled the horse to a walk and straightened. Nomi slumped back against him, her cheeks wind-chapped and her body a whirl of electrified nerve endings.

"Where to?" Malachi asked in her ear.

The thrill of the ride wore off quickly, her fears for Renzo swarming back. She pointed to the bank of coal-dark smoke lingering against the far silhouette of the mountains. "Factory Row."

Her stomach lurched. Nostalgia slammed into her with each breath of Lanos's dirty air. She'd been gone a few months. It felt like years. Like lifetimes. Nomi was a new person, but the city hadn't changed.

The closer they got to her family's small, dark apartment on Factory Row, the faster Nomi's heart beat. She was so scared for Renzo, so afraid she wouldn't be able to find him. But she was about to see her parents. Her mother, who, for all her harsh advice, gave the softest, most comforting hugs. And her father, who had told her gruffly, in a private moment as she boarded the train to Bellaqua, that he would miss her.

The horse's hooves clicked and clopped on the cobbles. They reached the central piazza, and Nomi could almost see Serina standing before the fountain with the other prospects from Lanos. She could remember with brutal clarity Signor

Pietro saying Serina's name, and how her own stomach had clenched in the anger of that moment.

She directed Malachi to her street, seeing the shabbiness and rust and cracked concrete with new eyes, with the Heir's eyes. Arriving at her door took an age and only a moment.

Malachi slipped from the horse and then helped her down, his eyes constantly scanning the street. It was early; soon the bustle of the morning commute would begin, when all the workers would walk to the factories. Her parents would be leaving any minute.

"No sign of soldiers," Malachi murmured. Just as he said it, the first doors opened and the first men and women stepped into the street. He tied the horse to a lamppost and turned to Nomi.

With a deep coal-clogged breath, she knocked.

When her father came to the door, would he give her a hug? Would he give her a chance to explain?

What would her parents think when they saw the Heir, presumed dead, alive and well at her side?

She waited a long time, but her father didn't come to the door. Malachi put his hand on her lower back.

She tried the knob. It opened easily, and she wondered why her father hadn't locked it. He usually did.

"Papa?" she called as she stepped inside. "Mama?"

The words caught in her throat and poisoned her on their way down.

The living room was in shambles. Chairs broken, the table on its side, dishes shattered on the floor. And bodies.

Two bodies, broken like the plates.

Nomi stumbled into the room, tripped on the torn-up carpet, and fell down beside her mother's still form. There might have been blood, dried into the carpet. There might have been wounds, dark, gory breaches of flesh and bone, but she didn't see. All she saw was the soft blue of her mother's dress, the warm chestnut of her hair.

There might have been the smell of death and rot.

Nomi bent forward and sobbed.

Two bodies.

She forced herself to raise her head. The other body. Was it—?

Her father, not Renzo.

The realization wasn't comforting. It was more grief, more pain piling onto her chest until she couldn't breathe.

Her parents were dead.

Dead.

Like Malachi's father was dead.

Had Asa tortured them himself? Or had he let his soldiers do his dirty work while he toyed with his new Graces in the palazzo?

Where was Renzo?

"Nomi," Malachi said quietly, from behind her. "I'm so sorry. I thought they might ask your parents some questions, but I never imagined . . . I never *dreamed* Asa would order them to . . ."

She cried harder.

He crouched down beside her and wrapped her tightly in his arms. For a while, she lived in the darkness and the horror and the pain. He left her for a few moments and returned, his arms tightening around her again.

"I looked in the other rooms. Your brother isn't here," he said at last. "There's still a chance he's alive. We need to find him."

"What makes you think Asa hasn't found him already?" she asked, her voice breaking. Her *heart* breaking. She pulled herself out of his arms, the room springing to horrible clarity around her again. "He—he killed my parents. I can't—I don't—"

She couldn't put herself back together.

A strange sight caught her eye, stopped her brain from spiraling further. A book, precisely centered on the floor in the middle of the room. It was open. No torn pages, not like the others. No bloodstains.

She crawled to it across the ripped and crusted carpet.

Why did it look so pristine?

When she saw what it was—*the book of legends, it's the reason for all of this, oh, help me*—a moan curled up her throat. How cruel.

It was open to the first page, "The Lovebirds."

Long before our ancestors' ancestors were born, there was no land here.

There was no land beneath Nomi either. She was falling into darkness.

"Look," Malachi said, crouching down beside her, pointing to a faint scratch of ink in the corner of the page.

Nomi held the book up to the light filtering through the dusty windows.

The moon loves a man, and a bird almost dies. A tattoo and a ghost, and a sister who lies.

Her brother's handwriting, cramped and hurried, curving the tiny words along the letters printed on the page.

"What does it mean?" Malachi asked. "Is it some kind of clue?"

At first, Nomi had assumed the book was a message from Asa. But this was Renzo's writing. One of Renzo's riddles.

The moon loves a man, and a bird almost dies. A tattoo and a ghost, and a sister who lies.

He was talking about the stories in the book—the lovebirds, the moon and her lover, the tattooed woman who got revenge from beyond the grave. It wasn't a clue. It meant nothing beyond that, nothing . . .

A strange memory surfaced, one she hadn't thought about in years. She and Renzo were twelve and had just read the book of legends for the first time. They'd had the brilliant idea to disguise Nomi in boys' clothes and sneak down to the river on the night of a full moon, to see if they could attract the moon's affections. So silly—

But they'd made it to the river, grabbing Luca, Renzo's best friend, on the way. They'd stood on the riverwalk and stared at the moon, and the boys had told ghost stories. Renzo had actually convinced Luca she was a distant cousin named Felicio. Nomi had lied shamelessly, playing up the deception, telling him she had a tattoo the entire length of her back. The stories she told that night! And then—and then a constable had come, and they'd hidden beneath the bridge, among the river grasses. Nomi had gotten her borrowed pants wet, and Luca had almost fallen into the river. He'd shrieked like a banshee until Renzo had pulled him up onto dry ground.

Nomi's pulse pounded in her throat. Could it be? Could he possibly have been thinking of that night? He couldn't have known she would find this, read this . . . Could he?

But it was something. And the smell, the dried blood, the reality was starting to seep back into her mind. She would happily grasp at the slightest straw.

"I think I know what this means," she said. "We—we should go."

Malachi helped her to her feet. She stared helplessly at her parents. "I—we can't leave them. They should be cremated; they shouldn't be here, out in the open like this—"

"I know," Malachi said gently. "But we can't help them now. Asa's soldiers may be watching the house, in which case we may now be in danger ourselves, and even if they're not, we can't call for the magistrate. He'll know this was foul play. He'll want to question us. We have to find your brother."

He was right. She knew that. But the tears fell again as they left, the book of legends cradled to her chest. She turned right out of the door and started walking, forgetting the horse.

"Nomi," Malachi said, reining her in. He took the book gently and carefully put it into their one small bag. Then he helped her onto the horse. The sidewalk was full now, curious faces turning toward them.

A sudden fear pierced Nomi's haze. What would happen if someone recognized her? She spent most of her life in the house, but her father had often had his fellow foremen to dinner. How would she explain why she was here? What would she say if they asked about her parents? Surely someone wondered why they hadn't shown up for work. How long had her parents been there, alone and left to rot?

And what about Asa's soldiers? Wouldn't they still be here? Watching? Waiting?

"Malachi, hurry," she whispered, her throat raw from crying.

He urged the horse down the street, following her whispered directions, vigilant for any hint of soldiers. Nomi was vigilant too; she kept expecting Asa himself to step out from every shadowed doorway, his handsome face twisted into a monster's devil grin.

NINETEEN

SERINA

The sun rose through the lingering smoke, bloodred and magnificent. Most of the southern tip of the island was destroyed. Small fires flared here and there, but the bulk of the conflagration had burned itself out. Part of Hotel Misery still stood, but the wing that had held the firearms had collapsed. Val thought the ammunition must have caught fire, causing an explosion. Serina stood at the edge of the rubble, overwhelmed. Fox and Twig picked through the crumbled concrete, but there were no weapons to salvage, no injured women to rescue, only bodies. Nero and Diego were dust. A couple of the girls had died too.

Cliff kicked a broken brick. "What are we supposed to do now?"

They had little food, few weapons, and the island had become nearly unlivable; ash ran in the stream, and most of the citrus trees were burnt husks. To the north, the island was untouched, but there was little there to sustain them. If the boat was even a few days late—

Anika ran up the path. "Grace!" she yelled.

Serina turned to her.

"They're coming," she said grimly.

At that moment, Serina didn't know how to feel. The boat was a prayer answered and a curse too, when they were still picking themselves up and taking stock.

"How many boats?" she asked. Was it possible that this was a regular prison boat? Or had Asa seen the fire and immediately sent soldiers to investigate?

"Just one that we can see," Anika replied. "We've little time to prepare."

Serina took a deep breath. When she'd left the compound this morning, she'd seen nothing but discouraged, scared faces. Everyone knew most of the firearms had been lost. Everyone knew there was no water, little food, and the Superior's soldiers would be coming.

But it was only one boat.

"Let's gather everyone in front of the compound," she said. "Even our lookouts."

Anika yelled for the others.

They hurried down the path, dodging the fallen, smoking corpses of trees. Serina reached the compound and stood outside while Anika went to gather everyone. While she waited, she took a few moments to close her eyes and breathe.

Anika was fast. The clearing filled with women quickly.

Val hurried out of the building to meet Serina. "We've got seven working firearms, with enough ammunition for maybe ten rounds each."

"That's not a lot," Serina said, heart sinking.

"No, it's not," Val said. "But if we station shooters on the cliffs like we planned, it should be enough."

Serina looked out over the women, most of them dirty, exhausted, with soot-streaked faces and pursed mouths. Their defeat was palpable. Maris slumped against Helena's shoulder. Ember stood at the rear of the crowd, hands clasped behind her back, her face stone. Fox kept shaking her head, her gaze fixed to the blackened ground. Serina focused on other familiar faces: Claw, the older woman from the Cave who'd introduced herself by telling Serina she'd clawed out a man's eyes. Mirror, her spiky hair streaked with soot. Shard, one of their markswomen, and Tremor. No one returned Serina's gaze.

"You know, when I got here," Serina began, pitching her voice loud enough so everyone could hear, "one of the first things anyone called me was *dead girl*." She glanced sidelong at Val, who had the grace to smile sheepishly. "And then Oracle called me *iron*. She told me strength was currency here. She told me I'd have to fight. I didn't know anything about fighting . . . I'd been taught my whole life to be soft and accommodating. Obedient. Submissive. Beautiful." Serina swept her aching body into an exaggerated curtsy. A few eyes lifted, a few mouths quirked. "Well, I'm not beautiful anymore. Or submissive. Or obedient. Or accommodating. I'm not even iron, because iron is strong but brittle, unyielding. And sometimes you have to yield. Sometimes you have to adapt."

She gestured to the destruction behind her. "Nero and Diego burned down the one place we felt safe. They killed our friends. They destroyed most of our weapons. And they alerted the Superior that something is wrong on this island. All of that is true, and it's all bad. *But.* Nero, Diego—every single one of those guards paid with their lives. They'll never leave Mount Ruin. *We* will. We still have weapons. We have a few firearms, yes, but we have *ourselves* too. We have our homemade knives and our spears and our fists and our strength. We have our *currency*. We have earned our way off this island. We have paid for our sins and the sins of the men who put us here. We have *paid our dues*."

Serina's voice hummed into the silence. No one was looking at the ground now.

"We're going to set up our markswomen on the cliffs. We're going to give them all the ammunition we've got. And the rest of us are going to wait at the head of the path, out of sight. When the bullets run out, it'll be our turn." She glanced once more at Val, her expression fierce. "Because I *refuse* to be a dead girl."

A shout tore through the crowd.

"We are getting off this island!" Serina yelled.

A roar answered back.

"Let's go," Serina said to Anika and Val, who flanked her.

Anika nodded and added her voice. "We will take our due!"

The women of Mount Ruin raised their fists and their voices. Serina didn't see defeat anymore. She saw defiance.

By the time they retrieved their weapons from the compound and marched en masse down the path to the pier, the sun had risen fully and the boat was nearly upon them. Val handed out the firearms to the women he deemed the best markswomen, including Maris, who stepped forward with the others, her chin held high.

"Thank you," Serina said. "Thank you for being a part of this."

Maris's lips trembled, but her dark eyes held Serina's gaze steadily. "If I have to kill more people to keep Helena safe, to protect us from Asa, I'll do it."

Serina nodded.

Helena pulled Maris to her, tangling her hands in her black curtain of hair, and kissed her. When they separated, Maris's ivory skin was flushed and her eyes bright.

"I love you," Helena said.

Maris smiled. "I love you too."

Maris's glow reminded Serina to tell the women with firearms to darken their skin so they wouldn't stand out against the cliff. With all the ash and char, no one would have to go looking for mud.

"All right," Val said. "Markswomen, take your positions. Everyone on the cliffs."

Val hefted his own firearm. Serina took a cue from Helena and threw her arms around his neck, pressing her face into the hollow of his throat. When she raised her head, he kissed her, a promise, not a goodbye.

Please, not a goodbye.

"Be safe," he said softly, and then left to get into position.

Anika handed Serina a homemade blade, this one with a sharp point and ugly serrated edge. "You should be able to do some damage with this," she said, with an equally pointed smile.

"You seem to welcome violence," Serina replied. It wasn't that she envied Anika, exactly, but Serina felt so scared all the time. She wished she could forge ahead without thought, without fear. "How do you keep the fear at bay?"

Anika laughed, but it wasn't a joyful sound. "I don't. I'm terrified."

"But—" Serina started, eyes widening.

"Despite what you may think, I hate fighting," Anika said. "But violence has saved my life and the lives of my sisters. So I do welcome it. If fighting—killing—keeps me alive, if it gives me the chance to make my life my own, to someday save my family, then I'll do it with a smile."

Serina didn't know what to say. She squeezed Anika's arm briefly, then headed down the hill.

Her makeshift army halted at the stretch of path where the whirls of lava rock looked like the surface of the moon. She held up a hand, and the women behind her stopped. Then she crept forward to get a better vantage of the pier.

Serina crouched low behind a small outcropping, studying the cliffs for any hint of her shooters. She didn't see anything. *Good.*

The boat was nearing; it was close enough now that Serina could hear the rhythmic pounding of the steam engine. She couldn't see onto the deck yet. But soon.

The engines slowed.

Slowly, the boat approached the pier.

A crowd of people stood on deck. Serina's heart moved to her throat and started to choke her. Three rows, ten deep. But not of prisoners. There were no women aboard.

Asa had sent troops. He'd seen Nero's signal. Every hope she'd had that this was a regular prison boat evaporated. The shriek of the boat hitting the pier split the quiet apart. Smoke still hung in the air, a haze that gave the sunlight a strange quality, like looking through dirty glass.

"What do we do?" Mirror whispered. "There are so many of them."

"We stick to the plan," Serina replied, her heart sinking. "Markswomen first. Then—then we fight."

Serina had hoped, prayed, it would be easy ... a few sailors, a couple of guards. A quick victory.

The troops jumped onto the pier. Thirty men on the concrete slab—they overwhelmed it. Two of them tied off the boat. They all held firearms. These were not sailors, not like the men who'd brought Nomi and Maris from Bellaqua. These men were prepared for trouble.

Before the soldiers could head for the path, the women hidden in the cliffs began their assault. The gunshots echoed against the stone, louder than the crash of waves.

Several soldiers fell where they stood. Others lifted their weapons and returned fire.

Curls of smoke rose from the firearms. The cacophony swelled.

Blood screamed in Serina's ears. Her girls, Val ... they were up there. They were targets. She prayed the cliffs would keep them safe, keep them invisible.

Bullets flashed. Several dinged against the pocked concrete. Chunks of rock crumbled, falling back onto the pier.

More soldiers fell. Serina tried to count—four bodies, no, maybe six. Ten? The smoke and the chaos blinded her. Beside her, Mirror trembled with nerves.

Serina's hand was slick on her knife. Such a small weapon against bullets and brute strength. But there were more women waiting in the shadows behind her than there were soldiers. And that boat meant freedom.

Gradually, the gunfire from the cliffs slowed. Then, abruptly, stopped.

No more bullets.

Serina swallowed. There were still at least fifteen soldiers standing. Maybe more. And *they* had plenty of bullets.

The men on the pier realized they were no longer being targeted. They paused, waiting.

Serina raised her knife and roared.

TWENTY

NOMI

Nomi held on to the horse's mane with both hands, newly dizzy by the height and the grief pounding in her chest.

"We need to walk from here," she said once they reached the street that fronted the river. She hoped Renzo was sitting on a beach in Azura or another far-off country. She couldn't bear the thought of finding him torn apart, just as her parents had been. If he wasn't here by the river, could she believe the best for him? That he was safe? Or would this numbness that had crept over her, freezing her hands, her tongue, her heart, be with her forever?

"Nomi?" Malachi asked. She couldn't respond.

Her parents were dead.

He tied the horse's reins to the iron railing overlooking the water. Nomi didn't pay attention. She stood at the river's edge, hands tight around the cold metal rail, and tried to orient herself. Where was the bridge? Where had they stood that night, with the moon shining down and the ghost stories walking in their mouths?

Would her parents haunt her?

The sun's touch couldn't brighten the murky green of the river. Nomi stared down into the swirling water as her grief battered at her. She needed to move. She had to find the bridge. But it was difficult to fight the sense that it was hopeless, and that made every movement feel like a waste, a useless denial of the truth.

Her parents were dead; how could Renzo not be too?

"Nomi, is this the place?" Malachi asked. "Do you think your brother came here?"

"No," Nomi replied dully. She looked around again—shops lined the riverwalk, mostly cafés and bakeries. To her right, beyond a butcher and a clock repair shop, a stone bridge rose over the river. "There. Over there."

She turned and walked toward the bridge, ignoring the man with white hair in front of the butcher's window who gave her a strange look. Maybe her face was too pale, or her expression too stricken. Maybe he didn't like that she was walking ahead of Malachi or that she didn't bow her head when she passed him. Maybe he recognized her. She was long past caring.

Malachi seemed to realize this, because he never tried to step in front of her or call her back. They reached the bridge a few minutes later. A steep moss-slicked stone staircase led to the muddy riverbank. Shadows and the angle of the bridge hid what, if anything, lurked below.

"Wait," Malachi said, taking her arm. "Let me go first. It looks slippery. You could fall."

Nomi stopped. She knew something was wrong; her body didn't feel like hers anymore, and a haze had fallen over her mind, making each thought difficult to call up. She could barely speak, barely move. Maybe this was what being poisoned felt like.

She thought about the evil cardinal whom Queen

Vaccaro had killed. Had he felt like this? Like each limb was separating from his body, one by one, until nothing would be left?

Nomi followed Malachi down the stairs. Yes, she remembered this. The night she'd snuck down here with Renzo and Luca came back to her so clearly—the moon on the water, the slippery riverbank, the sound of Renzo's voice telling ghost stories.

But this time, the shadows were empty. No one was here.

Malachi put his big, warm hand on her back. "There are more places to look."

"Like Asa's dungeon?" She stepped away from his hand, up to the edge of the water, where the ground was muddy and slick.

"You said you wrote to your brother using his friend's address. What about there?" Malachi suggested. "Could his friend be sheltering him?"

Nomi stared at the ripples of water meeting the shore. "And what if Luca and his family have been slaughtered too?"

"Then we mourn. But there is still hope, Nomi."

She turned to face him. "My parents are dead. How can you speak of hope?"

She had no tears left. But she did find something in the emptiness, in the haze. Something deep inside, a candle flame that grew, burning hotter and hotter.

Every moment that passed, her fury rose.

Asa had done a lot of terrible things. And now he had killed her parents, and probably her brother too.

Nomi's grief became sharp as a knife's edge, and just as dangerous.

"Nomi?"

Nomi looked up. At the base of the slick concrete steps, backlit by the wavering morning sun, stood a figure as familiar to her as her own.

Her too-big boots slipped in the mud as she scrambled to reach him.

Renzo.

"Renzo! Is it you? Are you okay?" she practically screamed. Her hands swept across his cheeks, his crooked nose, his worn wool jacket that smelled of old books and fresh bread.

Renzo's questions tripped over hers. "How are you here? How did you find me? Are *you* okay? Oh, Nomi, I've been so worried—"

She pulled back slightly so she could study him in the low light. "Did you go home?"

His face fell. "Yes. I—I got there too late. You went home too?"

Nomi nodded, her throat closing.

"But how did you find me?" Renzo asked. "I was so careful . . . I tried not to leave a trail. I thought it would be safe . . ."

"I saw your note in the book of legends," Nomi scratched out. "I remembered coming here with you."

Renzo's eyes widened. "That was a message for Luca. Did you see him? I was afraid Asa would go after him too. I went by his house as soon as I got back to Lanos, but he had traveled to the coast with his parents."

"I haven't seen him," Nomi said. She squeezed Renzo's shoulders, over and over, to reassure herself he was real. Not a ghost.

"You're here. You're alive." Her heart was still broken, but one small portion was slowly knitting itself back together. "I'm so sorry, Renzo. I never meant to get you involved in all of this. I never meant . . ." She couldn't continue.

Behind her, Malachi cleared his throat.

"Your—your Eminence." Renzo bowed, eyes wide. "*You're* alive!"

"I'm sorry for your loss," Malachi said softly.

"And I, yours," Renzo returned. "Your brother . . . he has destroyed many families, I think."

"He must be stopped," Malachi said with a grave frown.

Renzo tightened his grip on Nomi. "I'm so glad you're okay. I didn't know what happened to you, Nomi. I thought . . . I thought he might kill you."

"He tried," she said, and the fury paced her, a constant, blazing flame in her chest. "He sent me to Mount Ruin. Renzo, the island was nothing like I thought. The women were forced to fight, and Serina . . ."

Renzo's eyes widened, and in the sea of grief still threatening to drown Nomi, she found joy in the good news she could impart. "Renzo, Serina staged a rebellion," she said. "When we arrived on the island, it was entirely run by the women prisoners, and *Serina* was in charge. You should have seen her, hair wild and face dirty, ordering people around and giving speeches. I've never seen anything so incredible in all my life."

Renzo shook his head. "Serina? *Our* Serina? But she's so sweet, so . . . obedient. I can't believe—"

"It's true. She is a warrior now." Nomi's voice rang with pride.

The image, as unbelievable as it was, seemed to please him, drawing a smile. He looked behind Nomi. "Where is she? Is she here?"

Nomi shook her head. "She and the other women are taking refuge in Azura."

"Why didn't you go with her?" Renzo asked. "You shouldn't be here, Nomi. It's too dangerous."

"Malachi and I were going to find a regiment loyal to him and stop Asa. I didn't think I'd be able to find you, and Malachi said he would protect you once he was Superior. But the troops weren't there. And so we went to see Papa and Mama, we thought maybe they might have heard from you—" Her voice broke.

So much sadness in his eyes. She knew her expression mirrored his.

Nomi stared hard at her brother, studied every feature. She'd missed him so much. She could see their mother in his soft cheeks, their father in the quirk of his lips, and herself in his warm golden eyes. His hair was longer, shaggier than usual. She used to cut his hair.

She stared and stared, memorizing.

"What about Asa?" Renzo asked.

Nomi glanced at Malachi, who said, "I will take care

of Asa," with a hint of the chill she remembered from the Superior. "You two should go back to Porto Rosa with me. Take the small boat or buy passage on a merchant ship and go to Azura. Go to Serina. It's the only safe place for you right now."

That wasn't what Nomi wanted to do. A shiver of something ran through her, but it wasn't fear. It was resolve.

Instead of answering Malachi, she turned to Renzo. "Are you living here?" she asked, glancing around the muddy riverbank. There were no signs of habitation, no belongings.

"I have a small room above the shop across the street. It's got a back entrance and a window where I watch the bridge. And the soldiers." Renzo straightened his jacket, plucking at the cuffs.

He was nervous.

"There've been soldiers? Are they still looking for you?" Nomi stared at her brother's rounded cheeks, his clear amber eyes, his tall, sturdy frame. *He is safe. He is alive. You found him.*

"After they—" He swallowed. "After they went to our home, they kept an eye on the place for a couple of days. I snuck in by way of the roof soon after I returned, but I was too late. They don't watch it anymore. I don't know if they've given up, or if they're paying the neighbors to rat me out if they see me."

Nomi's stomach dropped. Who had seen her there this morning?

"Come on," Renzo said. "It's damp down here. We'll be safer—warmer—across the street."

Nomi and Malachi followed Renzo up the crumbling stairs, across the street, and along the narrow alleyway that led to a small door half-hidden by overflowing barrels of trash. Nomi breathed through her mouth until they'd ascended the building's narrow stairs and slipped into Renzo's apartment.

But calling it an apartment was a bit of a stretch. It was nothing more than one small room with a pile of blankets on the floor under the window, a heap of clothes in one corner, and a tiny washroom separated from the main space by a stained curtain. One exposed light hung from the ceiling.

"Signor Stefano owns it," Renzo said.

Nomi's eyes widened. She knew that name. "Papa's friend owns this building?"

"He knows about what happened to them," Renzo replied, nodding. He rubbed his arms, as if warding off a chill. "He plans to wait a few more days and then pay a call. He'll 'discover' them and have the authorities, um, put them to rest. Father had just visited him . . . He has to make it seem natural, waiting between visits, so no one will think he was tipped off."

Malachi moved to the window and stared down at the bridge.

"We should leave before he discovers them," Malachi said. "The farther away we are, the safer we'll be."

None of us is safe.

No one would be safe until Asa was dead.

But, Nomi realized, a weight settling on her chest, Asa's death had become more than a grim necessity to her. It had become a desire. She *wanted* him dead. She wanted him to suffer.

She wanted to be the one to make him suffer.

TWENTY-ONE

SERINA

Serina's battle cry echoed across the pier and was taken up by the women charging forth behind her, until the banshee shrieks vibrated in her ears and the blood pounded in her temples. She and the others swept down the path toward the soldiers.

The men scrambled to change their focus, but most of them didn't have time to reload and re-aim their weapons before the wave of women crashed over them.

Serina tried to shut off her brain, tried to focus on the muscle memory of Ember's training and the fury of revenge. She tried not to be afraid.

To her right, Ember slashed with her two long knives, her face hardened to marble. A spatter of blood stood out against her pale cheek. Mystifyingly, the man before Serina swung his firearm at her head instead of shooting it. She blocked the blow with her arm and thrust her knife into his belly. He tipped forward, groaning. She yanked the blade free and clambered over him.

The next paused for a split second before raising his weapon, and it was all Serina needed to strike him down. Beside her, Mirror screamed in a soldier's face. His eyes widened, but he didn't immediately attack. What was he waiting for? As with Serina, the hesitation gave Mirror time to mount her own offense, spearing him through the throat.

It was like that with many of the men; it was as if they'd been caught flat-footed, not really expecting a fight. Maybe they hadn't been prepared for their enemy to be female. Whatever it was, their doubt—their hesitation—was costing them their lives.

Serina dodged a half-hearted punch and drove her own fist into a man's groin. He collapsed, clutching himself, and she slashed his throat.

From above, the markswomen urged them on. They had no ammunition left, but a couple threw rocks down at the soldiers on the outskirts of the skirmish. Serina noticed at least one man fall after a chunk of stone struck his head.

Someone grabbed her by the shoulder, his fingers digging into her old, half-healed wound. Her knees threatened to buckle. He drew back his other hand as if to punch her, but then he paused too, confusion washing across his features. "Why are you like this?" he said, sounding oddly distressed. "Women don't fight."

Serina thrust her knife into his stomach and swept his legs.

"*We* do," she muttered, moving on.

A flash blinded her. She whirled, just as Mirror sank to her knees clutching her arm. A soldier's firearm smoked. Helena leapt forward, driving her heavy staff down on his head. He staggered back, and she followed, pummeling him over and over, the heavy wood connecting hollowly with his skull. When she was done, Serina couldn't see the man's face anymore for the blood.

Serina grabbed Mirror under the arms and hauled her to her feet. The girl's face was deathly pale under her freckles.

"Ember!" Serina screamed. She threw her arm up, blocking a punch by a gruff-faced soldier. The older woman appeared, her knives dripping blood. Serina kicked the soldier into Ember's murderous embrace.

Mirror sagged in Serina's grip.

"Come on," Serina pleaded. "You need to walk."

With a groan, Mirror found her feet. Serina aimed for a gap in the fighting near the cliffs. Ember paced them, her blades flashing anytime a man got too close. Serina tired quickly, but she braced herself and kept staggering forward under Mirror's weight. Blood sluiced from the wound on the girl's arm, soaking through Serina's shirt in seconds. It was too much blood, too fast. Panic poured through Serina's chest. Finally, they reached the base of the cliff, a short distance from the fighting. Serina helped Mirror lower herself to the pockmarked concrete. Ember stood between them and the battle, her weapons raised and ready.

Serina yanked at the hem of her pant leg. Her hands were shaking so badly it took her two tries to tear the fabric. Mirror leaned her head back against the rough cliff base, her face ashen. She cradled her injured arm in her lap. The blood still flowed, staining her blue prison uniform black and red. Serina inspected the wound. The bullet had torn through Mirror's upper arm, leaving a gash down to the bone. But the bullet hadn't lodged in the wound. A small mercy.

Serina had nothing with which to clean the wound, but it wouldn't matter anyway if she couldn't stop the bleeding.

She twisted the scrap of her pants above the wound as tightly as she could. Mirror cried out, her eyes rolling back until the whites showed, but she managed to stay conscious.

"It's just a scratch, Mirror, just a scratch," Serina said, over and over as she prayed for the blood to slow, for some color to come back to Mirror's face.

The girl gave a shaky laugh. "Scratch?"

Serina brushed Mirror's hair out of her eyes. Her forehead was clammy, much cooler than the warm Mount Ruin weather warranted. *Just a scratch. Just a scratch.*

She tried to convince herself.

Behind her, the sounds of fighting echoed off the towering wall of stone. Ember kept guard, but there were few soldiers left to bother them.

Serina shifted so she could follow the battle.

"Go," Mirror whispered. "We need that boat."

Serina shook her head. "I need to keep pressure on your wound. No being a selfless hero on my watch." Her eyes widened as she surveyed the pier. "Besides, they don't need me."

The wave of women washed across the pier, and soon the last remaining soldiers were caught, pulled deep into its fierce undertow. Blades, spears, fists . . . with their training and their anger, with their homemade weapons and their bare hands, the women brought the soldiers down.

To Serina, it looked like a miracle. And maybe it was. But it was also because these men hadn't been prepared for the fury or the organization of the women of Mount Ruin. It was obvious they hadn't been expecting a battle.

But Serina and her army had given them one.

Val and the markswomen climbed down from the cliffs.

Mirror wasn't the only one with a serious injury, and four of the female warriors had lost their lives. The soldiers lay in a bloodstained heap, their eyes unseeing. The few survivors, all with significant injuries, were killed. No one wanted another Nero or Diego to ruin them, not this close to freedom.

The ship bobbed next to the pier, its engine still belching steam.

Serina knelt beside Mirror and fought back tears of relief to see her still breathing, still conscious. Blood had leaked through the makeshift bandage on her arm, but it appeared to be slowing. Mirror gave Serina a wobbly smile. "I think I might survive."

Serina smiled back. "You will."

Ember took over with Mirror so Serina could wash her hands clean of blood at the edge of the pier. She searched the ocean for signs of another ship, for the next danger. It was hard to imagine the threat was over, that after everything, they'd achieved their goal. A ship, an escape route. Serina had greeted the dawn in defeat, so much of the island burned to its lava-black bedrock. Now they had everything they needed.

Anika came up to Serina with her firearm in her hands. She looked as flabbergasted as Serina felt. "Did we just . . . win?"

"It doesn't feel real," Serina replied. She didn't know what to do with her hands, now that she had no need to use them as weapons. She rubbed the back of each, wincing at the bruises and torn skin.

Val joined them, his face still covered in the soot he'd used to camouflage it. "The Superior underestimated you. Only thirty soldiers."

"I would have been happy with a boat full of prisoners and only a couple of guards," Serina replied. "But we made it."

His teeth gleamed when he grinned. Serina returned his smile. Her shoulders relaxed, but her chest was still tight, her throat sore from the smoke and all the screaming. Her body swayed toward him, aching for a quiet moment, an embrace.

"We still need to get off this island." Serina forced herself to focus. There would be time for embraces, for quiet moments, when they reached Azura. "And we have injuries to tend to. We'll prepare today and leave tomorrow at first light."

Anika stared out at the silvery water, wonder in her voice as she said, "We're leaving Mount Ruin."

Serina raised her chin. "Yes." Something suspiciously like joy stole through her. "We're leaving Mount Ruin."

TWENTY-TWO

NOMI

Nomi found Renzo's schoolbooks underneath the pile of clothes he'd salvaged from the house. She ran her hands across the leather covers and opened his small composition book to read his slanted handwriting.

"Two more months and I could have applied to university," Renzo said, glancing at the books. He sighed.

"I'm sorry." Nomi cradled the composition book to her chest. "I shouldn't have involved you in all of this. If I hadn't—" Her voice broke. The image of their parents' bodies was constant and unrelenting in her mind. She would never be free of it, or the murderous rage she felt toward Asa.

She'd made a lot of mistakes—trusting him, writing to Renzo—but it was *Asa* who'd committed murder. It was *Asa* who'd ordered her parents killed.

It was *Asa* who deserved to die.

"How long will it take for us to get to Azura?" Renzo asked, sliding down to the floor to sit on his collection of blankets beneath the window. "Will Serina arrive first, do you think?"

"I hope she's already there, and safe," Nomi said. She sat down too, near him. She couldn't stop staring at him, couldn't stop assuring herself that he was here. He was alive.

"You could be in Azura in a fortnight if you take the small sailboat," Malachi said. "If you buy passage on a merchant vessel, four days. Maybe five." He stood near the window, staring out into the street.

Nomi wished she could see his expression. He'd been quiet ever since they'd found her parents. Perhaps it was his way of giving Nomi and Renzo space to reconnect. But she had the odd feeling it was more than that. Because he wasn't just quiet. He was restless too, moving around the small room as if it caged him. He'd already disappeared for an hour, to sell the stolen horse since they'd be taking the train back to Porto Rosa.

"We don't have enough money to buy passage with a merchant. And I don't—" Nomi stopped. She wasn't sure what she meant to say, what she was thinking. Only that going to Azura felt like running away, and she wanted to stay and fight.

"We have money." Renzo dug into his pocket and held up a silk pouch that jingled invitingly. "It's the money Father got for your selection as Grace." He handed it to her. "He didn't spend it, not a silver."

Nomi's heart seized. "But why not?"

Renzo shrugged. "I don't know. Father spoke of Mama retiring, of buying a little house outside the city walls if Serina became a Grace. But when he heard it was you, he put the money in his desk and never spoke of it."

Nomi stood up, the weight of the purse heavy in her hand. Her father had lashed her often enough as a child when she'd railed and rebelled. He'd taught her, whether she liked it or not, how to hide her defiance. Was he ashamed that she'd been chosen instead of Serina? Or had he guessed how unhappy she would be?

Why hadn't he spent the money?

He was dead now, and she would never know. She slammed the flat of her hand against the floor.

"Nomi?" Malachi put a hand on her shoulder.

"I'm fine," she said, shrugging him off. "No, I'm not," she amended, forcing herself to look him in the eye. "Promise me that you'll make your brother pay."

He didn't blink or back away. "I swear, Nomi."

But the words didn't fully satisfy her. *She* wanted to make Asa pay.

It wasn't until hours later, when they'd eaten a small supper and decided that they would leave the next morning, that a dangerous idea took root. As Nomi drowsed, propped up against the wall, she scratched her leg and her fingers snagged against the rough handle of the knife Serina had given her. It was an answer to the question she'd been asking herself since she saw her parents' broken bodies.

She tilted her head to look at the Heir. "Malachi, back on Mount Ruin, you spoke of secret passages. Ways the women could access the palazzo without detection. Will you use that route with Dante's troops?"

Malachi rubbed the back of his neck, his head cocked to the side. "I don't know. It depends on how many join us, what Asa's defenses look like when we get there. The passages are narrow and hard to access. Why?"

"And if you must go alone?" she asked. "If Dante doesn't get your message?"

His attention sharpened. "Yes. Then I would definitely use the tunnels. There's one that begins in a baker's basement. My father showed it to me. There's a relief of a fat man on the wall, and if you press his belly, the door opens. That passage goes directly to the palazzo's sleeping quarters—the Graces, mine and Asa's rooms, the Superior's. *Why*, Nomi?"

A passageway straight to the Superior.

A fine tremble began in Nomi's fingers.

"Does Asa know about the tunnels? Surely he does," she deflected, staring at her boots. She didn't want Malachi to know why she was really asking about the passageways, and yet she found herself wondering at his answer all the same. "Your brother had me sneak out to meet him, but he never told me about any tunnels. I was wondering, you know . . . if there was a reason he didn't tell me."

Probably he thought her getting caught not worth sharing the secret.

"He didn't tell you because he didn't know," Malachi said, surprising her. "My father only told me."

"What were the tunnels made for, then?" Nomi asked.

"For escape," Malachi said. "To protect the Superior. Just after the Floods—"

"You mean the coup to overthrow the queen of Viridia," she corrected. It was his own fault—he'd given her a book detailing the *true* history of Viridia . . . now she knew the

Floods were not the natural disaster they'd been made out to be, but a deliberate effort to sabotage the country and the queen's power. Her advisors had overthrown her, and the first Superior had taken her and her two daughters as his first Graces.

The story still made Nomi feel sick.

Malachi cleared his throat. Renzo looked up with a "What?" but they ignored him. "Yes, after the *coup*," Malachi continued. "The palazzo was rebuilt, but the Superior and his advisors were worried about retaliation. He made sure there was an escape route."

"And he oppressed the women of Viridia in every way he could, so there never *would* be retaliation." Nomi stood up and paced, her heart beating too fast.

"What are you talking about?" Renzo asked, his gaze flicking between the two of them.

"The history you were taught in school wasn't entirely accurate," Nomi said, but she didn't explain further. She had too much to think about, too much rage pumping through her veins.

By twilight, Nomi had made up her mind. Malachi was not the only one desperate for revenge. And she didn't need to wait for a regiment to help her get it.

"Dessert?" Renzo asked, holding out a pastry.

She shook her head. In the guise of tidying up, she took stock of Renzo's belongings as she folded them: three linen shirts, his wool jacket, one heavy cloak, two pairs of pants. His schoolbooks, notebook, and one graphite pencil. Three blankets, a single pillow, his boots. The money purse. She and Malachi had a bag, a flagon, her prison clothes, and a few silvers between them.

Renzo insisted that she take the pillow when they settled down to sleep. Nomi chose a spot on the floor near her brother, and she hugged him tightly and kissed his cheek before they lay down.

"It's not long now, don't worry," he said, mistaking her clinginess for nerves. "Tomorrow, we'll wait until everyone is at work and then head for the station. No one will bother us. Porto Rosa by midday, and on a merchant vessel by nightfall if we're lucky."

"We should leave some money for Signor Stefano," she said. "For Mama and Papa . . . and for his silence."

Renzo nodded. "We will."

Malachi fell asleep sitting up, his head back and his mouth open. Nomi curled up and buried her face in Renzo's blanket, forcing her breath to slow. When Renzo started to snore, she crept to the stack of clothes and grabbed a few items.

She snuck into the small washroom and changed into the pants and shirt she'd worn on Mount Ruin. Then Renzo's heavy wool cloak. If she pulled up the hood it hid her hair and most of her face. She put a few of the coins from the silken money purse into her pocket, leaving the rest for Renzo. Silently, she slid her feet into her boots, adjusted the jagged blade Serina had given her, and picked up Renzo's composition book.

The moonlight through the uncovered window provided just enough light.

Dear Renzo,

The tattooed woman may become a ghost, but she exacts her revenge all the same. Take the train to Porto Rosa, the ship to Azura, and be safe. Give my love to Serina.

I'm sorry for everything.

Love,
Nomi

She placed the note on the floor by her brother's head, where he would see it when he woke. Then she crept for the door.

A hand gripped her arm. She swallowed back a scream.

Malachi turned her to face him and whispered, "What has gotten into your head?"

She raised her chin, her lip trembling, and hardened herself. "He killed my parents, Malachi."

His hand tightened on her arm. "He'll kill *you*."

"It doesn't matter," she murmured. "I'm the one who gave him this power. *I* will be the one to take it away. My parents deserve justice."

"No." His expression cracked. "He's my brother. He's *my* responsibility."

Nomi couldn't bear his protests. She felt like a jockey just before the Premio Belaria, full of anticipation and terror.

His lips parted, but she didn't give him a chance to speak this time. Driven by instinct, by grief and longing, she stretched up and pressed her lips to his. Tears leaked out of her closed eyes. He stiffened for an instant, and then he melted into her, his hands snaking up to tangle in her hair.

This moment was all they had. It was all they would ever have. So Nomi let everything else go, just for the space of a breath. The distance of a kiss. She didn't worry about what Malachi wanted from her. She wanted *this* from him. This one moment. This chance to sink into him, to bask in the warmth of his mouth, to let herself feel.

When she pulled away, her face was wet with tears. "Go find Dante. Bring your regiment. Be there to finish the job if I fail."

His sharp face filled with pain. If she'd been a little less broken, it would have wrecked her completely. "Nomi—"

"I *have* to do this, Malachi," she whispered, her chest tight. "I can't live with this fury inside. I have to let it out."

And then, before Malachi could argue, she slipped away.

TWENTY-THREE

SERINA

Serina helped haul the dead soldiers to the southern cliffs, where the sharks were plentiful. When the last soldier had disappeared into the sea, and while everyone gathered their belongings and Mirror and the other injured were tended to, Serina and Val explored the boat.

The deck was long and wide, just large enough to fit everyone, Serina thought as she walked from end to end. She tried to imagine the crowd in the amphitheater transplanted here. A bit of a crush, but they could make it work.

She followed Val into the small room at the bow of the ship. A giant wheel stood in the center, with various other mysterious gauges and instruments along the wall.

"Do you think you can navigate this?" Serina asked, her stomach sinking. She had no idea what any of the equipment was for, beyond the wheel. A ladder led to the engine room beneath them.

"Gia can," he said. "She knows far more about boats and navigation than I do."

Serina pulled him to a stop before he could leave the wheelhouse. He paused, his gaze questioning, until she tipped up to kiss him. He slipped his arms around her, and they stood for a moment in the quiet privacy of the little room. Serina rested her head against his chest, listening to the steady, reassuring beat of his heart.

She traced her fingers down the muscles of his upper arm; the feel of his skin ignited little sparks in her fingertips. In her training to become a Grace, she had learned how to please men, how to be alluring. She'd never known—never imagined—how much pleasure *she* would find, when the man was someone she actually cared for. No one had told her she could feel attraction and pleasure too.

Serina leaned up for another kiss, reluctant to leave this moment behind. Val's mouth was so warm and gentle, and she loved the power it gave her, to nip at his lower lip, to tighten her arms and draw him closer.

Her fingers curled into his soft, unruly hair. Her mouth opened, and a heat spread through her, as thrilling as it was unexpected.

Val drew away, a strange look on his face. "Serina?"

She laughed a little. "I don't know what's come over me. I think I'm a little giddy. We're going to escape, Val. This is really happening."

He grinned, a larger, happier smile than she'd ever seen. It lit him up, erasing the weight that usually hung behind his eyes.

He kissed her again, and she lost in herself in the swirl of their tongues and hands and heat.

But they hadn't escaped yet, and there were a lot of women waiting for their freedom.

Serina drew away reluctantly. As they left the wheelhouse, hand in hand, she asked, "What happens when we get to Azura? With you and me, I mean?"

It was a question she hadn't had the courage to ask before, out of a superstitious fear that naming a future would put it out of reach. But they'd won. She could let herself imagine the possibilities.

Val squeezed her hand. "Whatever we want." He shot her a quick, almost shy look and cleared his throat. "In Azura, you can work, own your own belongings and property . . . You will be able to choose the life and, um, the companion you want. If you want one."

"It sounds like a fairy tale, not a real place." Serina had never really thought about what she wanted, beyond what she was expected to want: to become a Grace. And when she'd arrived here, all she'd wanted was to survive long enough to see Nomi again.

She smiled up at Val. She wanted him. She wanted to learn to read, like Nomi. And she wanted her family to be safe. Beyond that . . . beyond that she didn't know. But she loved that she'd have the opportunity to figure it out. For herself. The bubble of joy grew inside her, full of light and air, until she felt as if she might float away.

———

By dawn, they were ready to leave Mount Ruin.

"All right, is that everyone?" Serina shouted. She helped the last couple of women onto the boat, then looked behind her at the empty path snaking up the hill toward the prison compound. Mount Ruin was really a ruin now, blackened and smoking, full of nothing but ghosts. She waited for a moment, but of course no one else hiked down the path.

They'd counted and recounted . . . carried the injured down first, assigned buddies. Anika had even done a final sweep of the north side of the island—the parts still accessible, anyway—to make sure no one was left behind.

Serina climbed onto the boat, closed the gate in the railing, and shouted at Val that they were ready to go. Val was belowdecks feeding coal into the engine. Gia and another girl, Bellweather, who was also from a boat village, were navigating.

Ember stood at the stern of the ship, her arms on the gunwale, staring back at the island. Serina guessed she was thinking about Oracle. She wished she could offer some comfort, but she found it was hard for her to leave too. As relieved as she was, she did feel as if she was abandoning the women who'd died here—Oracle, Petrel, Jacana, Doll, Val's mother, and all the others. Too many others. Maybe one day the volcano would erupt again, and all the women who'd been committed to it would become part of whatever the island became next.

"How are you doing?" Serina asked Maris, who was standing nearby, her hands curled around the railing.

"The memories of my voyage here are a little too fresh," she said with a small grimace. "But at least we're going in the opposite direction."

"And there are no chains," Serina said, smiling. "This victory is yours, Maris. You helped us when we needed it most. Thank you."

Maris raised her chin. When she'd come down from the cliffs, her hands had shaken so badly she could barely hold her firearm. But she'd shown no inclination to hide or wallow.

Helena put her arm around Maris and leaned her head on her shoulder. Together they watched Mount Ruin shrink behind them.

Serina moved down the deck, checking next on Mirror and the other injured girls.

"How's your arm?" she asked, nodding toward the more official bandage that was now wrapped around Mirror's bicep.

She made a face. "Hurts a lot. But it's stopped bleeding. One of the girls from Hotel Misery stitched me up. She wasn't sure . . . Well, it was deep. We'll see how it heals."

Serina put a hand gently on her shoulder, careful not to jostle her. "There'll be proper doctors in Azura. They will make sure it heals as it should."

Anika stood at the opposite rail, her back to Mount Ruin. Serina wove through the press of bodies to reach her. Anika didn't acknowledge her.

"I know it feels like we're going in the wrong direction," Serina said. "But you'll get back to your family, Anika. I believe that, I truly do."

Anika closed her eyes and let the sunlight dance across her face. "Right now," she said, "I'm just happy to be moving. This is the first time I haven't felt imprisoned, maybe in my whole life." She opened her eyes and turned to Serina. "I want my sisters to feel this way."

Serina gave her arm a brief squeeze. "I know."

She moved to the wheelhouse, where Gia stood at the ship's wheel, white knuckled, her face a twist of concentration.

"How long do you think our journey will take?" Serina asked.

"Two days, give or take," Gia said. "We can't move too fast with this large a cargo, but we'll get going a little faster as the fire burns hotter. We should have more than enough coal to get us there." The worried look she'd worn since they'd first arrived had eased; it was amazing how much more relaxed all of them were now. They'd all shed years—the tense gray complexions of constant terror had been replaced with a hint of bright-eyed hope.

Serina was about to lower herself down the ladder to check on Val when they rounded the western point of the island and the full wide ocean spread before them.

Gia gasped, frozen at the controls. Serina's hopes crumbled to dust.

Five ships. No, seven. Flying the Superior's flag.

TWENTY-FOUR

NOMI

Nomi walked through Lanos City with her head down. Not like a woman, she hoped, but like a man who had no time or patience for interruptions. The hood hid her hair, and the night hid her face.

She had been to the Lanos City train station only once, when she and her siblings had departed for Bellaqua. In the dark, the streets lost their familiar colors and sounds. She couldn't find the corner market with its bins of orangey-pink peaches and rich brown chestnuts, where they'd turned left, or the shop-lined street with the old man who sang and played an organetto near the entrance to the station.

Instead, she found a piazza filled with wrought-iron tables and old men drinking wine, their boisterous voices and expansive gestures undeterred by the chill midnight air. Nomi faltered. Should she ask one of these men for directions? Perhaps it was best to test her disguise now— if they saw her for what she was, despite the cloak and darkness, there was no way she could fool anyone at the train station.

She was about to step into the piazza, when a handful of soldiers spilled into the clearing from a side street. The men at the tables stopped talking as soon as the thud of boots sounded on the pavement. They buried their faces in their wine glasses. Nomi stepped back into the alley, out of view.

Breath held, she listened and prayed the soldiers wouldn't come this way.

They asked the men something—only a few words filtered through the dark: *seen ... the Superior ... questioning*. Were they looking for someone?

What if they were looking for Renzo?

Nomi's legs trembled. Heart pounding, she backed down the street away from the piazza. She couldn't ask directions, couldn't draw attention to herself. If those soldiers were looking for someone, they'd take a close look at her, and that was dangerous.

She'd walked several blocks in what she thought was the wrong direction, and was beginning to consider hiding in a doorway until dawn so she could ask for help without raising suspicion, when a strident whistle pierced the air.

A train whistle.

She fixed the sound in her mind and chased it, practically running. The streets were dark, lit only by the moon and streetlights placed so far from one another that she felt like a frog attempting to hop between bright stones, only to fall each time into the deep.

At last, she turned down a narrow lane bordered by squat brick buildings and there, at its end, was a wide piazza and the soaring edifice of the station. She hurried through the main archway, clutching her cloak close to her body and darting glances around, worried more soldiers would appear.

The train station was just as she remembered: large and echoing, with tall girders and the constant stench of coal and thick haze of steam. There were few travelers this late at night, and the lack of bustle gave it a hollow feel.

A few men and women shuffled through the large ticketing area, but only the rumble of male voices filled the lofty space. That, and the click-clack of the departures board. Nomi looked up—there were two trains to Bellaqua listed. One was an express that left just before dawn, the other the six-day regional train she'd taken with Serina and Renzo. It didn't leave until midday. Renzo and Malachi would surely see her waiting for it when they came for the train to Porto Rosa.

Nomi took a steadying breath. Then she headed for the ticket counter.

Her hand tightened on her cloak. A man walked by her, almost close enough to brush her arm. Could he tell what a fraud she was, how obviously she was trying to disguise herself?

She couldn't bring herself to glance back to see if he paused or turned to look at her.

When she reached the counter, an older man with heavy white brows and a bulbous red nose asked for her destination.

"Bellaqua," she croaked.

"Regular or express?" He stared down at his timetable.

"How much's the express?" Nomi asked, praying she had enough. She thought of her father hoarding this money, the money he'd been paid for her life. Why hadn't he spent it? Why hadn't he told Mama she didn't have to work anymore, or looked into buying Renzo a bride? She wished, more than anything, that she could ask him.

"Eight golds," he said. "Two golds, ten silvers for the regular."

Nomi drew out the collection of coins from her pocket and stared down at the glint of gold. She had little sense of the cost of things, never having been allowed to carry or spend money. But even so, she knew eight golds was dear. It was the reason they'd taken the slow train the last time, and why she'd assumed Renzo would need the full six days to travel to Bellaqua before the ball.

But there were far more than eight gold coins in her hand, even after leaving most of the money with Renzo, so she paid for the express. Whatever reason her father had for keeping the money, she was sure he'd never imagined Nomi would use it to avenge his death.

"The express leaves at five. Platform two. You'll arrive in Bellaqua tomorrow morning, just after eight." The man took her money and held out the ticket, and then called for the next customer in line. He never once looked at her face.

Nomi was so she relieved she could have cried. Instead, she cleared her throat in what she hoped was a manly fashion and stomped away from the counter.

Then she looked for platform two.

She followed signs, testing her luck once more at a kiosk selling espresso and pastries. She found a bench, settled back into the voluminous folds of the cloak, and shoved two pastries into her mouth, one after another. She ate because she knew she had to, because she needed her strength and a clear head to survive this journey, to execute her plan. But the sugar and fat sat heavily in her stomach after more than a week on the austere diet of Mount Ruin and the sailboat. How quickly it had forgotten the rich food of the palazzo.

A train left the station a few minutes later, and then it was quiet for hours. Nomi dozed uncomfortably on her bench. A man swept stray leaves and trash from the cracked tile floor. A few drunken voices echoed to the vaulted roof, but no one bothered Nomi.

Near four o'clock, a train pulled in with a shriek of brakes and a cloud of steam. Men in fine clothes disembarked, interspersed with a handful of women, their gazes fixed to the floor demurely. Nomi wanted to jump up and scream at the women to run, to escape, to fight back.

But the truth was, most of them didn't look unhappy. They didn't cringe away from their husbands or brothers or fathers; they didn't frown or fidget.

Nomi remembered how Serina had taught her to smile, even when she seethed inside. She remembered Mama's lessons on the importance of masks.

Contentment was a hard emotion to fake, and yet she saw it everywhere.

Mama had been content, Nomi thought. She might not have *wanted* things in Viridia to change. She'd loved that Serina had been chosen as a prospect. She'd been as ambitious in training Serina as any man would have been. Nomi had never seen any hint that it bothered her to have her wages paid to her husband, or her body broken down by the long hours at the factory.

Nomi didn't know how to resolve her feelings—the anger, the resentment—with that contentment. She couldn't judge her mother for not wanting more. But she couldn't be happy that her mother never got to see Serina liberate an entire island of women either.

Nomi had seen Serina as a prospective Grace, and she'd seen her as a warrior.

Warrior Serina won. And now Nomi would become a warrior too.

No, not a warrior.

An assassin.

A new throng of people swept onto the platform, and suddenly, there in front of Nomi, a whole group of soldiers appeared. They surveyed the platform with narrowed eyes, and her heart plunged to her feet.

Trying not to be obvious about it, Nomi pulled the hood even further around her face and crossed her arms over her chest, bending her head as if she were napping, as Malachi had done on the coach.

Nomi's breath came in small, silent gasps, and it took all her strength not to flee. She kept her eyes closed, to preserve the illusion of sleep and because she couldn't bear to see them come toward her, to see her deception laid bare.

A loud voice echoed across the platform. "Well, hello there, flower. Aren't you a vision?"

Nomi's eyes snapped open. A soldier stood in front of her, but his attention was directed toward a girl waiting with her father a few feet away. The other soldiers whistled and made kissing noises.

"The Superior likes sweet young faces like yours," the soldier said, approaching the girl. The *child*. He grabbed her chin, forcing her to look up at him. Her body shrank at the same time, cringing toward her father.

Nomi watched in disbelief.

The girl's father stiffened. "She's fourteen," he said in a low voice. "Not nearly old enough—"

The soldier made a dismissive noise. "The Superior decides who is old enough to be a Grace. It is an honor that your daughter will be considered."

"Please," the man said, more quietly.

The flame of Nomi's anger flared to life. The father was *begging*.

The soldier put his large, heavy hand on the girl's shoulder. "What's your name, flower?"

She was shaking too hard to answer.

Nomi thought she might be sick. She looked around. Someone would do something. Why wasn't anyone doing anything?

She saw a few faces turned toward the spectacle, a couple of frowns. But no one moved.

The Superior's power is absolute.

These men, all the people on this platform, would let the soldiers do whatever they wanted. After all, the soldiers were the Superior's men. They carried his power in their hands.

"Her name is Talia," her father said softly. "We are on our way to Silver City to visit her uncle, who is ill."

"Well, now you're on your way to Bellaqua. Isn't that nice?" The soldier pulled the girl toward a bench and sat her down. The girl never cried. She didn't scream or try to get away. And that broke Nomi wide open inside.

The soldier jerked his head toward the shiny black train. "Go on, Papa. Your train to Silver City is about to leave."

The father stood frozen in the middle of the platform. A cloud of steam gave him an insubstantial air, as if he were becoming a ghost right then and there. But his agonized eyes never disappeared into the haze. He wasn't honored to have his daughter ripped from him and taken to the palazzo. This wasn't how Graces were chosen. This was a travesty.

A tragedy.

And Nomi couldn't bear it.

The train whistle blew. In the silence afterward, she stood up, pointed to the far end of the platform, near the engine, and yelled in a low, gruff voice, "There's someone on the tracks!"

Every soldier turned to look at her.

She kept pointing and ran a few steps closer to the train. "I saw him fall! Did no one else see him? He'll be crushed!" Fear and urgency coated her words. Maybe that would sell the lie. The fear was certainly real.

The soldier holding on to the girl glanced toward the train's engine, now belching steam with exuberance. The tracks disappeared into a cloud of dirty white. The wheels started to turn.

"Hurry!" Nomi yelled, in desperation. "Save him!"

Her throat threatened to close. Her gambit wasn't going to work. She couldn't breathe.

And then, to her amazement, someone down the platform started yelling too. The soldiers turned as one and jogged toward the front of the train.

Nomi ran to the girl and grabbed her arm. She pulled her to her father and pushed them both onto the train. "Hurry, hurry," she murmured, forgetting to pitch her voice low.

The wheels started to churn, and with a great rumble, the train slowly moved forward. But the soldiers were running back this way. They were yelling at the conductor to stop the train.

Nomi's heart pounded in her ears.

Panicked, she leapt onto the train after the father and daughter and shoved the door closed behind her. She watched from the window as the soldiers milled around angrily, shaking their fists at the train as it rapidly gained speed.

It hadn't stopped.

The conductor hadn't heard.

Nomi didn't breathe until they'd passed beyond the end of the platform and on through the outskirts of the city.

A hand touched her arm. Nomi turned, expecting to see the father's haunted face.

Talia stood before her, eyes wide. In a soft voice that shook with emotion, she whispered, "Thank you."

———

Nomi rode to Silver City. There, she switched trains for another express to Bellaqua. She'd arrive later at the palazzo, not until midday the following day, but her impulsive gesture hadn't cost her much in the end except a small delay.

It was worth it for Talia's smile. The girl's father said nothing during the journey, didn't even acknowledge Nomi, who huddled into her cloak at the back of the nearly empty carriage. But Talia smiled at her when they disembarked, and her father kept her protectively curled into his side. He retained the haunted look of someone who'd almost lost everything.

In the Silver City train station, Nomi bought a meat pie, a bottle of mineral water, and a small book of stories at a kiosk. On the train to Bellaqua, she slumped in the back of the sleep carriage and read her book.

She had never read openly before, without the fear of discovery weighing heavily on every word. And now it actually helped, adding authenticity to her disguise. Here in the quiet darkness of the sleeping car, the occasional snort or snore the only sound, she could let her gaze move across the rough pages, shaping letters and words, distracting her from the finality of her destination.

All through the night she read, until she reached the end of the book. Then she ran through her plan, over and over again in her head. It had a beginning, middle, and an end.

Find the bakery, sneak into the basement, find the tunnel. Go to Asa's room. Kill him with Serina's knife.

Nomi thought there was a chance she might actually succeed. It helped that Asa didn't know about the passageways. But she wasn't trained. She wasn't *really* an assassin. She was sure Asa would raise the alarm, or one of his soldiers—Marcos maybe—would be in the room. Even with the secret tunnel, she knew it was unlikely she'd escape.

Marcos would kill her, or Asa himself would. Maybe they would die together, their matching mortal wounds a poetic sort of justice for all the plotting and betrayal.

As the train clattered into Bellaqua, Nomi stared out the window and thought about endings. About Asa's last breaths, and her own.

TWENTY-FIVE

SERINA

The night and the rim of the island had hidden the Superior's ships, but now Serina could see them racing forward in horrifying detail.

"I can't outrun them." Gia groaned. "We're too heavy—"

"And we can't fight," Serina murmured, reality clawing up to choke her. They'd left most of their knives and spears behind, and there was no ammunition left for the firearms, which they'd only brought to trade in Azura anyway.

Serina ran out onto the open deck. What could she tell these women, who'd put so much trust in her? Horror rippled through the women quickly, as those close to the bow spotted the ships and passed the news to those in the stern.

"What do we do?"

"What *can* we do?"

"How stupid to think we could be free."

Serina's heart broke again and again.

Within minutes, the Superior's ships penned them in. Soldiers threw ropes and cinched the boat to its brothers before Serina could even begin to consider a defense. From all sides, firearms were raised and waiting.

One of Jungle Camp's fighters screamed and leapt the gunwale toward the soldiers, her makeshift spear held aloft.

They shot her and shoved her body into the ocean. Unlike the men who'd arrived on Mount Ruin, these soldiers didn't pause. They didn't blink.

Serina stood with Ember and Anika, every scrap of joy, every ounce of determination draining from her. She racked her brain for a way to fight back. But she was frozen.

She stood dumbly as they shackled her, stared blankly as they beat Val senseless for betraying his fellow guards. Fox jumped overboard before they could bind her. She didn't know how to swim. The other women watched, some screaming, as she bobbed along the side of the boat and eventually disappeared beneath. Deep down, deep inside, Serina screamed too. But the numbness held her captive, trapping all the outrage, all the fear, all the horror. She couldn't breathe.

They didn't try to move the women to the other boats. The soldiers just took command, steering the ship away from Azura and back to Bellaqua.

Everything they'd suffered and all they'd fought for had been for nothing. There would be no escape, no rallying of reinforcements in Azura. There would be no battle for Viridia's soul. Serina had given every one of these women hope, including herself . . . and it had been an empty promise.

The journey took three agonizing hours. Several of the women were seasick. The soldiers let them move to the rail, the only concession they made. They moved through the women, binding wrists together. Yanking on sore shoulders. Laughing.

No one tried to fight them, not even Anika. They were all in shock.

It was past noon by the time they reached Bellaqua. Serina crouched by Val, who'd dragged himself to a spot along the gunwale. One of his eyes had swollen shut, and his lip had split. Ugly streaks of blood dirtied the front of his shirt. Serina knew there were hidden bruises too, because every time he moved he winced in pain. With her arms bound, she could do little more than hold his hands.

The boat docked at the palazzo's pier. Serina had expected they would be taken to another prison somewhere, but the spark of surprise at their destination barely touched the haze of defeat engulfing her. The soldiers marched them through the baking sunlight to a cooler hallway at the rear of the palazzo. Servants steered well clear of the line of prisoners, their eyes going wide.

Serina twisted to search for Mirror and the other injured women, who were all weak and likely to falter. One of the soldiers cuffed her on the shoulder. "Keep moving," he growled.

Her heart pounded in her throat. She felt sick. She'd thought she was through with violent guards.

The line of women moved slowly through narrow hallways and down a steep dark stairwell to a dim passage that smelled like a newly dug grave. They passed a wine cellar, storage rooms, and several closed doors. Even lit, the corridor was as confining—as terrifying—as the lava tube. Serina took tiny, too-quick breaths, the weight of the palazzo pressing down around her.

At last, at the very end of the hall, they were herded into a room. Unlike where Serina had been held after she was caught with Nomi's book, this cell wasn't merely dim and sparsely furnished. It was dark and dank, with weeping stone walls. *This* was the dungeon.

And it was far too small. The guards shoved and yanked until every woman was squeezed inside. Somehow Val made it into the room too. Serina wondered if they'd meant to keep him out, to punish him as a traitor and insurrectionist. Execute him, like they'd executed his father. But in the press of bodies and confusion, he managed to stay with her, for which she was painfully grateful.

There wasn't room to sit. The cool dark heated quickly, and the constant pressure on all sides was nearly more than Serina could bear. It was worse than the cave on Mount Ruin. There was no air, no space. They'd been buried alive.

"Please, please," a voice whispered into the darkness. "Please deliver us."

"Just kill me," someone near Serina muttered, and she recognized it as Anika's voice, but this time her defiance was laced with desperation.

Serina wanted to offer a rousing speech, a word of comfort, anything—but the voice of her own defeat drowned everything else out. Val leaned into her and kissed her temple, but he had nothing to say either.

For hours, they were left alone in the dark. There were no windows to give them a sense of passing time. No water, no food. A couple of the girls swooned. It was difficult to help them in the tight confines.

Serina dozed standing up for a little while, hounded by nightmares, and she spent her waking hours internally debating where this interminable day stood in the pantheon of her worst life moments. Was it better than the night Petrel died? Worse than her fight with the Commander? At least that debacle had ended with them taking Mount Ruin. Of course, Oracle had been killed.

At some point, Serina realized she was quietly becoming hysterical, her own frantic panting breaths echoing in her ears. She closed her eyes and imagined vast ceilings and tried to slow the chaotic pace of her heart.

Hours or days later, a distant clank heralded someone's arrival. A light clicked on above them, bathing the exhausted, terrified women in its sallow glare. Serina found the strength to push to the front of the room, by the iron door. Anika took the place at her shoulder, Ember on her other side. Serina knew Val stood behind her, with all the women who'd fought so hard to create a new life for themselves. The numbness broke apart under that unforgiving light.

The door creaked open.

Four men stood in the hall, three in black uniforms, their hands on their firearms.

The fourth—

For a split second, Serina was staring at the ghost of a memory. She was climbing a long staircase, two handsome brothers looking down from the top. One was severe and intense, the other rumpled and distracted.

Asa had dropped the act. There was nothing disorganized or endearing about him now. His eyes were dark as ink, and the twist of his mouth betrayed his cruelty.

Did he recognize her? She couldn't tell. His gaze passed over her without pausing. He surveyed the press of women and smiled. "Ah. My little insurrectionists."

Ice razored down Serina's spine.

"You know, my father underestimated you," Asa said conversationally. "He threw you all on an island and gave his guards free rein. He forgot about you. But you wouldn't be forgotten, would you? You're smarter than he gave you credit for."

He smiled. Serina thought she might be sick.

"I'm different," he shared, his eyes glittering. "I appreciate a woman's intellect. Her propensity for deceit."

Asa shifted his weight. Behind him, the guards waited patiently.

"One such woman, very beautiful, very intelligent, joined your ranks not too long ago. Nomi, where are you?" he raised his voice, calling into the cramped room.

"She's dead," Maris snapped, from somewhere behind Serina. "Just like your brother."

Asa went still. "That's too bad," he said quietly, knives in his voice. "With you here, I thought I'd get the chance to kill her myself."

Serina's whole body went cold. She had never been so grateful to be separated from her sister than she was at this moment. With any luck, Nomi and Malachi were on their way here already, along with Malachi's army. Asa would be surprised when they arrived. Serina almost smiled, imagining it.

"As I was saying," Asa continued, a little louder, "My father did not fully understand the dangers posed by defiant women. I am not so disillusioned." His gaze passed over Serina again and paused. "Which is why you will not be moved to another prison. You will all be executed."

A collective gasp rose. Serina's jaw dropped open. Should she be so surprised? Nomi had warned her.

"One by one," he said. "Every morning, beginning tomorrow. We'll draw it out. You, my flowers, will be my examples. A new Superior needs a show of force. You will be mine."

Silent tears burned Serina's cheeks. She had brought them to this.

"Who's your leader?" Asa asked. "Do you have one?"

Serina swallowed. At least she could take responsibility. She raised her chin. His eyes met hers.

Someone knocked her out of the way.

"These are my women, and I will die before you hurt them." Ember stood nose-to-nose with Asa, her every muscle tense with rage.

"Ember, *no*!" Serina cried, shock draining every useful thought from her brain. With her bound hands, Ember pushed her farther back into the crowd, without breaking contact with Asa's sinister glare.

"Oh, you will die," Asa said. He grabbed Ember's chin, and for a moment, Serina thought Ember was going to slam her head into his and make him kill her now. "Tomorrow morning."

He tried to push her away from him, but she didn't flinch or falter. It was a crack in his authority, a slight misstep. For a split second, Ember had the power. Then he snapped a finger and one of his soldiers shoved her into the room.

Serina and Anika used their shackled arms to hold her up. They wouldn't let Ember fall.

I have to fix this. It should be me, Serina thought, but Asa was already closing the door.

Tomorrow. I'll make him take me. Not Ember.

The door stopped creaking. Asa lingered, his gaze caught on someone behind Serina. "Maris, dear," he said. "You look well, considering."

Serina spun around. Maris and Helena stood behind her, their hands twined together.

"That's . . . interesting. I think I'd like you for a Grace after all," Asa said. "I suppose your execution will have to wait. Aren't you grateful?"

Mutely, Maris shook her head. Helena pressed closer to her.

Asa snapped his fingers again.

The guards shouldered into the room and grabbed her. She wailed and tried to worm away from them, but there was nowhere to go. Helena spit at them and hit them with her shackled hands and shouted at Maris that she loved her as the men dragged her out of the room.

The door shrieked closed on their screams.

TWENTY-SIX

NOMI

Nomi found a small café near the Bellaqua train station and hid in the back with a cup of espresso. She placed her book on the table and pretended to read, keeping her face deep in the cowl of her cloak. She couldn't walk through Bellaqua in midday without attracting suspicion. It was hot and sunny out, not wool weather at all. Even here in the café, she sweat inside the cloak's heavy folds.

All through the long afternoon, Nomi waited. When the proprietors of the café started giving her looks, she moved on to another establishment. If she'd brought her dress, she might have walked more freely through the city. Then again, soldiers loitered on every corner, and she saw no women walking alone, so perhaps not.

The day slowly, inexorably tilted toward twilight. When the streets had started clearing and Nomi felt as if she might crawl out of her own skin, she headed out into the heavy, humid early evening.

She skirted the central piazza—too busy—and snaked down twisting cobbled streets and arching bridges toward the palazzo.

Malachi had spoken of a bakery, somewhere near the grand canal.

At last she made it to the waterfront. She studied each shop she passed. A tiny yarn store, a butcher with hare and hog carcasses hanging out front. She bought an apple at a little fruit market, keeping her head down and her voice low.

Few shoppers were out this close to nightfall, and the ones who were moved quickly, almost furtively. The only women Nomi saw were elderly wives with baskets for the goods their husbands would buy. No young female servants, no young daughters, no young wives. Bellaqua was keeping its girls close.

Nomi remembered the spectacle of Malachi's selection ball. There'd been little girls throwing flower petals, dreaming of becoming Graces as the beautiful prospects floated across the canal on golden gondolas. Serina had worn a gown, had smiled as if she could never want for more than the Heir's attention.

A group of soldiers turned onto the street a few yards down. Nomi's stomach twisted. She ducked into a shadowy stationery shop, just before the shopkeeper could lock up.

"Excuse me," he muttered.

"I—I apologize," Nomi said in her deepest, gruffest voice. "I'll just be a moment." From the corner of her cloak, she kept her gaze on the street outside the window, waiting for the soldiers to pass.

The stationery store smelled of ink and leather and musty paper. Nomi feigned interest in a stack of heavy cream paper with a gold foil border of twisting vines. A soldier appeared before the window on the street outside, so she moved to the back of the store, hidden from the door by a towering, precarious stack of boxes. In a dusty corner, she found a small, cheaply bound journal, with smooth blank pages and a coarse leather cover. She lingered over it a few more minutes, until the shopkeeper pointedly cleared his throat. On her way to the register, she noticed a jar of thick graphite pencils, each with a small razor for sharpening tied to it with twine.

"How much?" she asked gruffly, holding out one of the pencils and the little journal to the shopkeeper. She hoped she sounded like her brother, and not like a girl playing dress-up in her brother's clothes.

"A silver," the man said.

Nomi kept her head down as she rummaged in her pocket, never meeting his eyes. She had no clear idea what he looked like, only how he sounded: nasal and vaguely disapproving. Nomi slammed a silver on the counter and snatched her items up. She whirled and headed for the door before he could get a better look at her.

A peek down the street revealed that the soldiers had disappeared. She slipped out of the shop, the clank of the shopkeeper locking the door behind her loud in her ears.

It took her another twenty minutes or so to find the bakery Malachi had spoken of.

The store's lamps were lit, and a small stream of customers slipped in and out, hands filled with paper boxes of cornettos and almond cookies, loaves of fresh bread and rich chocolate tortas. Nomi's stomach grumbled painfully.

She slipped in among the shoppers, quickly surveying the layout along with the baskets of breads and pastries. The front room was small, but a glass divider showed a glimpse of the baker's ovens in a room beyond, where his wife and daughter were busy cleaning. A hallway led away from the front room to a back door she could just spy the edge of, along with several darkened doorways. Perhaps one led to the basement. Nomi reached for a small round of savory cheese bread, paid for it as quickly as she could, and hustled outside.

She found a spot deep in the alley across the street, dark enough that her cloak made her disappear, and sat down on the damp stone. There was no breeze here, nothing to cool her overheated skin, but she didn't brush the hood away from her face. She curled into the heavy night, ate her bread, and waited, comforted, at least, by the food.

Eventually, the owner of the bakery ushered the last customer out with a hearty "See you next week, Claudio!" and locked the door behind him.

Nomi snuck a little closer and watched the owner's wife and daughter finish cleaning up the shop. She waited until, at long last, the lights went out. A few minutes later, the windows on the upper floor brightened. And then, another hour after that, those lights went out as well. Nomi listened for footsteps, any sign that someone was out on the street. When she was sure she was really, truly alone, she scuttled across the street and down the narrow walkway beside the worn stone building. The rear of the shop backed up to the main canal, and soon the smell of brackish water and dead fish overtook the more appealing scents of bread and melted chocolate.

Nomi's pulse raced. She glanced across the water at the glitter of the palazzo. She took a deep breath and closed her eyes. She wouldn't lose her nerve now. She couldn't. Her parents deserved justice.

With a last look at the palazzo, she turned around. The back door of the bakery was also locked. She wrapped her arm in the thick folds of her cloak.

You've already broken the law. You learned to read. You escaped prison. This is child's play.

Nomi tried to imagine what Serina would do.

She wouldn't hesitate.

With that thought, Nomi slammed her elbow into the glass panel in the top half of the door. She had to do it a couple of times to break the glass, and the loud crack sent horror coursing through her. She ducked away from the door and waited, breath held, for the baker to rush down and investigate the commotion.

Endless minutes passed.

Eventually, she accepted that, miraculously, no one was coming. She carefully reached through the small ragged hole to unlock the door.

As quietly as she could, she slipped into the bakery, the broken glass crackling under her boots. She put out her hands to feel for the doorways she'd seen as she shuffled down the hallway, her heart clamoring loudly in her throat.

At last, her hand caught on a door handle.

It squeaked faintly as she opened it. Stairs, down into a velvet darkness.

She crept into the black. Why hadn't she bought a lamp? Or a box of matches, anything to help her. She put her hands out, feeling her way. Malachi had said there was a secret door behind a relief of a fat-bellied man.

When she reached the bottom of the stairs she knelt, running her hands along the lower half of the wall, pushing and testing the wood. Nothing. She moved down and repeated her actions. Again, and again. She wriggled between the legs of a table, hands trailing the wall, only to crack her head painfully on a chair set up at the other side.

Nomi moved the chair out of her way, shuddering as it scraped loudly across the floor. She'd made so much noise . . . surely someone would come soon. She tried to hurry, but the walls seemed to go on forever, smooth and featureless.

The darkness pressed close.

And then it didn't. A flickering glow bloomed behind her. Heart in her throat, Nomi turned around. There, in the doorway, stood the baker's wife, a lamp in her hands.

The woman looked at Nomi.

Nomi opened her mouth. Shut it again. Her throat closed. Panic made her vision wobble. She needed to breathe. The hood of her cloak had fallen away from her face. This woman could see her, could tell she was a girl, could describe her when the constables came, even if somehow Nomi escaped.

"Are you loyal to the new Superior?" the woman asked, her voice hoarse and strangely uncertain.

Nomi started to say yes, but something in the woman's face, something in the tight worry of her mouth, made Nomi pause. She thought of the girl she'd seen through the window, helping this woman clean up. A daughter. Young, with a sweet round face. Nomi blurted out the truth instead. "I am loyal to the rightful Heir. Malachi."

The baker's wife didn't respond. Nomi held her breath until her vision sparked at the corners.

At last, the woman held the lamp a little higher, until the whole room was lit, and inclined her head. Mutely, Nomi turned to look where the woman indicated and saw it. The little fat man.

Then the baker's wife disappeared, taking the light with her.

Nomi let out her breath. She scurried to where she'd seen the relief.

When her fingertips brushed across the fat belly, she felt a tiny bump in the center and pressed it. With a click, part of the wall opened inward. A wave of stale air wafted up at her. She gulped.

TWENTY-SEVEN

SERINA

"Ember, you can't do this," Serina said. She couldn't grab the taller woman's shoulders, with her hands still shackled, but she wanted to. She wanted to shake her. "It has to be me."

Ember shook her head, her expression resolute. Not defiant, not anymore. "Grace, I have watched too many women die," she said, with a strange, sad acceptance. "I will not watch another one."

The grief was too heavy, too much. Serina couldn't bear its weight.

It was the only reasoning she couldn't argue against. How could she deny Ember this? Ember, who had watched Oracle die right in front of her, who had seen so many of her friends killed in the ring?

Serina's throat burned with tears and misery. "You know it should be me."

"It will be soon enough," Ember replied, her voice flat.

We're all going to die.

The door creaked again. The guards shoved several buckets into the room, sloshing water across the floor.

Women rushed to use their cupped hands to drink up water from the buckets. In their thirst and desperation, they splashed and grunted.

Like animals, Serina thought. *That's what they've made us.*

"All right, come on," she said, her voice hoarse. "We've got to take turns. Everyone gets some."

The guards never brought them food or turned off the light, but the water helped a bit. With the light to see, they were able to arrange themselves so that most of them could sit down. Val kept his arm pressed against Serina's, and she leaned into him, her heart heavy.

Many of the women cried, heavy sobs of hopelessness, but Helena's keening wail vibrated deep into Serina's bones. To be reunited with the person you love, to have hope for the first time, only to have it all torn away . . .

"All I wanted was to be with my sister," Mirror said, burying her head in her hands. "We'd never been apart, and then, in a moment, that was it. I'll never see her again now."

"I have a daughter," Blaze said, her voice gravelly with emotion. "I was put in Mount Ruin just after she was born. She'll never know anything about me. She won't remember me. But I remember how small her hands were, her little fingers . . . I burned down my own house, killed my husband, because he looked at her as something he could sell, as money he could make. I couldn't stand it. I thought I'd escape with her. I thought we'd run away together, that she'd have a better life. But they caught me and took her away. Now I'll never find her. My Lucia. My light."

And then they were all telling their stories.

"I wanted to get to Azura so badly. I have nothing here, I never did. I've always wanted to leave Viridia," a girl from Jungle Camp said.

"My best friend died on Mount Ruin a year ago," another said. "And I've had nightmares ever since. I miss her so much. I think maybe she took part of me with her, and I'll never be whole without it. Without her."

Serina leaned against Val, his heat the only thing keeping her from falling completely apart. During a lull, his deep rumbling voice filled the room. "I went to Mount Ruin to save my mother," he said. "I had a plan . . . I was going to get a job as a guard and get her out of there. But she'd already died by the time I arrived. She was already gone. And now I've watched so many more women die."

So much sadness. So many lost chances and so much longing. Serina wished more than anything in the world that she could change these stories, that she could give all these women the happiness they deserved.

It was good that Nomi and Malachi had left. Maybe they'd find Dante, maybe they'd get here in time to save a few girls. Malachi would take all of this, all of Asa's power from him. There was a certain faint comfort in knowing Malachi was alive, while Asa assumed he was not.

"I killed my father's best friend." Anika's voice had lost its hard edge. "He wanted to marry me, even though I was seventeen and he was forty-five. He wanted me to bring my younger sisters with me as my maids. But I always knew what he really wanted them for. The night before the wedding, he came into my room. He didn't want to wait. I didn't want him at all." She drew in a shuddery breath. "My father didn't protect me. He didn't say the death was an accident, or hide the body. He told the magistrate about me. I wish I'd killed him too. I wish I'd taken my sisters and my mother and fled. I might have made it. I don't know where they are now or what happened to them."

So many lost sisters. So many broken families.

"I never had a family," Ember said gruffly. "Only Oracle."

Serina remembered what Ember had asked her before they left Mount Ruin, about whether she'd be able to find Oracle when she died. The memory cut straight through Serina's heart, the burning metal of an arrow. She hated the thought of Ember dying tomorrow, still holding on to that fear.

"You and Oracle will always have each other," Serina said, her voice thick with tears. "When all the battles are over, you'll be together. You'll be free. Wherever you want, with no one forcing you to fight, no one driving you apart. Do you . . . do you know where you'd want to go?"

Ember tightened her bound wrists around her knees and stared at the ground. "I love the ocean. Sometimes Oracle and I would sit on the beach for hours, talking. Not about our sad pasts, or the horrors of the next fight. We'd stare at the water and talk about where we'd go, what we'd do, if we could go anywhere. If we could do anything."

Serina was really crying now. "You're going to get the chance, Ember. I *know* it. You're going to see everything, be everything. All those dreams, you'll dream them forever. You and Oracle. You'll be together. I know it."

Val's breath hitched. She turned her head into his chest and closed her eyes. It was her hope for them too, that in death she and Val might find each other again.

The women of Mount Ruin held vigil through the long night, with their stories, their prayers, their regrets and hopes filling the space between them, until it didn't really feel like space at all.

TWENTY-EIGHT

NOMI

When Malachi had plotted with Serina to bring her army through these very passageways, Nomi's heart had thrilled at the thought. But now, as she wormed her way down a narrow tube in complete darkness, knowing the weight of the canal hung above her head, feeling the drips of fetid water stream down her face, Nomi had no illusions left. Secret passages weren't exciting or romantic; they were slimy and terrifyingly dark.

When the tunnel finally tipped upward, its weeping walls giving way to drier stone, Nomi began to focus her mind on her task and not on how loud her panicked panting breaths sounded in the silence. It was the middle of the night. Asa would be asleep. Malachi had said there were entries into all the family's rooms, and the Graces' chambers as well. She just had to find the right one.

A faint prick of light caught her attention. She shuffled forward, as quietly as she could, as more pinpricks pushed through the black. She crouched to look through one of the small holes and stifled a gasp. A lone serving girl sat at a table in what looked like the kitchen, stirring something as her head tipped forward drowsily. A loud bang startled the girl—and Nomi. A large man strode into view, shouting, "Get that bread to kneading, missy. I need it rising for a good two hours before I can bake it, and you know what happens if the Superior's breakfast is late. If it's not ready to pop in the oven when I return, you'll be lashed. You hear me?"

The girl nodded frantically and turned the dough out onto the table. Nomi snuck forward, moving from point of light to point of light. Most of the other rooms she passed were empty, storerooms and staging areas for the palazzo's meals. Her eyes strained to see through the dimness, and she almost ran into the ladder in the deeper shadows at the end of the passageway.

Slowly, carefully, she climbed. The second-floor passageway was long, with tiny holes into guest rooms and sitting areas. She wondered if the Superior had used this method to spy on his guests and servants—perhaps he'd come to value the secret passages for more than as escape routes. Eventually, Nomi found the ladder to the third floor and was once again bathed in total darkness.

There were no peepholes into the Graces' or royal family's chambers. Nomi squeezed her body carefully through the tight space between walls, her hands pressing, searching. Were there secret latches? Panels that would swing open? What if she pushed on the wrong place and the wall gave, tumbling her right out at Asa's feet?

Nomi's heart pounded. There was no air in this dark, and her thick woolen cloak, so useful as a disguise, dragged at her shoulders, warming her past the point of comfort. The cloak itself was a torture device, pulling at her throat and drenching her in sweat. Finally, when she could stand it no more, she unhooked it and let it drop to the floor. The stuffy air suddenly felt cool against her skin.

She moved silently, precisely. She took tiny, measured sips of air. She tried to orient herself based on what she knew of the palazzo, but couldn't sort out where in its heart she might be. So she slid through the darkness and pressed her ears to the walls and listened. Her fingers drifted, seeking out latches or other anomalies. Her mind filled with images of Asa, asleep in bed, her jagged knife poised above his heart.

A few yards to the left of the ladder, with her ear pressed against the wall, Nomi caught the faint cadence of a woman talking and the lap of water. Perhaps she was near the Graces' bathing chamber? As she retraced her steps, she bumped into an odd little lip of wall. No, it wasn't part of the wall. It was a *hinge*. She dropped to her knees and felt every inch of wood, praying. Her fingers snagged against a small, round nub. She tugged at it, and slowly a panel opened toward her. She peeked through the gap and found herself looking at a potted fern. She was about to open the panel a bit more when the sound of voices grew louder, and two sets of slippered feet glided past. She was sure now. This was the Graces' chambers.

She slipped the panel closed, memorized the feel of the tiny doorknob, and noted the distance back to the ladder. She shuffled down the passageway until she came upon another small door, this one opening to Malachi's silent bedroom.

Her pulse fluttered wildly in her throat. She slipped a hand to her boot, reassuring herself of the knife hidden there. The next small panel led to the Superior's chambers.

Nomi pulled the door open a sliver. She took a deep breath and held it.

Listened.

In her mind, she saw her parents' broken bodies, the bruises on Serina's face. She saw Renzo's haunted eyes. She was doing this for them. And for herself.

But it wasn't quiet in Asa's room. His voice, low and dangerous, murmured, "That's not good enough."

Terror razored through her. The memory of his dagger slicing into skin, the way his eyes turned ugly, came back to her.

He was awake. Someone was with him. She couldn't kill him now.

Nomi closed the panel in silence, the blood pounding in her ears.

He wasn't alone. She lowered herself to the ground and sat against the wall for a long time. How long should she wait? What if it took him hours to sleep? What if he'd heard her in the walls? What if he sat on the edge of his bed, even now, waiting for her?

In the spiraling darkness, the door to the Graces' chambers called to her.

Was Angeline there? Was she okay? What about Rosario and Cassia and all the rest of the older Graces? Nomi shook her head. Once Asa was dead, those women would be free. Malachi was probably already on his way, hopefully with Dante's regiment.

But he never promised to release the Graces.

She was sure he would. But, suddenly, she couldn't spend one more moment hidden in the walls of the palazzo like a forgotten secret, buried alive.

She needed to breathe.

Nomi snatched up her cloak and found the panel that led to the Graces.

Slowly, holding her breath, she pulled it open. The dim light that snuck through the crack touched her face like the hand of a friend.

This time, no one walked past.

As quietly, as carefully as she could, Nomi slipped inside the hallway, silent and marble-floored, that led to the bathing room.

It was the middle of the night. The girls would be asleep. The Superior's men would walk the halls. If she wasn't careful, they would find her.

Nomi shut the panel, pulling it into place as quietly as she could. She made sure she could open it again, that she could remember which panel, of all the identical panels along the hall, led to the tunnels. Led to freedom.

Led back to Asa.

She was sneaking through the quiet rooms toward the hall of bedrooms, when a commotion sent her running for cover in the shadows behind a decorative urn.

"Thank you for your time, flower," a voice, instantly recognizable, said.

Nomi heard a shuffle of feet, a quiet cry.

"I look forward to seeing more of you." Asa wasn't being polite. He was issuing a threat.

A whisper of fabric, and a door slammed. Then, a quiet sobbing.

Nomi peeked around the corner. On the floor next to the opulent couch in the round central room, a figure curled into a ball, her face hidden by a curtain of long silvery-blond hair.

Nomi's gut twisted. "Cassia?"

Malachi's third Grace lifted her head, saw Nomi, and opened her mouth to scream.

Nomi darted to Cassia and covered her mouth, hissing, "Hush, hush, it's me."

The girl grabbed at Nomi's shoulders, her eyes wide and terrified. She said something against Nomi's hand, the words muffled. Carefully, Nomi let her go, poised in case she tried to scream again.

"You're not a ghost?" Cassia whispered. Her skin was pale and dry, without its luminous glow. She wore no cosmetics that Nomi could discern; her shimmering pale gold hair hung loose and limp down her back, and gray-purple shadows clung beneath her eyes. Nomi had never seen her so undone.

"No," Nomi said. "I am not a ghost."

Cassia gripped her suddenly in a tight, desperate hug. "I thought you were dead. Maris said you were dead! I asked and she said—"

"Wait, *Maris* told you I was dead?" Unease coiled in Nomi's stomach like a venomous snake, ready to strike. "When did you see Maris? *How?*"

"The Superior brought her here earlier today."

Nomi couldn't comprehend what Cassia was telling her. There was no possible way Maris was here, among the Graces. She was on her way to Azura, with Helena and Serina. She had to be. Cassia was mistaken.

But they couldn't talk about it here. The silent men who patrolled the Graces' chambers would come on their rounds. They would be here any moment.

"Is there somewhere I can go? Somewhere safe?" Nomi whispered. "Is Angeline still here?"

Cassia bit her lip and nodded. She took Nomi's arm and led her to the door with the sad-faced deer carved into it. Nomi's old bedroom. Cassia opened the door and slipped inside, pushing Nomi first, just as heavy footsteps sounded around the corner.

Inside the room was dark, lit only by moonlight.

"Angeline?" Nomi whispered. Cassia still had a hold on her arm. "Cassia, whose room is this now?"

Sheets rustled on the bed. Nomi shuffled over to the cot by the washroom. "Angeline?" she said again, a little louder. What if the girls asleep in this room woke up and screamed?

The figure on the little cot sat up so abruptly Nomi almost screamed herself.

"What is it?" The voice was thick with sleep, but Nomi recognized it.

She sat down on the cot next to Angeline.

"Angeline, it's me, Nomi," she said quietly.

In the moonlight, the girl's eyes widened. *"Nomi?"*

Like Cassia, Angeline threw her arms around her, but this time Nomi found it much less disquieting. Angeline had shown affection toward her in the past, unlike Cassia, who'd always seen her as competition.

Cassia lowered herself to the cot as well, wincing.

"Are you well?" Nomi whispered, remembering Cassia's tears after Asa had left her. Remembering Asa's *That's not good enough* to someone in his room. Had he been speaking to Cassia?

Cassia rubbed at her face. A faint bruise marred the side of her chin, the shadow caught in the pale glow of moonlight. She didn't answer.

Cassia was so changed, Nomi could hardly account for it. Her confidence, her statuesque beauty had been stripped away. She looked like a frightened girl, someone vulnerable and broken. It made Nomi hate Asa even more.

"How can you be here, Nomi?" Angeline asked. "Maris said you were dead."

Nomi's hope that Cassia had somehow been mistaken crumbled. A new urgency swept through her. If Maris was here, where was Serina? She stood up. "Do you know what room she's in? I need to see her."

"Stay here. I'll go get her." Angeline stood up, drew a worn robe around her nightdress, and snuck from the room.

When the door clicked shut, the sheets on the bed rustled again. "Angeline?" came a quiet voice. "Is it time to get up?"

With a sigh, Cassia switched on the light. "Ria, flower, Angeline stepped out for a moment. But all is well."

The small figure who sat up slowly in the bed wasn't a young woman. She was a child, even younger than Talia. Ria's pale blue eyes were swollen and rimmed in red, as if she'd fallen asleep crying. "Who are you?" she asked Nomi, her expression caught between fear and surprise.

"I'm Nomi. You're a Grace?"

The little girl nodded.

Nomi's horror turned to bile at the back of her throat. Suddenly, her mind conjured Asa's hands around her own waist, his lips pressed to hers, and the memory was a cage she couldn't escape.

She'd welcomed his embrace, and she'd been stupid enough to think her willingness mattered to him. But he was just as his father had been, eager to impose his will on others.

Eager to tame the unwilling ones.

The door opened again, and Maris appeared, Angeline behind her. As soon as Maris saw Nomi, her face crumpled.

Nomi hugged her, panic wrapping sharp claws around her throat. "How are you here?"

Anguish flashed across Maris's face. "We were captured. All of us from Mount Ruin. They're all stuck in a cell in some sort of dungeon. Asa noticed me and brought me here. Said this is where I belong." Her mouth twisted. "He saw me with Helena . . . I think he did it because of that. He wants to torture me."

Nomi wondered how many shards of her heart were left to shatter. "Serina, is she . . . Maris—"

"She's alive. I don't think he recognized her. But it doesn't matter." Maris dropped her gaze to her dirty boots. "He is going to execute them all."

The words echoed in Nomi's mind.

Rage filled her veins, burned through her chest, set her pulse to pounding in her temples. She grabbed her cloak and started for the door. "No, he isn't."

"Nomi, what are you—" Maris started.

Someone knocked on the door. Nomi froze, her hand on the knob.

"Hurry," Angeline hissed. She doused the light and pushed Nomi, Maris, and Cassia into the washroom. They hid, holding their breath, listening to the muffled voices in the bedroom. Only a few seconds passed before Angeline opened the washroom door.

"Ines says we're all to get dressed." A deep furrow dug its way down the center of her forehead. "The Superior has ordered his Graces to observe the execution at dawn. We must dress and be ready to go."

Nomi muffled a scream with both hands. There was no time. No time to kill Asa, no time to search for Serina. But she couldn't just let her sister die.

What was she going to do?

"I don't want to watch anyone die," Ria said as Angeline helped her into a soft pink dress with ribbon accents. Her voice choked on unshed tears. "Why do we have to go?"

"The Superior demands it," Angeline said in a broken whisper.

Cassia left to go to her own room to dress, but Maris stayed. She sat at the dressing table and stared at her reflection with the vacant, hopeless look of someone who has lost everything. Nomi had seen that look on her face before, after Malachi had chosen them as Graces. All her time in the palazzo, Maris had been locked in the grief of not knowing what had happened to Helena.

Today, the woman she loved would die.

"I'm going too. There may be something—*something* I can do," Nomi murmured. "If I can get close to Asa . . . if I can just . . ." The words caught like sand in her throat. She'd come so far. It couldn't end this way.

"But someone will see you—" Angeline started.

"I'll be careful. I need . . . I need . . ." *I need to kill him. I need to save Serina.* "I need a dress. Please, Angeline."

Angeline found Nomi a dress. Nomi took the soft gray gown and went to the washroom to change. The skirt was long enough to mostly hide her boots. She wouldn't have minded a different pair of shoes, one that fit better, but these provided a good hiding place for her knife, and she wasn't about to give that up. She drew it out and stared at the thin jagged blade.

This is yours, Asa, she thought. *You deserve it.*

TWENTY-NINE

SERINA

Ember was waiting by the door when the soldiers came for her.

"Let's go," one of them said, yanking on her arm. She stood, immovable as a mountain, until he released her. Before he could hit her or shove her into submission, she moved forward steadily, her chin held high.

Serina prayed that when it was her turn, she could face it with Ember's brave serenity, but she was fairly certain she'd be screaming.

"You all are coming too," the guard growled. "And don't try anything. We'll kill you if you do, Superior's orders."

Serina followed Ember out of the room, Val beside her. He moved stiffly, his face bruised and swollen.

A long line of women unspooled behind them. She wondered how many of them were left. One hundred? How many days would Asa last before he got impatient and killed more than one of them at a time?

They climbed the slick dark stairs and moved into a lovely mosaic-floored walkway, and then out into the sun.

The morning was so bright it stung Serina's eyes. Everything looked bleached out, faded, not quite real. The soldiers led them to the front of the palazzo. Across the canal, a crowd stood in silence, shoulder to shoulder.

Serina was grateful they didn't cheer. Maybe they would when the deed was done.

She wormed her way to Ember's side. She reached for Ember's hands. Every cell of Serina's body screamed out in horror at this injustice. At the waste, the agony of this moment.

"Let me do this," Serina begged, the words ragged. "Please."

"I think you're right, Grace," Ember said, with a tiny, tired smile. Her hands were warm and solid in Serina's. "I think Oracle is waiting for me."

Serina tightened her grip, held her hands, until the moment she was torn away.

A guard stopped in front of Serina, his big body blocking the crowd. "Halt," he ordered.

Serina spit in his face. She expected him to hit her, but he didn't move.

Another soldier led Ember to a wall near the grand staircase. Her boots sank into a patch of soft green grass. They turned her so she faced the crowd, her back to the wall.

Above her, at the top of the stairs, Asa appeared. Even from this distance, Serina could see his sharp-edged smile.

He raised his arms in a welcoming gesture to the crowd. After a moment, a smattering of applause filled the air. It died quickly.

"Good morning to you all," he said. "The group of women you see before you has committed grievous crimes against our great country. I know my father had certain . . . qualms . . . about the execution of women, but it is vastly important to me that we hold these women accountable for their actions. Their brazen disregard for the norms and laws of Viridia cannot—*will* not—be tolerated. Today, the leader of this group will pay the ultimate price. She has committed treason, and she shall die for it. The rest of these women will pay, one a day, one death at a time."

Treason.

Serina choked on her own sobs. She didn't know what to do, but she had to do something. She *had* to.

He stopped speaking. Gave the signal to his soldiers.

And Serina sang.

Fire, breathe

Water, burn

Terror, wane

Your reign is over.

Gunshots ripped through the air. She closed her eyes.

Fire, breathe

Water, burn

Stars, lead the way

Your sister is here.

THIRTY

NOMI

Nomi couldn't get close to Asa. She tried to hang back as the Graces were led down the hall, looked for ways to slip away as they filed out onto the terrace, eyed the male servants as they corralled the women outside. There was no opportunity to run.

She was pushed out onto the balcony by the press of bodies, hidden among the Graces. Safe from recognition but rendered utterly useless. Helpless.

Asa stepped out onto the head of the palazzo stairs. Too far away to try to throw her knife.

He spoke of treason, of daily executions. He said the leader of the rebellion would die today.

Oh, Serina.

Nomi couldn't keep herself together, she couldn't breathe, she was going to scream—

In the grass before the palazzo, the soldiers lined a woman up against a stone wall near the grand staircase. She stood steadily, her red hair bright in the sun.

Bright red hair.

It wasn't Serina.

The women of Mount Ruin and the crowds in the piazza were deathly silent.

Nomi's heart shuddered in her chest. Relief and shame filled her in equal measure. Serina wouldn't die today. But that woman would. Somehow, she'd taken Serina's place.

Asa gave a signal.

And then one single, shaking voice began to sing.

Nomi knew that voice. It had sung her the lullabies that had soothed her throughout childhood. It had told her stories. It had admonished her when she rebelled.

And not too long ago, it had called for a vote.

More voices joined Serina's, but they couldn't drown out the gunshots, sharp cracks that tore the morning in two.

The red-haired figure jerked like a marionette, and then, strings snapped, she fell.

The women sang on, loud as cathedral bells.

Nomi didn't make a sound. The hurricane raging inside her was too big—if she screamed, she'd never be able to stop.

One thought kept her from breaking apart.

Tonight. Asa would die tonight.

THIRTY-ONE

SERINA

Serina had never wanted anything more in all her life than to see Asa suffer. She wanted his country torn from him. His *life* torn from him. Nomi was right. He was so, so much worse than his father.

Serina shuffled through the hallways back to the dungeon, surrounded by dead-eyed women. Val held her hand, their shackles clanking together. If they hadn't been chained, Serina would have told everyone to fight ... firearms or not, her women could have overwhelmed the guards. And if not, well, they were all slated to die anyway. Why drag it out?

Serina stared straight ahead, images of Asa being flayed alive playing on a loop in her mind. She killed him over and over again in a hundred different ways. She had no power here, no hope for her own life, but she could still control her thoughts. And, in her thoughts, she eviscerated him.

The man himself was waiting by the door of their prison. He smiled mildly as the women shuffled into the room, and Serina could see a hint of the manipulator who had so fooled her sister. He looked kind, earnest even. And yet he had just ordered Ember killed.

As Serina passed him, she spit at his feet.

He held up a hand, and one of the soldiers stopped her, shoving Val into the already crowded room.

Asa looked Serina up and down.

"Ah," he said. "Of course. You're Nomi's sister."

"And you're a murderer," she growled. "You're a fraud, a traitor, a liar, and a—"

"And you're next," he said, cutting her off. He didn't raise his voice, but color had come to his cheeks, staining them red. "Tomorrow morning, it's your turn, Serina. Your family is waiting for you."

A cold wind blew through her, clearing out every thought. Her chin jutted forward. "What's that supposed to mean?"

He just smiled.

Serina swung her shackled hands at his face with all the force of her hate. His head whipped back, and blood spurted along his cheekbone. He shouted.

An animal roar exploded from her throat. She lunged at him again. Rage overwhelmed every other thought, every other feeling. She would kill him, here and now.

One of the guards struck her across the face, driving her back. The roiling mass of women, packed tight into the hallway, shifted and surged, and for a moment, Serina thought they might stage a revolt after all. But the guards started hitting them with their weapons, shoving and pushing until everyone was squeezed back into the dank hole of the dungeon, the wave taking Serina with them.

She lifted her heavy hands to her face and the swollen, sore place there.

"Are you okay?" Val asked, pushing through the crowd to reach her.

She leaned her forehead into his chest, her anger spent. Now she was just tired. So tired.

"He's chosen me for tomorrow," she said softly. It was too difficult to repeat what he'd said about her family. Her parents, Renzo . . .

But Asa had thought Nomi was here, with the women of Mount Ruin. Maybe . . . maybe Nomi had escaped. Maybe her sister would survive.

The day passed slowly, mostly in silence. Everyone had told their stories the night before. Serina spent her final hours pressed into Val's side, their hands clasped tightly together. He tried to talk to her once or twice, but she didn't have the heart for it.

"Don't let me haunt you" was all she said. "Promise me."

He pressed his face into her shoulder, the wet of his tears soaking through the thin fabric of her shirt.

A guard brought more buckets of water and a couple dozen small loaves of bread. Twenty-four rolls for one hundred bodies. Serina didn't eat. Why, when she wouldn't need the nutrients for much longer? Val didn't take one either, even after she begged him to.

Some of the girls fell asleep. Some cried in their dreams. Helena drummed a foot against the floor and twisted her hands into her stomach. No one had seen Maris at the execution. The soldiers hadn't returned her to the dungeon. "She's probably with the other Graces," Serina offered, but Helena didn't find comfort in the thought.

Serina wasn't much comforted either.

"Do you think Malachi will be able to fix all this?" Serina asked.

"Not *this*," Val said. "But maybe Viridia, in time."

"Nomi will help him. She'll make sure he remembers us." Serina let her eyelids droop closed. Her head swam. She felt untethered, as if part of her had already left her body and was drifting, ready to leave all this behind. But a deep, heavy pit in her stomach told her the panic was only lying in wait. That she wasn't as accepting as her body would like her to believe.

"Nomi will make sure," Val agreed.

"She'll be sad," Serina said faintly as she drifted. "We were supposed to save each other . . ."

Hours, her *last* hours, passed too quickly and too slowly all at once.

THIRTY-TWO

NOMI

Nomi spent the day feeling as if she were about to climb out of her skin. She hid in her old room, running through her plan over and over. It was simple. Wait until late at night, sneak into Asa's room, kill him in his bed. Just as she'd hoped to do the night before. Except this time, no matter what she heard, she wouldn't hesitate.

By some miracle, she'd not been noticed by Ines or any of the guards during the execution, but she couldn't take the chance again. So she was trapped in this room, trapped by the daylight. She prayed for the sun to move more quickly through the sky, for the world to plunge into darkness.

For a few groggy hours, she curled up on Ria's bed by the window and slept, driven awake again and again by nightmares.

Late in the afternoon, Angeline brought Nomi some food. Cassia and Maris followed her into the room, their faces shadowed with worry.

"I want to know what's happening." Cassia sank to the edge of Ria's bed. "*Why* did Malachi kill his father and leave us with his vile brother? Do you know, Nomi?"

Ria had spent most of the morning being fitted for gowns. Now she lay stretched out on her back, staring at the ceiling, her small body barely denting the coverlet.

"Malachi didn't kill his father," Nomi replied. "Asa did. He framed Malachi for the crime, then stabbed him and sent him to Mount Ruin to die. He used me in his machinations, and then he made me disappear so I couldn't tell anyone what I saw."

"And he sent me away to die too," Maris added. "Because I saw what he did."

"But none of us died," Nomi said. "Not yet anyway. Malachi is gathering troops and will take his rightful place as the Superior soon. And Asa will die tonight." She got up and paced again, ignoring the food Angeline pressed upon her.

Cassia cast her gaze to the floor. "Your story sounds like the sort of thing that should surprise me, but it doesn't." She looked up, her mouth pinched into a straight line. "The new Superior is cruel. I never expected this palazzo to feel like a prison."

Nomi had always seen it that way. But there were, she was learning, different degrees of captivity.

Ria drew her limbs together, curling herself into a ball. As if she could protect herself from these revelations, or from Asa himself. "I just want to go home," she whispered.

"There's a secret passage," Nomi said. "In the hall that leads to the bathing pool. Count ten panels down on the left, behind a fern. It leads to a bakery on the other side of the canal. If I fail . . . if Malachi doesn't come, sneak out of here and go home. Get as many of the girls out as you can."

Ria's eyes widened. Cassia ran her hands through her hair.

Angeline pushed a pastry into Nomi's hands. "Let's hope it doesn't come to that."

———

By twilight, Nomi had taken to staring out the window. She watched the excruciatingly slow sunset as the last streaks of pink faded to a dark, inky blue.

Cassia and Maris had gone back to their rooms.

Ria sat at the dressing table, her hands quiet in her lap. She looked so young, her limbs too long, her face still round and soft. Asa hadn't demanded her presence yet, but she lived in fear. Nomi could see it in the hunch of her shoulders, the way she hid behind her reddish-blond hair, just like Maris used to.

"Is it time for you to go?" Ria asked, looking toward the darkening sky.

"Not for a while." Nomi climbed down from the high cloud-like bed. She wished she'd been able to sleep more. At least the food Angeline had forced upon her had revived her. She would need all her strength tonight.

She used the washroom and changed back into her prison clothes. The pants gave her more range of motion and made her feel closer to Serina. Next she put on Renzo's cloak. It would help her blend into the darkness.

She wished she could search the dungeons for Serina, but the best she could do for her sister right now was kill Asa. And who knew? Maybe she wouldn't be killed by Asa's men right away. Nomi would try to find the dungeon after the deed was done, if she could.

But she didn't expect to leave Asa's room alive.

She checked the knife in her boot. She slipped her hand into the pocket of her cloak and found the sharpened pencil and small journal she'd bought in Bellaqua. She left the writing tools there. They were a strange comfort, a reminder that she knew more than she was supposed to.

Angeline twisted her hands into her apron. "I wish I could go with you. I want to help."

"You *are* helping," Nomi reminded her. "You know about the escape route. You can help Ria. You can tell the others. But wait a day or two if you can. Malachi will come. He will help."

Maybe he wasn't bound by the concessions she and Serina had demanded of him. But she'd seen his disgust when he'd discovered how Asa was collecting Graces. These women would be safe in Malachi's care.

She folded the handmaiden into a hug. "Be careful."

Angeline's arms tightened around her. "You too."

Nomi sat at the dressing table while Angeline and Ria prepared for bed. She waited, skin crawling, until the room was velvet with night, until at long last, their breathing had slipped toward slumber.

Now it was time.

Nomi picked up the small lamp Angeline had found for her. Then she opened the door slowly, just an inch or two, and listened. Memories of the night she'd snuck out to see Asa the first time threatened to drown her. How naive she'd been, to plot Viridia's downfall without suspicion, without fear.

Looking back on that night, on her misplaced trust, Nomi could entirely believe her stupidity. She'd been desperate. Guilty. Sick with worry for her sister. Rightfully so, it turned out. And she had made the wrong call.

But this, killing Asa, she knew deep in her bones that this was the right decision. She was plotting again, but this time it was for Viridia's soul.

It was almost as if the night knew it too. Nomi slipped out of the room and down the hall uncontested. No footsteps followed her or echoed down adjoining corridors. She saw no guards at all. The secret passage would allow her to bypass any soldiers or servants in the halls. She remembered Malachi having one stationed outside his door—she was sure Asa did as well. Probably Marcos, the man he seemed to trust most. The one who'd given Nomi his messages. The one who'd shoved her onto the boat to Mount Ruin.

But when she turned the corner, Nomi froze. A figure waited by the secret panel. Right in front of it, as if she knew it was there.

"I saw you on the terrace this morning," Ines said. Her curves shimmered in a white silken robe that caught the moonlight. "I wondered if this was how you came in."

The older woman's serenity had cracked. Her age had seemed to find her in the weeks Nomi had been away; fine lines framed her eyes, and she was frowning, something she'd once told Nomi Graces never did.

"Malachi said only he and his father knew about the tunnels." Nomi crossed her arms over her chest. The cloak enveloped her completely; she was a shadow to Ines's light.

"Malachi had such potential for kindness," Ines said, and Nomi was struck again by the sense of age, of exhaustion, that clung to the woman. She had suffered in the past few weeks. Whatever else, Nomi believed that. "He should have been Superior."

"He will be," Nomi said. "He is still alive."

Ines took a step back. "You are lying."

"Asa tried to kill him, but he failed. He *did* succeed in killing the Superior, though. Malachi didn't to that. Asa did."

Ines stared at Nomi, her eyes two black shadows in the dim hall. "And what are you planning to do?"

Nomi took a breath. If she told the truth, would Ines let her go?

"I am a Grace," she said at last. "I am going to visit the Superior."

Ines's hands clenched at her sides. She didn't speak. But after a moment, after another wordless stare, she lifted her gaze above Nomi's head as if she were suddenly invisible, and walked down the hall. Nomi watched her go, but Asa's mother never turned around.

Nomi didn't wait. She pulled the panel open and slipped into the tunnel.

THIRTY-THREE

SERINA

The dungeon door ground and squealed too soon. Serina sat up, dazed and thirsty, and not ready.

She'd been determined to accept her fate as calmly as Ember, but now that the moment had come, she found herself desperately clutching Val's arm.

"Serina?" a whisper carried across the sea of bodies.

Serina stood up at the voice. A figure was framed in the doorway, and it wasn't Asa.

"*Renzo?*"

He saw her, and his whole face changed, opened up. He beckoned.

"Come on. I've got the keys for the shackles. And a firearm. We need to hurry."

Serina wove through the women, all of them shaking off sleep and beginning to stand, their chains clanking. Dumbly, she asked, "How are you here?"

Was she dreaming?

"The Heir told me how to get into the palazzo through the tunnels," he said. "There was only one guard outside. I took his keys and his weapon." Renzo put his hands on her cheeks, studying her as if she were a stranger. The bruise on her face stung. "*Serina*. I hardly believed Nomi when she told me. But you . . . you are a warrior."

"The Heir . . . Nomi . . ." she mumbled. "How . . ."

A cloud passed across Renzo's face. "They found me."

"So . . . so you're all here together? With the regiment?" A small tendril of hope unfurled within her.

"No," Renzo said. He unlocked the shackles around her wrists. "But I hope the Heir is on his way."

Serina rubbed at her sore wrists, shock making her slow. Her mind was still muddy. "And Nomi?"

"She snuck away on some fool mission to go after Asa. I came after her to help, and then I heard about the women captured from Mount Ruin and the executions. So I figured you might need help too," he replied. He looked different too, older, without his cheeky grin. Serina couldn't stop staring at him. "I was afraid for you."

Serina threw her arms around him. "Asa said you were dead. I thought—I can't believe you're here."

He hugged her tightly but drew back before she was ready.

"Our parents *are* dead," he said softly, his dark eyes shining with tears. "His men got to them before I could."

Serina's throat closed. That's what Asa had meant. *Your family is waiting for you.*

She looked down at her hands, callused and dirty, bruises marring her wrists. The last time she'd seen her mother, Serina's hands had been soft and smooth, the nails perfectly shaped, not a single mark on her skin. So much had changed.

Without looking up, she said, "We're going to take the palazzo. We're going to kill him."

Asa, his soldiers, this country . . . she would burn it all to the ground.

"Good," Renzo said.

She took the keys from him and got to work. Unlocking a shackle, moving to the next, passing the key to hands beyond her reach. "Hurry," she said quietly.

She turned back to Renzo. "You said you have a firearm. Any knives or swords? Silence is a weapon. We need to avoid firearms as long as we can."

He nodded. "I've got two knives. But that's all."

"We'll get more." She glanced past him to the guard sprawled on the hallway floor. He was starting to move.

"Didn't you kill him?" she asked. Her mind was sharp now, clear as it had ever been in her life. She knew what she had to do. She knew where this would end.

Renzo looked over at the guard. "I, uh . . . I knocked him out. I'm not really the killing type."

Serina used one of his knives and did what had to be done.

Renzo stared at her with wide eyes.

"This is war," she said, her voice calm, her mind calm. She was going to get her battle, her rebellion, after all. And it began now. "If the guards live, they can sound the alarm or attack us from behind. They have to die. Do you understand?"

He nodded, but his face paled.

When everyone was free from the heavy metal cuffs, Serina addressed the women, low and urgently. "We planned to go to Azura, but plans change. All of you who wanted to fight back, this is your chance. We're going to take Asa down. Kill any guards or soldiers you get your hands on, but don't touch the courtiers and servants. Collect all the weapons you can. Every soldier you kill, take his firearm, his knife, whatever he has."

Anika sidled up to Serina and took one of Renzo's knives. "You think we can do this?"

"We fight back." Serina tightened her hand on the hilt of her knife. "Always."

She'd rather die fighting than on display, like Ember. This was *for* Ember.

And for her family.

Serina and Anika slipped into the hall, leading Renzo, Val, and the rest of the women of Mount Ruin out of their prison. And together, when a guard rounded the corner, Serina and Anika took him down. Anika grabbed his firearm, Serina his dagger.

They were just getting started.

THIRTY-FOUR

NOMI

Nomi's slither through the secret passage went faster this time, with the lamp to guide her. And yet, her feet dragged all the same. Her heart beat so loudly she was sure the people in the rooms she was passing would be able to hear it.

She reached the ladder and kept walking. She counted the doors. Dusty, cobwebbed. Small square panels, tall thin ones, all with tiny doorknobs. She stopped before the final faint rectangle, the entrance to the Superior's rooms.

She took a deep breath. Closed her eyes, thought of Serina. Of Renzo, safe on his way to Azura. Of her parents, dead on the floor of their apartment.

She thought of Malachi and the hope she held in her heart. Hope that he would be a different kind of Superior, that he would help the women of Viridia. *Please*, she prayed.

Then she doused the lamp and opened the door.

Moonlight shone into the Superior's bedroom from a doorway that led to an open terrace beyond. A vast bed took up the right half of the room. A gilded armoire loomed against the other wall below a display of dangerous-looking weapons that gleamed in the dim light. The bed was hung with sheer gold-flecked curtains, partially obscuring the bed itself. She couldn't tell if Asa was inside, nor if he was alone. What would she do if he wasn't alone?

A shiver whispered along the back of her neck.

She slipped the knife out of her boot and stepped silently into the room. Nomi knew Serina was better suited for this task, seeing as Nomi had no idea how to use a knife. But even if her sister had been standing next to her, Nomi would have shouldered the duty of this undertaking. She had given Asa his opportunity, if not his power. She had to be the one to take it away.

She snuck up to the bed curtains and peeked inside. The silken sheets—black and shimmering—were smooth, unwrinkled. No one was in the bed.

Nomi's stomach flipped. She'd been so prepared to see Asa asleep in this bed, his dark hair mussed. She'd expected the memories to come flooding back; she'd braced for weakness and doubt. She'd imagined it would be difficult to see him in the flesh again, to resolve the capricious murderer with the man who'd promised her the world.

But he wasn't here.

She backed away from the bed, toward the secret passageway. She'd have to wait for him to return. She wasn't abandoning her mission now. As she turned, a flicker of movement caught her eye.

There, through the doorway . . .

She slipped out of her boots, knife in hand, and padded barefoot across the cold marble. Before she reached the doorway, she could hear his voice: soft, persuasive.

She snuck a glance around the corner.

Asa stood on the balcony beyond the doorway, facing a girl with a curtain of black hair, her head bowed. His hand rested at the joining of her neck and shoulder. Even from the other side of the terrace, Nomi saw the tension running through her.

Oh no. Maris.

"I saw you," Asa was purring. He was taller than she was by a few inches, and he used that height to loom, to assert his power. In his shadow, Maris cowered. "You belonged on Mount Ruin, didn't you? You had your own secret. Your own . . . aberration."

Nomi bit back a gasp.

Maris said nothing, but her hands clenched at her sides.

Asa's lips thinned. He twisted his hand into her hair and *yanked*, driving her head down. Maris stumbled to her knees, crying out.

Nomi tightened her grip on the homemade knife and charged.

The short distance benefited her. *Slap, slap, slap . . .* three footfalls and she'd reached them. He was just turning toward her, mouth opening, when she used her momentum and her fury and all her broken pieces to drive the knife into his gut, to the hilt.

Asa staggered back a step.

But he didn't falter the way she expected him to. Infuriated, he launched himself at her, yelling and cursing, his eyes wild as an injured animal's. Her legs caught in her cloak as she tried to back away.

She fell down, and he followed, sprawling on top of her, her knife still protruding grotesquely from his side.

He wound his hands around her neck. Suddenly, painfully, she couldn't breathe.

"Nomi," Asa growled. "Good. I so wanted to kill you myself."

Nomi's fingers scrabbled uselessly at her throat. She wriggled beneath him, but his legs and the billows of her cloak pinned her to the ground. Black spots danced across his twisted face. She should have slashed his throat, she should have . . .

Maris threw herself at Asa. Her weight toppled him, and for a few seconds, Nomi could breathe. Maris tried to scrabble out of the way, but Asa crawled after her, the knife still buried in him, still not slowing him down. Maris sobbed as she tried to escape.

Nomi clambered after them and shoved Asa as hard as she could. He listed to the side with a furious groan. But he recovered quickly, backhanding her across the face. Nomi fell to her knees. He got his hands around her neck again and drew her up.

"You know," he grunted, pulling her closer to him, "I really did want you as my queen. My beautiful queen, kneeling at my feet." His eyes, those eyes she'd once thought gentle and mischievous, added a perverse cast to the image. "But then you backed out of our plan. You turned on me."

His face twisted, the murderer showing through.

Nomi raised her knee and slammed it into his groin. He wobbled, but he didn't let go.

Her right hand knocked against her cloak. No, something in the pocket of her cloak.

Hand shaking, she drew out the pencil, sharpened savagely to a point, and drove it into Asa's eye.

He fell back, ramming into the balcony railing. A strange, savage moan left his lips. His other eye stared at her fixedly. Slowly, its light went out.

His body tipped backward, overbalancing. Nomi gave him an extra, furious push.

Time seemed to slow as she watched him fall, his black silk dressing gown fluttering all the way down.

A moment later, a percussive thud. No screams or shouts of alarm. No one had seen him.

They would soon enough.

Nomi coughed weakly, her throat burning. She collapsed to the floor next to Maris and took several deep, painful breaths.

"Nomi, Nomi . . ." Maris put her arms around her and held on tight.

"We need to get away," Nomi murmured. "His guards will find us. I don't know if I can fight them off."

"I'll help however I can," Maris said, her voice surprisingly steady. "I helped on Mount Ruin."

They staggered toward the secret panel. Nomi had expected Asa to be guarded, or to call for Marcos when he saw her. She hadn't expected the chance to walk away. This time, before his men found his body, this was a gift. She needed to use it to find Serina and get the women of Mount Ruin out.

Suddenly, a roar echoed from somewhere deep within the palazzo, clinging to the walls, shaking the foundation.

It was the roar of a hundred female voices, all of them full of rage.

It was a battle cry.

Nomi and Maris bolted into the corridor and followed the sound. Maybe Serina wouldn't be hard to find after all.

THIRTY-FIVE

SERINA

The lower levels of the palazzo were a maze, as labyrinthine as the Graces' chambers but on a much larger scale. It wasn't all cells and dungeons down here either; among the soldiers, each dispatched swiftly to avoid raising the alarm, servants and maids scurried to and from stock rooms, cold storage, and wine cellars. It was one of these maids—a round, doughy woman in a stained apron—who saw Serina, with her blackened eye and her army of women, and screamed until her face went purple.

Serina grabbed the woman's arm. "How do we get upstairs?"

The woman didn't stop screaming.

"Please," Serina added. "We just need to get out of here. We're not going to hurt you."

The woman's voice petered out. She didn't speak, but her eyes flicked toward a corridor on her left.

Serina patted her shoulder and headed down the hall. Behind her, the tide of women flowed through the passageway and up the narrow stair.

"We need to find the Superior," Anika said. "If he goes down, they all will."

"The soldiers will guard him heavily," Serina said grimly. "We find them, we'll find him." *And Nomi, hopefully before she gets herself killed.*

292

She sent Val and Renzo to the back of her army—Val to protect them from behind, and Renzo to keep him safe. As safe as possible, anyway. She didn't want either of them on the front lines. "You stay out of the way, you hear me?" she told her brother, shaking him by the shoulders. He nodded and made no argument.

As Serina entered a long gallery, she got her first glimpse outside—it was full night, with a streak of moonlight gleaming on the ocean. Beautiful.

She rounded the corner and skidded to a stop. The wide walkway was full of Asa's men, all of them with weapons held aloft. They must have heard the servant's scream. And it wasn't just a handful of guards either. This was a regiment.

But they were still fewer than the women of Mount Ruin.

Serina shared a split-second glance with Anika. There was no fear in the other woman's eyes. She was ready for this. And suddenly, so was Serina. These men, with their weapons and their big looming bodies and their blank faces, they represented all the men who had oppressed her, judged her, hurt her. They were the men who had done the same to the women standing behind her.

They were the enemy.

A scream built in her chest, the same wild pressure that she'd released every time they committed a body to Mount Ruin's volcano. Every time she had to bear witness to another senseless death, another life wasted. Another Oracle and Petrel and Jacana. Another Ember. All around her the scream built and amplified, echoing off the gilded walls of the palazzo. The men before her hesitated. As the scream grew, they seemed to shrink. Until they were small, unimportant. Powerless.

At the height of this miraculous alchemy, Serina, Anika, and the army of Mount Ruin attacked.

The men got a few shots off before the women reached them. The girl to Serina's left went down. But Serina didn't falter. She stabbed and slashed. She shoved. She gouged eyes and kicked groins. She carved a path through the men, pushed at them, tore firearms from hands. Her brain shut off, all analysis reduced to *stab, slash, shove, gouge.*

The soldiers stumbled back, trying to force enough space so they could use their firearms. Or maybe they were scared.

The wave of women crashed over them, washing them out of the hallway and onto a patio. Voices screamed. Chairs crashed to the tiled ground. For a moment, Serina was disoriented by a small gathering of men in colorful suits and waistcoats, smoking pipes.

They scattered, or tried to.

Lights were strung above the assembly, revealing the battle with excruciating detail.

Soldiers and female fighters tumbled over each other, into the men with their pipes and their finery. Serina shoved a portly man in purple velvet out of her way.

"Move!" she roared.

In the chaos, Cliff raised two stolen carving knives to fight a soldier, but someone behind her rammed into her, throwing her off her target. Instead, her knives impaled a man in a blue jacket huddled beside a table. His mouth dropped open as his body collapsed. Cliff stepped back, her face a mask of horror. She raised her hands, still holding the knives wet with his blood, as if to beg forgiveness.

The soldier she'd missed raised his firearm. Serina screamed, trying to warn her. But the battle was too loud, too chaotic. Her voice disappeared into the din. He shot Cliff at point-blank range. She crumpled to the ground beside the twitching body of the courtier.

Serina's head pounded sickeningly as she turned away. A soldier stood before her, so close she could pick out the silver in his pale blue eyes. He raised his short fighting sword. Without thinking, she drove her head into his stomach, shoving him into several other soldiers. Anika bounded after them, striking them down before they could regain their feet.

A massive soldier with a thick blond beard and heavy fists appeared in front of Serina. Before she could react, he punched her, sending her to the ground. Her ears rang. It was obvious this one didn't *need* weapons. *He* was the weapon.

Her head spun. The screams and shouts of battle wobbled in and out. The giant kicked her in the side, angering her broken rib. She curled into a ball, hands protectively covering her head, and gasped for breath. She couldn't withstand another kick like that. Her ribs would snap, she would break in half.

She looked up in time to see three women launch themselves at the mountainous soldier, their voices raised in a banshee cry. They had no weapons but their ragged fingernails and their desperate strength. She didn't recognize them—their faces and hair were streaked with blood.

Serina scrambled to her feet, ignoring the fire in her cheekbone and the flames in her side. When she was sure the women had the large soldier in hand, she helped Mirror fight off another man, this one more reasonably sized but still deadly, with a firearm in one hand and a short sword in the other.

Mirror slammed him in the head with a heavy iron platter she'd found somewhere, and Serina finished the job with a knife to the throat.

"What are you doing, Mirror?" Serina hissed. "You should be hanging back with the other injured women."

Mirror showed her teeth. Grimace or feral smile, Serina couldn't tell.

"I will not cower," the girl said. Then she yanked the firearm from the fallen soldier's hand and fired it at a man running at them. He sank to his knees, blood blooming across his chest.

More bodies fell: both men and women. Gunshots cracked through the night. The lights swung wildly above them. It was difficult to make sense of the jumble of movement and blood.

Serina used her knife and her fist and her knees. At some point, Val pushed through to her side. He discharged the firearm he held and tore another one from his waistband, firing again.

There were more women than soldiers, but more men kept appearing, called to the battle by the sound of gunshots. In the haze and confusion, Serina looked for a way to get out, to get to Asa, but never saw an opening.

A large, wide-shouldered man with an air of authority appeared and started shouting orders to the soldiers. They made an attempt to regroup, but Serina and her forces didn't give them a chance. These women were the survivors, the ones who'd won battles in the ring—they knew how to divide, debilitate, distract.

Serina spared a thought for Renzo; she hoped he was staying out of the way as she'd told him to. She couldn't let herself search the melee for him. Her own survival was constantly in question with every soldier who raised his weapon or his fist to strike her.

She and Anika went for the big man, the one trying to take charge.

He reminded her of Commander Ricci; his eyes were full of the same hatred, the same disbelief. Even now, even as she shoved her blade into his stomach, he didn't see how these *women* could possibly be a threat.

She and Anika showed him exactly how.

The last thing he saw as he fell was Anika's grimace, her face streaked with blood, as she slashed his throat.

THIRTY-SIX

NOMI

Nomi skidded down the hallway to a long, twisting stair. Down two stories, to the ground floor. She could hear Maris panting behind her. They emerged into a long corridor dimly lit with sconces. Nomi listened for another shout or the sounds of conflict. Where was Serina?

"Nomi," Maris said. "Look."

A thick streak of blood arced along the wall like a garish arrow, pointing the way. Nomi ran. Around the corner, a body sprawled across the hallway, a pool of blood congealing beneath him. The soldier stared sightlessly at the ceiling. Nomi swallowed down bile. She carefully stepped over him, Maris sticking close behind her.

There were more bodies. They became a macabre trail, leading Nomi and Maris on. Soon, the sounds of fighting filtered back to them. Nomi prayed she wouldn't come across Serina's body.

Maris found a firearm in the arms of a dead soldier. Nomi snatched a dagger next to a dead woman in prison blue.

No living soul appeared. The rooms they passed—luxurious sitting rooms, an airy art gallery, a library—were all empty. Abandoned.

The next hall was filled with bodies, several deep in some places. Nomi skidded to a halt, realizing for the first time that she was still barefoot. The carpet was damp, soaked with blood. Beyond the carnage, the terrace opened to a wide patio. She could see figures moving, hear gunshots.

Here was the battle.

To her surprise, Maris charged forward without hesitation, picking her way to clear ground. Nomi followed, wishing she'd put on her boots so she wouldn't have to feel the slick, rubbery give of bodies beneath her feet.

They stopped at the outskirts of the fighting. Nomi craned for a view of Serina, but there was too much movement, too much chaos. It was difficult to see who was winning, if anyone.

She wanted to climb up on a table and scream that Asa was dead, that they could stop fighting, but she knew it wouldn't matter. She was as likely to get shot as have anyone listen. Still, she had to do something.

Suddenly, Maris darted forward. Nomi watched, eyes wide, as the former Grace planted her feet, raised her weapon, and fired into the crowd. A soldier collapsed, revealing Helena. The girl was staggering, bent forward from the waist, one hand grasping the other—bloody—shoulder.

"Helena!" Maris screamed. She grabbed her and pulled her away from the fighting.

Helena wrapped her good arm around Maris's neck and buried her head in her shoulder.

Near the edge of the patio, where sand kicked up over the tiles, two round wrought-iron tables lay on their sides like shields. Nomi grabbed Maris's arm. "Look," she said. "Let's get her over there."

Together, Nomi and Maris helped Helena stagger to the tables.

On the other side, several other injured women sprawled in the sand. A man crouched over them. He stood quickly at the sound of newcomers. Nomi faltered, shock waves reverberating through her.

"Renzo!"

Her brother was disheveled and dirty, with a scrape down his neck and his bloody shirtsleeves rolled to the elbow. He helped them sit Helena down. As soon as she was settled Nomi stood up and heaved her fist at Renzo's arm.

"Why aren't you on your way to Azura?" she asked wildly. "You were supposed to be *safe*!"

He rolled his eyes. "You snuck out in the middle of the night to avenge our parents." He gestured past the tables. "And Serina's leading an *army*. What did you expect me to do?"

"Where's Malachi?" Nomi asked. "Did he come with you?"

If he was here, now that Asa was dead . . .

But Renzo shook his head. "He left Lanos when I did. He went back to Porto Rosa for Dante."

"I hope he found him."

A shout caught Nomi's attention. She peeked over the edge of a table. It looked as if the fight might be slackening. There were far more women standing than men. The soldiers were faltering. Some ran down the beach and into the water, swimming their retreat.

Nomi thought of Asa, broken on a tiled patio on the other side of the palazzo. These men had no leader, no one shouting orders or sending for reinforcements.

With a glance at Maris, who was oblivious to anything but Helena, Nomi ventured onto the patio. Renzo went with her. "I've been grabbing the injured women and trying to get them out of the way," he said. "I'm not a fighter. I don't know—I don't know how to do what Serina's done."

As they crept forward, they stepped carefully, walking the maze of clear tile between bodies. The moonlight turned the splashes of blood silver.

They found Serina in the center of the remnants of battle, knife raised, watching as the last soldier darted toward the waves. She was panting, sagging on her feet, her hand streaked to the wrist with blood, but she was still standing. She was alive.

Tears streamed down Nomi's face.

The night settled back around them, the echoes of gunshots fading.

Serina looked up and froze, mouth open, when she saw Nomi.

Nomi threw her arms around her big sister.

They held on to each other, so tightly, as if somehow this embrace could erase the last few hours, the blood, the death, and maybe the months before that too, all the time they'd spent apart, fighting to save each other.

Beside them, Anika fell to her knees, a hand to her stomach. Serina tore her arms from Nomi and crouched beside the girl. Nomi hurried to help.

"Are you all right?" Serina asked.

It was hard to tell in the dark, but Nomi thought Anika's skin seemed ashen, almost gray. The whites of her eyes glowed. She stood back up with Serina's help and then waved them both off. She picked through the bodies, her shoulders slumping, and collapsed into a delicate patio chair that had somehow avoided the carnage. She didn't answer the question. Serina followed her, panic showing on her swollen face. "Anika!"

Nomi trailed after them, trying to think of something she could *do*. She saw Val off to the side, exhaustion making him haggard.

Anika hissed in a breath. "I'm . . . I'm okay. I just . . . need to sit down."

"You need a doctor," Serina replied. She looked around, as if somehow one might materialize out of the night.

Nomi looked around too. But all she saw were the surviving fighters, the white splashes of the retreating soldiers, the moonlight. A few feet from where she stood, Marcos lay crumpled, his throat cut. She couldn't bring herself to feel guilty about the relief that flowed through her.

"Did we get him?" Anika asked weakly. "Did we bring down the Superior?"

"Not yet." Serina looked at Nomi, her expression shifting at whatever she saw in Nomi's face.

"Asa is dead," Nomi said. She'd been trying to ignore the pain in her throat, but her voice came out strange and hoarse, like she'd swallowed broken glass. She tried to keep from cracking . . . the look in his eyes as he strangled her, the sound of his body hitting the ground . . .

"Oh, Nomi," Serina said, and in those two words, Nomi heard that she was sorry, that she understood why Nomi's hands still shook, that she knew the nightmares that would carry them both.

They hugged again, and for a moment, the darkness seemed less absolute.

THIRTY-SEVEN

SERINA

Serina never wanted to let Nomi go. She couldn't believe she was here, that she was safe. She couldn't believe that her sister had killed the Superior.

Asa is dead.

The battle was over.

Serina was still standing.

She buried her face in Nomi's neck and breathed.

"We have a problem." Val's voice cut holes into Serina's growing peace. She drew back with a sigh.

Val put a hand on her lower back. "There are troops massing in the piazza across the canal. More than we can handle."

"Maybe it's Malachi!" Nomi said, some light coming back to her eyes. "Maybe he found Dante."

"Or it could be the Superior's reinforcements," Val said. "No one knows Asa is dead yet. Those retreating soldiers could have sounded the alarm to Bellaqua's garrison."

"So how can we tell?" Nomi asked, looking crestfallen.

Serina squeezed her arm. "Hopefully it *is* Malachi." She looked down at Anika, still clutching her stomach, her face taut with pain. Everyone looked exhausted. Defeated. This moment should have been a victory.

"We need time and a place we can defend while we

catch our breath." Serina wiped her clean hand across her forehead. "I don't know the palazzo very well. Maybe—"

Nomi put a hand on her arm. "I know where we can go."

There were as many women lying on the ground as there were men. A trail of bodies led into the hallway. Serina saw Gia, Tremor, and Cliff among the dead. The women who'd survived stood in clumps, their clothes streaked, their hair mussed. Blaze stood at the edge of the patio, looking out at the water and the path of moonlight.

Serina's bruised face ached, and her head pounded. She hadn't eaten anything in a couple of days, and her stomach suddenly felt *this* was the moment to twist and complain. But there was no time to worry about any of that.

"Most of the injured are over there," Renzo said, pointing to several tables upended at the edge of the patio. Serina went to see. Helena and Maris huddled together, and Mirror was there. She looked rough, but somehow she managed to spare Serina a smile.

"Renzo, you and Val help the wounded," Serina ordered. "Maris, you and Nomi collect as many firearms and as much ammunition as you can carry. Get the others to help you. Quickly, as fast as you can."

As soon as Nomi's hands were full, Serina helped Anika out of her chair. Her head lolled a little before she steadied herself. Serina tried to look at her wound.

"No," Anika snapped, brushing away Serina's hand. "Later."

Nomi led the way inside. Serina took a rough count of the women who followed—about seventy women had survived. They'd lost more than a third of their number in the battle.

Serina swallowed painfully. Many women had died tonight for a freedom the rest of them might never see.

Please let the troops be Malachi's.

What she didn't share with Nomi were her doubts. What would Malachi do about her little army? Could he really let them back into Viridia, free, after all this bloodshed?

"We all fought," Anika said, her voice hoarse.

"What?" Serina asked. They brought up the rear of the procession with the rest of the injured.

"I see you looking around, taking stock." Anika winced. Cleared her throat. "And I'm saying at least we fought. Thanks to your brother, we didn't have to wait for Asa to parade us out and kill us one by one. Even if we all die tonight, at least we fought for our lives."

Fight back. Always.

Petrel walked with Serina, even now.

"You're right," she said as they entered the hall.

They were the last to reach the Graces' chambers. Serina entered the circular room, hung with cream damask and velvet, and was immediately, uncomfortably aware of her dirty clothes, her bloody face and hands. This was a place of beauty, and she'd brought ugliness and grief inside. Women spread from the central room out through the arches and into sitting rooms and dining areas. They slumped onto soft settees and across the thick carpets warming the marble floor. They frightened the Graces, who emerged from their bedrooms in silken white nightdresses, their eyes wide.

Several white-clad men hurried past Serina and out the door. At least the Graces' attendants weren't putting up a fight.

A small reprieve. They needed to take advantage of it.

Serina helped Anika down onto a velvet chaise, checked to make sure she was still conscious and alert, and then made her way through the tightly packed rooms looking for Nomi.

She found her on a balcony. Nomi was staring out at the canal, where bobbing lanterns illuminated wide-bottomed boats shuttling soldiers to the palazzo. There wasn't a clear view the way the building was situated, and the Graces' chambers mostly faced the ocean. But here, on this balcony, part of the city and the canal were visible. Yet even this restricted view illuminated more soldiers than Serina cared to count.

"Malachi thought he might need to take his soldiers through the tunnels," Nomi said. "I don't know what it means that these men are coming in boats."

"We will hope they are Malachi's until they attack," Serina said. "We'll be ready, either way." It was a lie to make her sister feel better. There were too many soldiers. If they attacked, the women of Mount Ruin would fall. "But, Nomi, you must prepare yourself . . . Even if they *are* Malachi's men . . . Malachi might not be our ally anymore."

Her sister turned. She was still wearing the heavy dark cloak she'd appeared in down on the patio. Here, with the torches lit, Serina could clearly see the blood that stained Nomi's hands, the bruises that encircled her throat.

"What do you mean?" Nomi asked.

Serina gave a painful shrug. "Just that, if it *is* him, he has all the power. We've nothing to bargain with. We are a ragged force, too small now to be a threat, except perhaps to his legitimacy. He will have to decide what message to send to Viridia, as its ruler. And rebellions must be quashed."

Nomi shook her head. "Malachi won't do that, Serina. He . . ." Her voice petered out. A shadow passed across her face. She didn't think he would, but Serina could tell she wasn't *sure*.

"You . . . Asa . . ." Serina paused. "Are you all right?"

"I don't know," Nomi replied. "I didn't—it didn't happen like I thought."

Serina kissed Nomi's forehead. "When I was on Mount Ruin, I tried to imagine what you'd do. How you'd survive in the palazzo. You've always been such a fighter, Nomi. You did what needed to be done."

"I killed him for Mama and Papa," she said softly. "And for me. For us. I thought that the world would change somehow, magically, once he was gone." Tears slipped down her cheeks. "But an army is massing at our gates, we are still just rebels needing to be silenced, and no amount of murder will bring Mama and Papa back. I was a fool."

Serina brushed the wet from Nomi's cheeks with her thumb. Her heart was as broken as her sister's. "Viridia *will* change. It has to. They can't erase us."

Nomi sniffed and hardened her mouth to keep it from trembling. "Of course they can."

She turned back toward the balcony, her gaze on the

slivers of boats and soldiers visible around the edge of the building. Serina watched them too.

Ines appeared on the balcony. The woman was severe and implacable, just as she'd been when she'd caught Serina holding Nomi's book. She was clothed in a slim column of black satin. "I've ordered food and a medic to tend to the injured. The servants will do as I say."

Her face betrayed nothing.

"Thank you," Serina said, fighting the outdated impulse to curtsy. She was no Grace, after all.

Ines's gaze shifted to Nomi. "I assume the Superior is not in a position to object."

Nomi swallowed. "No, he is not."

———

Serina stationed Val and the strongest of the uninjured girls at the doors to the circular room. They stood guard, their weapons ready. She put Maris and Helena on the balcony, with orders to find her when the last of the soldiers had been ferried to the palazzo.

It was eerie how little urgency the army showed in their approach—they seemed unconcerned with the prospect of being attacked, as if they already knew the forces within were not a proper threat.

Serina ate a bit of bread and slowly sipped a goblet of water. Her stomach churned, but the food steadied her hands. She checked on Anika, who'd been grazed in the side by a bullet. According to the medic, it was a superficial wound. Anika growled at that. "It doesn't *feel* superficial."

The injured women were lying in real beds for the first time since they'd come to Mount Ruin. Even Mirror's color looked better, now that she was settled into one of the Graces' bedrooms, with a proper doctor to tend to her wounds.

Ines kept the servants jumping, bringing up food and extra medical supplies for the newcomers. She even ordered several servants to retrieve Asa's body and place it on a black sheet in the main entry, so there would be no dispute about the Superior's fate. The approaching soldiers would see their fallen leader immediately upon breaching the palazzo doors.

No one questioned her. Serina thought it had to do with the rigid set of her mouth and the fact that no one else was giving orders within the palazzo. Everyone, servants and Graces included, was waiting to see what the soldiers outside would do.

Serina, Nomi, and a few of the less injured girls bathed hurriedly and put on the clean, dry clothes Ines provided. Wide-legged linen pants and blousy shirts. Not exactly fighting clothes, but better than their torn and bloodstained prison uniforms.

Serina cringed at the way her callused palms caught against the fine fabric. It was strange to be dressed like this again. It felt natural and yet foreign at the same time, like the two sides of herself—the Grace and the warrior—were in constant opposition, both vying for control.

Nomi introduced her to a small tawny-haired girl named Angeline, the handmaiden who'd replaced Serina. The girl looked meek, but the first thing she said to Serina was, "I've herded all the Graces into the farthest dining room so they'll be out of the way if you need to fight."

She spoke like a soldier giving a report.

Serina nodded, and the girl hurried away.

Nomi finished braiding her wet hair and swung it over her shoulder. "We can try to get them out through the tunnel. I told Angeline about it, in case I didn't come back . . . in case Malachi wasn't able to help them."

"The passageways. Of course," Serina said, her mind racing. "Maybe we can all escape, if need be. Unless there are troops hiding in them."

They both fell silent at the prospect.

Renzo appeared in the doorway, a strange expression on his face. It almost looked . . . relieved. But Serina couldn't account for *that* at all, not with an army at their door.

"Are you well?" she asked, unease coiling within her.

Renzo stepped inside the room, revealing another figure. Malachi.

Unlike the soldiers in the palazzo, who had been dressed in the household uniform, the Heir was dressed for battle, in armor. He held his helmet under one arm.

"Hello, Nomi. Serina," he said.

THIRTY-EIGHT

NOMI

"M-Malachi," Nomi stuttered. Her heart ricocheted against her ribs. She didn't know whether she wanted to throw her arms around him or run away. Emotions churned so quickly through her mind she couldn't fix on any of them.

He looked so big and frightening in his battle gear, and his expression didn't offer any relief. His mouth had turned into a severe frown, his freshly shaven jaw sharp and unforgiving.

"I wish to speak with you privately," he told her gravely.

She glanced, half-panicked, at Serina, who nodded.

"Of course," Nomi said. She clasped her hands together to keep them from shaking as she led him to her old bedroom. She couldn't think of anywhere else that would give them privacy.

Ria wasn't there; all of Asa's Graces were gathered in a dining room, away from any possible danger. The bedroom was dark and cool. A breeze from the open window drew Nomi's gaze to the golden line along the horizon. Almost dawn.

Nomi switched on the light. Very carefully, methodically, Malachi placed his helmet on the bed, and then removed his armored gloves, one after the other. Those he placed on the coverlet as well. Finally, he turned to her.

"I went to my father's rooms first," he said, the rough slide of his voice sending tiny lightning bolts through Nomi's chest. "I was afraid I'd find you injured, or dead . . . but no one was there."

He cleared his throat.

"I killed him, Malachi," Nomi said before he went further. Before he was forced to ask. She swallowed back the impulse to apologize. She *was* sorry for the pain that revelation might cause him, sorry that he might never look at her the same way again, but she couldn't be sorry for killing Asa. "His body is in the front entryway. But you came through the tunnel, didn't you?"

Malachi raised his hand and let his fingers brush, feather-light, across her bruised throat. "He did this."

She nodded.

Emotions flitted across his face too quickly for her to identify.

"I would have happily carried that burden for you," he said softly. "He and I . . . There were things I would have said to him."

"Are you upset not to have the chance?" she asked.

He shook his head. "I'm upset that he hurt you. Only that."

"Those troops . . . massing at the gates," she said. She still couldn't read his face. Was he relieved? Was there more bad news to come? "Are they yours?"

He inclined his head. "As soon as you left, I went back to Porto Rosa. Dante had gotten my message. He was waiting." He glanced briefly out the window, where the first golden streaks of dawn climbed the sill. "He'd taken his force into hiding . . . The orders he received from Asa were ones he couldn't bring himself to carry out. Rounding up women, punishing anyone who tried to publicly mourn my father . . . He'd been assessing his options, had even considered attempting a coup maybe. He was happy to hear from me." A small wry smile touched his mouth and was gone.

He reached out for her, his fingers sliding against hers. But she took a step back, out of reach.

"That's . . . that's good," she said, her voice cracking. She took a steadying breath, pulling all her courage around her like a shield. "But this is our coup, Malachi. You should honor your concessions, the ones you made back on Mount Ruin. These women didn't fight for things to stay the same. You made us promises. You should honor them."

Nomi braced for Malachi's answer, her heart in her throat. He would prove he was worthy of her trust . . . her regard for him. Or he would betray her, just like his brother.

"No."

Nomi looked up at him, her heart crumbling to ash. Serina's words ripped through her mind.

Rebellions must be quashed.

"I should do *more*." Malachi took a small step toward her, but he didn't reach for her again. "Nomi, I don't *want* to be Superior."

"You—you what?" She couldn't process what he said. "But all of this—leaving Mount Ruin, finding Dante, killing

314

your brother, it was all about you regaining your birthright. Malachi, you *are* the Superior."

He took his own steadying breath. "I know that's where we started. But it's not so simple anymore, not for me. I want Viridia to change."

Nomi stared at him, agape.

"Tell me how to make this country better," he said. "What should I do? What should *we* do?"

Her heart clattered in her wounded throat. "What— what do you mean?"

"How can I fix this? Not just the concessions. I mean the very way this country is ruled. Whatever you say, whatever it is, I'll do it." She could read no deceit, no trickery in his eyes.

"But how *can* you change it, if you don't want to rule?" she asked. "This is your country. You are its rightful leader. You can't just ... That's—that's not how things work. Another man will not be better. You can't believe that."

He shrugged. "I'm not talking about another Superior, don't you see? There's been a coup, like you said. Asa's been killed. Only my men know I'm here. You and your sister won this fight, Nomi. *You* decide who rules, and how."

"Why?" she asked again, her voice scratching in her throat.

"You know why." The look in his eyes made her ache. Gently, he took her hands. "You won this fight, Nomi. This is your choice."

Her choice. The future of Viridia was *her choice*.

Once, she'd wanted the freedom to choose her own future. Now it was her job to choose a whole country's. It didn't matter that she thought Malachi had lost his senses. She was not going to refuse this chance.

Nomi didn't hesitate. "Okay. I know what to do."

THIRTY-NINE

SERINA

"They're the Heir's forces, right?" Serina asked, her hands tightening on the railing. She and Val had taken over the corner where Maris and Helena had been keeping watch. "Unless he snuck in through the tunnels."

Val craned to get a better look. There were troops numbering in the hundreds, maybe a thousand, some lined up along the lawn leading to the palazzo, others still in boats spanning the canal. One of the women from Jungle Camp had snuck through the palazzo to investigate the docks on the ocean side, only to find more troops there. They were surrounded.

"It looks like they're waiting for orders," Val replied. He glanced over his shoulder at her. "Although, if they're waiting for *Asa* to give them . . ."

Across the canal, the piazza was empty. None of the vendors had appeared with their carts, but Serina saw many faces at the windows of surrounding buildings. People were staying out of the way of the soldiers. They were waiting too.

"If they're Asa's, we'll have to protect the Heir," she said. "As long as we can."

Val turned fully toward her and slipped his arms around her. "Until the end," he agreed.

She leaned against his chest and listened to the beating of his heart. It was so surreal, standing here on this balcony in the palazzo with him. Being here was all she'd wanted as a prospective Grace. But now, as Grace of Mount Ruin, it felt uncomfortable and strange, like a dress she'd outgrown.

"I am happy I am not a Grace," she murmured. "But I do prefer embroidering fabric to sewing up flesh. *That* I miss."

"The fairy tale still calls to you," he quipped.

With a little laugh, she lifted up on her toes to kiss him. "And the handsome prince."

He kissed her back, igniting tiny hungry flames in her belly. Her hands wound through his hair.

"If you were in a fairy tale," he said, "there'd be no time to embroider *or* gallivant with the prince. You'd be too busy." His lips nipped at her smile. "A princess leading an army."

"How about a queen?"

Serina started at the sound of Nomi's voice and pulled out of Val's arms.

Her sister stood a few feet away. Her loose black pants and linen shirt hung in an elegant drape from shoulder and hip. Her braid curled over one shoulder. For the first time that Serina could remember, Nomi looked serene. Genuinely at peace, without a hint of fire behind her eyes. She really looked like a Grace.

"What are you talking about?" Serina asked, alarmed. Had killing Asa torn her sister from reality? And where was Malachi?

"The regiment outside is Malachi's," Nomi said. "They are men loyal to him, led by his closest friend."

Some of the tension in Serina's shoulders eased. But she was still wary. "What are his intentions? I will do whatever I can to protect these women—"

"He knows that." Nomi glanced over at Val. "Would you give us a few minutes, please? I need to speak with my sister."

He kissed Serina's cheek. "I'll be right inside," he murmured.

As soon as he was gone, Nomi took Serina's hands. A strange light shone in her eyes. "Malachi doesn't want to be Superior, Serina. He has told me to choose who rules. Because . . . well, we've led a coup. He says that means the country is *ours*."

Serina opened her mouth. Shut it again. She could think of nothing to say. It was entirely possible *she* was the one having a break from reality.

Nomi smiled at her, so brightly, all her love shining in her eyes. "Serina, the country is *yours*."

Serina started to shake her head, but Nomi continued, inexorable. "You are Viridia's next warrior queen, just like the first, Queen Vaccaro. You raised an army. You took the palazzo. This is your victory. You will be queen, and you will make this country into what it *should* be . . . a place where women aren't bought and sold. Where they aren't punished for reading or for using money; where they can earn their own wages. A place with no Graces, and no Mount Ruin either."

Serina could see the future written so clearly on Nomi's face. Her sister was there already, living in a world where women had as many rights and choices as men. *That* was where her serenity came from.

And it was that moment, that expression on Nomi's face, that reminded Serina of who Nomi was. What she wanted.

Serina looked her sister in the eye. "Nomi, you're in love with Malachi."

Nomi's beatific smile faded. "What does that have to do with anything?"

"It's true, isn't it?" Serina pressed. She needed to hear Nomi say it. She couldn't do this—she couldn't suggest what she wanted to suggest—unless she was sure.

"Even if I was, it doesn't matter," Nomi replied, emotions warring on her face. "This is about *all* the women of Viridia."

"But *you* can be his queen," Serina said, reaching for her sister's hands.

Nomi's brows rose. Shock slackened her jaw. "What? No. This is your victory, Serina. You should be queen."

"I don't *want* to be queen," Serina said gently, and felt the truth of the words in her bones. "What *I* want—what I've always wanted—is to protect you. And I will."

Mount Ruin had made her into a warrior, not a queen. Her place was by Nomi's side, keeping her safe. Serina had always cared more about protecting Nomi than anything else. That would never change.

"You and Malachi should rule together, as equal partners," she went on, her eyes never leaving Nomi's. She could see her version of the future unfurl in her mind, but it didn't have the same impossible, fantastical sheen as Nomi's.

Serina had always been the pragmatic one. "It will help the country transition. The magistrates will be mollified by Malachi's role, and you'll be able to do everything you can to make this country what it should be. You will show the men of Viridia that women deserve to be equal, and you'll show the women all the new possibilities opening to them."

Nomi looked at Serina as if she were speaking another language.

Serina shook her gently. "You can already *read and write*, Nomi. You know the real history of this country. You are educated, intelligent . . . You're what Graces should have been all along—the perfect example of *all* a woman can be."

"But . . ." She faltered.

"Marry him," Serina said, her heart full. "Be the queen this country needs. Side by side with Malachi, so there will be no doubt of your legitimacy and no need to deny your heart."

"What about you, Serina?" Nomi asked, sounding for an instant like the little girl she'd once been, curled into her big sister's arms.

Serina smiled. "I'll be here in the palazzo with you. There will be threats—I will protect you. I know how to do that now. This is what I want. What I've always wanted."

Nomi stared at her hands. "You want me to ask Malachi to marry me. You want *me* to be queen."

"Yes," Serina said simply. "But it's your choice. That's all *you* have ever wanted, baby sister, to choose your future. Don't be afraid."

FORTY

NOMI

Do I want to be queen?

Nomi thought about the queens in Malachi's history book. The warrior and her daughters. The thoroughness with which their enemies had erased them. The price the women of Viridia had paid over the past two hundred years. She thought about Asa and his father. All the Graces who'd lived in this palazzo, all the women like her mother who were never given a choice about anything. She thought about Serina, sent to Mount Ruin to die for reading, a crime she didn't even commit.

Yes. Nomi wanted to be queen. As long as Serina was here with her.

She hugged her sister tightly. "Tell our fighters at the door they can stand down. Get some more food from Ines. *Rest*, Serina. You deserve it."

Nomi returned to her old bedroom, where Malachi waited for her.

He was sitting on the edge of the bed. He'd removed his heavy armor now that the threat of battle had passed. The tight breeches and thin shirt he wore beneath clung to his muscular frame.

When she entered the room, he stood up. "Serina will need to organize a formal event," he said. "Invite all the magistrates. She'll set out Asa's crimes, make a show of force with her army, augmented by Dante's regiment, and then she'll take command. I'll disappear . . . We don't want any perceived threats to her rule—"

"Malachi, wait." Nomi took his hands.

He paused and raised an eyebrow. She studied his face. Somehow in the past few weeks it had changed in her eyes. He still had the same intensity, but she couldn't find the cruel set of his mouth she'd been convinced she'd seen . . . and she couldn't find the haughty dismissal she *knew* she'd seen. She remembered the day at the beach when he'd swum with her, holding her up when the water had scared her. That was the day he'd told her he was the one who'd left her the book about Viridia's secret history. He'd played at rebellion before that too . . . when he'd chosen her instead of Serina, defying his father and the magistrates.

She thought about how willing he'd been to give up his birthright to Serina. It was an honorable move, yes, but was that the only reason for it? Could he be afraid?

"What is it?" Malachi asked, bringing her back to herself.

Nomi took a deep breath. Well, if he was afraid, he wasn't the only one.

"Malachi," she said, and paused, and knew she was stalling. "Malachi," she repeated, more firmly. "You have a responsibility to this country. You can't give Viridia to us and leave it to us to fix it alone." It was easier to start here. To start with responsibility. Her feelings . . . those would be harder to discuss.

His eyes narrowed, and a flash of the old Malachi, the gruff, inscrutable one, returned. "I thought this is what you wanted. A queen. I was trying to fix this . . . It was your idea—"

"I know," she said. "I know. But Serina doesn't *want* to be queen."

"So what's the solution?" He crossed his arms over his chest. "We go back to the old system? The one you hated so much?"

Nomi took another steadying breath. Maybe she'd started in the wrong place after all. He was defensive now, and what she had to say, what she had to ask him . . .

It all came out in a big rush.

"You should be the Superior, and I should be your queen. Ruling together as equals. We should get married." She gasped in a breath. "Will you . . . will you marry me?"

He backed up a step, bumped into the bed, and sat down. Seated, they were almost on a level. She closed the distance between them. There was something in his shell-shocked expression that made her feel powerful. She'd surprised him. Genuinely shocked him.

"You want to marry me?" he echoed.

"No Graces," she said. "Only me. And we rule together, equal partners. We change this country. We open our borders, we teach women to read, we allow them to choose their own futures. Serina will stay in the palazzo as a sort of, well, a guard for me, I suppose. She says she wants to protect me. We'll—we'll call her an advisor. She'll help us navigate the hazards."

"I never wanted any Graces, not after you . . . You want to marry me?" he asked again, in wonder.

She hit his shoulder. "What is wrong with you? This isn't just about that. It's—"

He grabbed her around the waist and kissed her, his mouth urgent and hot and sweet. She melted into the embrace, soft and warm as candle wax. Their tongues slid together, and her hands slid around his neck, up into his silken hair.

When he drew away, all his sharpness, all his intensity, had disappeared, replaced by a lovesick grin. "You love me. You must, if you're willing to marry me. This wouldn't be your choice if it were just for Viridia. You wouldn't do that to yourself."

She smiled, feeling a little spacey herself. "You're right." She kissed him again. "I wouldn't."

"Then I accept your proposal," he said. "And your partnership." He kissed her, and heat flared between them. He pulled her slowly down to him, until they were both lying on the bed, their arms and legs entwined.

A strange mix of emotions flowed through Nomi. Love, happiness . . .

Hope.

She was going to marry Malachi. She was going to be queen. *She* was choosing her future. And she knew, deep in her soul, she was choosing the right one.

FORTY-ONE

SERINA

Serina smoothed her hands down her sparkling black-and-silver gown. It shone like a night filled with stars, and she loved the way it accentuated her curves. She drew up the hem and slipped the dagger hidden at her calf from its sheath. The twisted silver hilt fit her hand perfectly. It was a beautiful weapon, but just as sharp and deadly as the ugly, handmade knives she'd used on Mount Ruin.

"See? A warrior *and* a princess," Val said, his gaze lingering on her exposed calf.

She returned the blade to its hiding place and fixed her dress. Looking him up and down in his silver velvet coat and black breeches, she grinned. "And you look like a prince."

He bowed gallantly. "I suppose I am one now? As the paramour of the queen's sister . . ."

"Soon-to-be queen," Serina corrected. She moved closer; close enough to kiss him. He pressed into her, sending delicious shivers down her back.

When she pulled away, his eyes were dark and hot.

"Do you think there will be trouble?" she asked, slipping into silver sandals. She'd decided against the precarious heels of her prospective Grace days . . . Couldn't run in those.

"All the magistrates accepted Malachi's invitation. The rest of Asa's army has fallen in line." Val used a thumb to wipe away her smudged lip stain. "I think Asa's short but brutal reign opened a lot of eyes. Most Viridians seem ready for change."

"I hope you're right," Serina said.

She kissed him once more, then fixed her makeup. Val opened their door for her and followed her into the hall. A swirl of color and light greeted them.

In the weeks since the Superior's death, the Graces' chambers had become a place of refuge for many of the former prisoners of Mount Ruin. The laws hadn't changed yet, and many of these women couldn't return to their families without the risk of being forced into service or marriage. Serina and Nomi had agreed that they should stay at the palazzo until it was safe for them to rejoin Viridian life. Until they could choose their own fates.

In the meantime, Malachi had been working on bringing the female relatives of some of the women to the safety of the palazzo: like Mirror's and Anika's sisters. And Blaze's daughter, who had been harder to find.

Anika saw Serina and did a little spin, her red dress belling out around her glowing brown skin.

Serina laughed. "You look ready for your first ball."

Anika rolled her eyes. "I feel like a peacock." Her expression softened. "But you should see my sisters and my mother. They're beside themselves."

While Anika hadn't lost her sarcastic humor, the defiance had disappeared almost entirely from her eyes. Now that her sisters and mother were here with her, safe, and she no longer had to fight for survival, she'd become this strangely cheerful person who Serina loved even more.

Serina hugged her.

"Dancing is like fighting," Serina said. "Without the kicking and biting."

Anika laughed. But she sobered a moment later, lifting her hem to show her own leather sheath, her own dagger. "I hope all we'll be doing is dancing."

"Me too," Serina replied, her own smile fading.

Many of the women here had spent years fighting—it wasn't so easy to let go of that drive for survival, and the fear of danger around the next corner. It had been Nomi's idea to let the women of Mount Ruin continue to train, if they chose. They'd become a sort of protective detail for her, led by Serina, more effective because no one knew they were anything but well-dressed courtiers.

Hopefully, it would stay that way.

The Queen's Graces.

That's what Nomi affectionately called them. The thought made Serina smile.

She and Val headed for the circular central room. A lot of the women were already waiting. Maris and Helena sat on the cream divan in the middle of the room. They both wore green gowns, Maris's a shade darker than Helena's. Helena's hair had grown out a bit; she'd pinned it into little spikes with sparkling silver clips. Maris's black hair curled in a braid to her shoulder, silver ribbons threaded through it.

"It's almost time," Serina said. "Can you believe it?"

"No," Maris said, laughing. "But for the first time in my life, I'm actually looking forward to a ball."

Serina left the chambers, Val just behind her, and headed down the carpeted hall toward Malachi's room. When they reached the door with the carved fish, she paused. "You mind waiting out here for a moment?"

"Of course not," he said. He had his own weapons, a firearm and a dagger, strapped to his waist. He pivoted and stood with his back to the wall beside the door, like the guard he'd once been. He still had the straight shoulders and stiff bearing when he wanted to. It made her feel safe, knowing he was here.

She knocked on the door. Malachi opened it, resplendent in a white suit threaded with gold. "There you are. She's been waiting for you."

Serina patted his arm. "I forgot how long this getup takes," she said, gesturing to her dress. She headed for the large dressing room off the bedroom. She could hear Nomi humming.

There'd been no discussion about Nomi and Malachi moving into the Superior's chambers; Nomi couldn't forget the memory of Asa's body tumbling off the balcony, and Malachi was more comfortable in his rooms than in the opulence of the Superior's.

"Nomi?" Serina called as she entered the dressing room.

Nomi sat on a little stool, her huge periwinkle pouf of skirts surrounding it, as Angeline worked on her hair.

"Serina!" Nomi cried, meeting her eyes in the mirror.

"I'm sorry I'm late," Serina said. "My dress wouldn't cooperate."

"You look beautiful," Nomi said.

Serina smiled at her sister's reflection. "So do you."

Angeline slipped a sparkling pin into the twist of Nomi's hair. "All done," she said. "Should I wait outside?"

"Yes, please," Nomi said. "Thank you, Angeline."

Angeline had agreed to stay on as Nomi's handmaiden, her face flushing a brilliant shade of red when Nomi explained that she would be paid wages for her work. Ria and all the rest of Asa's unwilling Graces had gone home to their families. Cassia was still here—she hoped to catch the eye of one of Malachi's wealthy merchant friends.

"Are you ready?" Serina asked. She put her hands on Nomi's shoulders and stared at their joined reflection, remembering a moment long ago, when she'd studied their reflections just like this, wondering how Nomi had been chosen as a Grace and she had not.

"No," Nomi said, with a rueful grin. "But I won't ever be. Once Malachi announces me as queen, there may be riots and rebellion—it may feel, at first, like we're breaking the country apart. But there'll be no going back."

"No matter what happens, I'll be here with you," Serina said, grateful as she was every day that she'd survived this long, that she could be at Nomi's side.

Footsteps echoed behind them, and another reflection joined theirs in the mirror.

"And so will I," Renzo said, with his lazy grin. He looked so grown-up in his velvet jacket. Serina could hardly believe that he was her little brother, that her little sister was about to become queen.

"Do you think Mama and Papa would be proud of us?" Serina asked, because she couldn't *imagine* what they would think about this tableau, about where their children had all ended up. Their mother's one wish was to have a Grace for a daughter. Would she be horrified if she'd lived to see one of her daughters become queen instead?

"So proud. They always were," Renzo said softly. His eyes met Serina's in the mirror. "They were horrified when you were sent to Mount Ruin. Father petitioned the magistrate— he almost got himself arrested fighting to have you freed."

Nomi gasped.

"He did?" Serina's eyes watered.

Nomi lunged for a tissue and handed it back to her. Serina closed her eyes and took a shuddering breath, blotting to preserve the kohl liner she'd so carefully applied. She couldn't break down now. But her heart stitched itself a little more strongly together, knowing her parents had fought for her. She'd always assumed they had been ashamed.

"I always wondered what they would have done if they'd known I could read," Nomi whispered. "I wondered if they'd have turned me in."

"I wondered too," Serina said softly. So many of the girls on Mount Ruin had been sent there by their own families.

"Never." Renzo shook his head. "Nomi, Father knew. You were never very good at hiding it."

"*What?*" Nomi twisted to look him in the eye without the mirror between them.

He shrugged. "He and Mama loved us. They wanted us to be happy."

Nomi gave a little hiccupping laugh. "I'm so happy you're both here. That you're safe. I wish . . . I wish they could have been here too."

Renzo put his hand over Serina's on Nomi's shoulder. "There are a lot of people who should be here today. That's why you're doing this. To honor them, and to do better going forward."

They all shared shaky smiles. A little more of Serina's serenity returned.

Nomi stood up, her giant skirt billowing out. "Okay, *now* I'm ready."

Serina and Renzo followed her out of the room to where Malachi waited. When he saw Nomi, dawn broke across his face. Serina cast a sidelong glance at Renzo. He grinned back at her.

"Today, the people of Viridia will meet their queen," Malachi said proudly, taking Nomi's arm.

But as much joy and hope filled this room, there was answering darkness outside it.

They all knew the battle for Viridia's soul was just beginning.

Serina imagined what she would see when they entered the ballroom, the suspicion and disgust the magistrates wouldn't be able to hide. Even with Malachi and Nomi working together, there were sure to be challenges. Threats.

That's why Serina was happy for her dagger, for Val and Renzo, and for the Queen's Graces. Between them all, they would keep Nomi safe.

Serina, Val, Renzo, Malachi, and Nomi walked through the quiet corridors to the gallery just outside the ballroom. Ines stood before the big carved wooden doors in a shining violet gown, her back straight and her eyes full of pride. Anika, Mirror, Maris, Helena, and several other women from Mount Ruin stood with her, as graceful in their colorful dresses as their hidden weapons were deadly. Beyond the doors, their guests waited.

Val and Renzo took their places at the head of the procession as Ines's escorts. Serina and the rest of the Queen's Graces fell in line behind them. Serina twisted to catch a glimpse of Malachi and Nomi, their arms linked, their chins high, waiting to enter last.

For a moment, everyone stood in silence, the only sound the faint rumble of voices from the other room.

Then, at Malachi's nod, the liveried sentries swung the double doors wide.

Serina laughed softly to herself as she entered the brilliant light of the ballroom, flanked by Anika and Mirror. Somehow, she had become a Grace after all.

FORTY-TWO

NOMI

Nomi paused in the doorway of the ballroom. Musicians were playing a quiet, lilting song, and the chandeliers tinkled in the breeze from the open terrace. The room was full to bursting. Everyone of importance had come to hear Malachi's announcement.

Nearly every courtier and magistrate in the room was staring at Nomi.

Two rows of soldiers formed a clear route across the dance floor to a raised platform adorned with flowers at the far side. Upon the dais sat two chairs instead of one.

The nearest soldier inclined his head toward Malachi, his mouth set in a thin line. Dante. He didn't approve of what Nomi and Malachi were about to do.

Nomi picked out Renzo in the press of people. He watched her, smiling proudly. Serina stood to the side of the dais and watched everyone else.

"Are you ready?" Malachi pressed her arm gently into his side.

"There are so many ways for this to end badly," Nomi murmured. She was caught at the surreal point between fantasy and nightmare and for good or ill, the dream was about to begin.

"Have you changed your mind?" he asked.

Nomi steeled herself. "No, I have not."

Together, they walked into the room.

The musicians played a fanfare. The soldiers saluted, even Dante. His glare twisted Nomi's heart. How were they to convince the country, when they couldn't convince Malachi's closest friend?

It will take time, that's all.

Nomi raised her chin and glided across the floor. She didn't lean on Malachi or let herself be caught up in his shadow.

We are equal.

I am not a Grace.

When they reached the dais, Nomi and Malachi turned slowly to face their subjects, the silver beading of her voluminous periwinkle gown glinting in the light. Serina and the other women curtsied deeply. Some of the magistrates bowed. But not all of them.

The musicians finished with a flourish.

Every breath hung on a knife's edge, each movement careful and contained.

"Good evening. Thank you for being here," Malachi began. "Tonight we have come together to acknowledge and celebrate a new chapter in Viridia's history. One that I am honored to be a part of and that gives me great hope. Our country has suffered deeply. My father's murder and my brother's ascension caused strife and unease throughout Viridia. But when I speak of suffering, I speak of more than Asa's brief, brutal reign and my father's death. Viridia has also suffered for its lies."

A low murmur broke through the crystal silence of the room.

Nomi continued, her voice steady and clear in contrast to her wild, unsteady heart. "In particular, the *women* of Viridia have suffered. We have been broken down, stripped of our choices, our agency, our dignity. We have paid a heavy price for fear. Women once ruled this country"—a gasp from the assemblage—"until they were erased. We have hidden our queens and subjugated their descendants. But no longer."

"As the rightful Heir to Viridia," Malachi stated, "I will take no Graces. Instead, I choose to align myself with a queen." He held Nomi's hand aloft for a moment, though no one cheered. Serina and Anika slipped through the crowd, their movements deceptively casual, as they tracked the magistrates, their aides, even the servants carrying trays of wine. Nomi's breath hitched, watching them move silently through the room.

Malachi continued. "Queen Tessaro will rule at my side, an equal partner. She will lead our efforts to bring all of Viridia's lies to light and usher in laws that give the women of this country the rights they've been denied these many years."

"The Superior and I will ensure that the men *and* women of our nation flourish," Nomi concluded. "We will make Viridia even stronger and more vibrant than it has ever been."

Nomi smiled into the faces of men who hated her. The florid courtier with red cheeks near Renzo, the magistrate from Sola, his golden cape jarring against his sallow frown. Dante. Even Signor Pietro, the magistrate from her own province, looked disgusted. She smiled at them all.

Together, hands joined, Nomi and Malachi bowed.

Music spilled into the silence. Serina curtsied before Signor Pietro and spoke a few words. Reluctantly he let her lead him into a dance. The rest of the Queen's Graces spread through the crowd, offering themselves as dance partners to the angriest of the men in the room.

Nomi and Malachi slid into the center of the dance floor, their heads held high.

"They will hate us," Malachi said, his mahogany eyes enlivened by the challenge.

"For a while," Nomi said as she flashed him a sharp, knowing smile. "But this is our history to write. We will do it well."

They spun until the lights swirled around them and the murderous glares disappeared.

ACKNOWLEDGMENTS

You would not be reading this book today without the insight, support, and enthusiasm of a whole lot of talented, generous people.

Thank you to Pam Gruber, Lanie Davis, Viana Siniscalchi, Polly Lyall-Grant, and all the editors and translators of the foreign editions of this series. To Katharine McAnarney, who has done a fantastic job of getting the word out and sends me the loveliest emails. To the rest of the LBYR and Alloy teams, whose enthusiasm and support for this book (and the series as a whole) continually gives me the warm fuzzies. To my agent, Linda Epstein, who always makes me feel like a star. With all of you on my team, I am one incredibly lucky author.

To the faculty and fellow attendees of the MadCap Writing Cross-Culturally Workshop, thank you for being so welcoming and generous with your perspective, advice, and friendship. Meeting you was life-changing.

Big hugs to my friends and fellow writers who have supported me, encouraged me, and reminded me to trust myself. Who've read early drafts, who've offered advice, who've shown up at events, and who've reminded me that my value as a person is *not* tied to the words I put on the page: Michelle Nebiolo, Dr. Jody Escaravage, Aimee L. Salter, Rachel Hamm, Natasha Fisher, Jax Abbey, Paige Nguyen, J.D. Robinson, Crystal Watanabe, Morgan Michael, April Anft, Kate Elliott, Kyra Whitton, Danielle

Boateng, Kaitlyn Sage Patterson, Dhonielle Clayton, and Natalie C. Parker.

Thank you to my family for all the support and enthusiasm, for getting your friends to read *Grace and Fury*, for driving hours to come to my events, for showing me in all the little and big ways that you're proud of me. To my son, Oliver, for telling anyone and everyone that his mommy is a "famous book star." To my husband, Andy, who listens to all my publishing angst and loves me anyway.

Thank you to the folks at Fairyloot, OwlCrate, and Cushy Crate for choosing to include *Grace and Fury* in their beautiful subscription boxes. And to all their subscribers, thank you for sharing the most gorgeous book photographs I've ever seen in my life. Bookstagram has become my happy place.

And finally, to you, the reader, *thank you*. Thank you for picking up *Grace and Fury*, for investing in Serina and Nomi enough to come back for more. Thank you for preordering, for purchasing, for borrowing from the library, for subscribing to book boxes, for telling your friends, for sharing on your social media, for reviewing, *for reading*. *You* are the one who gives a book life. It's magic, what you do, and I am so grateful you shared your magic with me.

READ THE FIRST BOOK IN
THIS EPIC FANTASY SERIES!

NOT ALL PRISONS HAVE BARS

GRACE
& FURY

TRACY
BANGHART

Photo © April Anft

Tracy Banghart grew up in rural Maryland, with a cornfield in her backyard and flying squirrels in her bedroom walls, and spent her summers on a remote island in northern Ontario. All that isolation and pretty scenery led to a reading addiction, writing obsession, and several serious book boyfriends.

Always a bit of a nomad, Tracy now travels the world army-wife style with her husband, son and sundry pets. Follow her adventures on Twitter @tracythewriter.